ASTRAY

A BIRCH FALLS NOVEL

POPPY FITZGERALD

CONTENTS

For my amazing husband, who supported this crazy dream of mine from the start.

TRIGGER WARNINGS

Astray is a dark romance, with dark themes, including gaslighting, manipulation, stalking, kidnapping, and sexual assault. I did my best to handle these topics with care and compassion for the victims, but please tread carefully if any of these subjects are upsetting for you.

Visit the National Sexual Violence Resource Center for more information or help if you have been a victim of sexual assault.

National Sexual Violence Resource Center
https://www.nsvrc.org

PLAYLIST

If you'd like to set the mood, and listen along to songs that fit the vibe of Astray, here is the play list I listened to constantly while writing this book.

Spotify Playlist

- Cover Me Up - Jason Isbell
- Wicked Game - Chris Issak
- Oh Darlin What Have I Done - The White Buffalo
- You've Got The Love - Florence and the Machine
- Drive - The Deftones
- Dancing Days - Stone Temple Pilots
- Plush - Stone Temple Pilots
- Everlong (acoustic) - The Foo Fighters
- Redbone - Childish Gambino
- It Was A Sin - The Revivalists

- Goodnight Moon- Shivaree
- Help I'm Alive - Metric
- And She Was - The Talking Heads
- Psycho Killer- The Talking Heads
- All Your'n - Tyler Childers
- Must Be The Whiskey - Cody Jinks
- This Tornado Loves You - Neko Case
- Ashamed - Deer Tick
- Tear Drop - Massive Attack
- Babe I'm Gonna Leave You - Led Zeppelin
- Every Breath You Take- The Police
- Ain't No Sunshine - Bill Withers
- #1 Crush - Garbage
- Where Did You Sleep Last Night - Nirvana
- The Promise - Sturgill Simpson
- Criminal - Fiona Apple
- Slipping Husband - The National
- Nothing Better - The Postal Service
- Falling Faster Than You Can Run - Nathaniel Rateliff

PART ONE
THE PROMISE

CHAPTER
ONE

ELOISE

"What do you mean you're not going to make it?" I glare disbelievingly at my phone while my friend Sara gives me an apologetic shrug through the FaceTime call. "It's girls' night! I've been looking forward to this for weeks. I haven't seen you in so long."

Sara cringes at the exasperation in my voice, that I usually reserve for my nieces and nephew when I'm on babysitting duty. "I know. I'm so sorry but Derrick and I had a big breakthrough in our lunchtime therapy appointment today and when I got home, he was already making dinner and had Liam in the bath. He's really trying, and I just want to keep this momentum going. I think I might actually get laid tonight."

I roll my eyes but smirk at her. "Fine. But you better make him go down on you until you're hoarse from screaming his name before you let him get his dick wet.

Housework isn't the only place he has room for improvement."

Sara chuckles, "Oh, believe me. He knows he has his work cut out for him. I have a feeling he is willing to give it his all tonight."

My heart shrivels at the idea of flying solo tonight, but I hide my annoyance at being ditched, and try to be happy for my friend for working so hard to repair her marriage. "Have fun then and don't do anything I wouldn't do."

"Ha, as if there isn't anything you wouldn't try at least once. I know what kind of books you read, you slut." I cackle before giving her the finger. "Bye bitch. Love you."

Blowing out a deflated sigh, I end the call and debate on if I should just get out my Kindle and be the weirdo at the bar reading, or just finish my drink and head home. I stare at the coaster depicting a blind pig wearing sunglasses, holding a white cane, debating my options. Just as I am getting ready to ask for my check, a deep voice rumbles next to me, "That's some sound life advice you were giving there. If her husband knows what's up, he should be thanking you."

Startled, I look to my right and feel my phone slip out of my grasp, and it clatters to the floor. The man sitting next to me is huge, gorgeous and smoldering. How the fuck I missed his presence next to me is dumbfounding. He gives off Big Dick Energy like a star going supernova.

The stranger is tall, even sitting next to me on the bar stool, broad, easily encroaching on the space on either side of his seat. He has long dark curly hair tied up in a messy man bun and a dark beard surrounding lush lips that gives him a rakish look. He wears a tight, long sleeved, dark gray Henley that is molded to his body like a second skin, and I can see swirls of black and gray ink peeking out of the sleeves onto the backs of his hands and up around his neck. His eyes are so dark they are almost black. All I can do is blink dumbly at him while my brain tries to process what life advice he was referring to.

"Excuse me?"

"You dropped something," he says, and before I can react, he slips off his bar stool and grabs my phone from the ground. Looking up at me from his crouched position in front of my crossed legs, he speaks again. "Licking her pussy until she's hoarse advice. Any man worth his salt should be clamoring at the chance to make his woman scream with her thighs wrapped around his head." The hungry look in his eyes, coupled with the mischievous smirk of his pouty lips, does nothing to stop the short-circuiting of my brain.

I can feel my cheeks heat as a blush creeps up my face, while his eyes drink in my dark aubergine hair curled around my shoulders, my breasts looking especially perky tonight thanks to my new bra and the dark burgundy lipstick that coats my mouth. I know I look good tonight, but it has been so long since I've been flirted with by a stranger, my usual sharp wit and sarcastic bite I typically use as a defense mechanism have abandoned me completely.

As he slowly stands back up my eyes track the movement. He is positively delicious looking, and he is so close I can feel his body heat radiating from him. The man feels like the sun and I'm afraid I will get burned if I touch him.

Clearing my throat, I turn away before I give into temptation. "Oh, you know, just trying to do my best to encourage better standards for my friends. We are too old to settle for the bare minimum in the bedroom." The chuckle that rumbles out of him sends another wave of heat rushing up my face and down into my core.

Mentally, I berate myself for engaging with the Khal Drogo look-alike. Logically, I know no good could come of this interaction. I am married, bored, horny, and more than a little lonely - a dangerous combination for a woman such as myself left alone in a bar.

"The name's Drew, can I buy you a drink?" Tall, Dark and Deadly (the nickname I have given him in my head) asks as he places my phone back on the bar top between us.

"Oh, um, I was actually just getting ready to leave..."

He quirks a dark brow at me and leans in closer, "You got somewhere better to be? It didn't seem that way based on your conversation with your friend." He has me there. I think about the dark, quiet house that was waiting for me if I left now. Caleb is out of town for work and won't be back until the morning. My closest friend has already bailed on me, so I literally have nothing better to do at the moment other than go home and finish reading the dark reverse harem romance I am in the middle of and take my favorite pink vibrator for a spin if I get to any good spicy scenes.

I think back to the last time I have truly done something fun or different in my life and cannot come up with any recent examples. Between pulling doubles at the hospital, Caleb going out of town for work very frequently, and my close friends all dealing with their own life shit, I can't remember the last time I did something spontaneous or fun.

I glance over at Drew and feel my eyes get trapped in the intense stare he is giving me as he waits for my answer. My pulse is racing, and I decide just for tonight I am going to live for myself in the real world and not bury my nose in a book looking for excitement. "You know what, you're right. I don't have anywhere better to be. You can buy me a drink. I'm Eloise."

I stick my hand out to introduce myself and instead of shaking it, he grabs my hand and pulls me so close his lips brush my ear as he whispers in my ear, "That's a good girl, now tell me what you're drinking." I couldn't have stopped the compulsion to lick my lips after that line if my life had depended on it. After only talking for less than five minutes this man already knows my kryptonite.

"Bourbon on the rocks, please."

The smile that lights up his face is blinding. He clutches his chest dramatically and declares, "A woman after my own heart." Drew flags down the bartender and orders two Blanton's Single Barrel, his neat, mine on the rocks. As we wait for our drinks his stare does not lessen in intensity and it feels like there is a solid chance I will spontaneously combust if he doesn't look away.

"So, Eloise, for a woman who seems so sure of her worth, why do you not have anything worth going home to tonight?" Drew glances pointedly at my ring finger where my wedding ring glitters under the low bar lights.

I debate on not answering him, guilt swirling in my gut, but I think back to the clipped conversation that Caleb and I had early that morning. The one where I begged him to talk to his boss about doing less travel for work. He brushed off my plea by saying it was only temporary, and that he'd be done traveling soon.

A reassurance he's been spouting at me for the last year and a half every time he leaves for another week away. I know his boss is taking advantage of Caleb's childless status and inability to say no. Caleb feels like he owes Harold everything, since Harold had taken a chance and hired him straight out of college, and promoted him up the ranks quickly, giving him a leg up on all of his peers right out of school. But what good is a job when all you do is work and have no life outside of it? I know my husband's heart is trying to be in the right place, but unfortunately that place is not in our marriage.

Fortunately, the bartender reappears and deposits our drinks in front of us. I swirl the amber liquid around the sphere of ice in my glass, while I consider my words before coming up with, "My husband is as married to his work as he is to me. Maybe more so lately. He says it's temporary, but it's been lonely with him gone all the time." The grin that creeps across Drew's face can only be described as feral.

"Well, his stupidity is working out well for me. Cheers." He tips his glass towards mine, and I tap his back.

"Calm down Casanova, I'm just having a drink with you, not going home with you." Drew just shoots me a wink and quickly downs his bourbon before signaling to the bartender to bring him another.

"Whatever you say, darlin'." He responds with a knowing grin.

Taking a sip of my bourbon, I let that comment hang in the air. I am not going to encourage that particular train of thought. I let the notes of citrus and vanilla linger on my tongue for a moment, as the heat from the alcohol sends a flush up my cheeks. "So, Drew, for a man who seems to know exactly how sexy he is, why are you here alone tonight? Seems like you shouldn't have to resort to flirting with a married woman to have a good night. I'm sure there is easier game afoot." I glance at the blonde sitting alone at the end of the bar in a barely-there red dress that has been surreptitiously shooting glances Drew's way since we started talking.

Drew follows my gaze and turns back to me with a quick dismissal of the blonde. "Who said I'm looking for easy? Maybe I just know good company when I see it and want to talk to the gorgeous married woman who looks like she needs someone to remind her of how sexy and amazing she is."

Nearly choking on my drink with that compliment, I

make a mental note to end this night after finishing my drink before I get myself into trouble. My inner romantic who is addicted to spicy romance books cannot handle this kind of intense flirtation.

Three hours later, two more bourbon drinks, and in the midst of a heated debate on the ranking of Cohen Brothers' movies catalog, the bar lights suddenly come up and the bartender announces last call.

"Shit, what time is it?" I glance at my phone and see it is almost 2 a.m. and I have two missed call notifications from Caleb. Fuck, I gotta go. "Drew, thanks for a fun evening, but I need to get home." Before he can object, I pull up the Uber app on my phone and order a ride home.

I attempt to flag down the bartender, but he grabs my hand, an intense fire burning in his eyes that leaves me feeling breathless, and says, "I've got this. I hope I did a good job reminding you of what you're worth, Eloise. Be sure to pass the message along to that fool of a husband of yours." With nothing to say to that, I nod and rush out the door to catch my ride.

Standing outside in the fresh night air I begin to feel like I can fully breathe again. The intensity in which Drew had been staring at me all night had started to muddle all my senses. I had to get away from him before I did something truly stupid, I couldn't take back. I pull out my phone to check on the status of my ride and while I am distracted a large hand firmly grabs my shoulder and spins me around, pinning my back against the light post behind me.

"What the -" before I can finish that sentence his mouth is on mine, his large body pressing against me, one hand gripping the back of my neck, fingers tangled in my hair while the other gently cups my jaw. A small gasp leaves my lips, parting them, giving him the opening he needs to thrust his tongue inside and he begins to devour me. His lips are soft, I can still taste the hints of charred wood and caramel from the bourbon he had been drinking on his tongue.

The way his tongue sweeps against mine reminds me of the way my husband and I used to kiss, when our relationship was still new and exciting. A moan escapes my lips before I can stop it and he takes it as a sign to double down on his efforts. His body presses more firmly against mine and I can feel the hardness of his cock against my belly. The hand that had been tangled in my hair slowly travels down my back until it is cupping my ass in a punishing grip as he pulls me tighter to his body.

Headlights flash in the street breaking the spell and I put my hands between us and shove against his chest. "What in the hell do you think you're doing?"

Whispering against my ear he responds, "Reminding you to not settle for the bare minimum, darlin'."

Rage flashes over my face and I shove Drew away from me. "I do not settle. Get the fuck out of my way. I'm leaving now." Drew throws his arms up in surrender and shoots me a wicked smirk as he steps to the side clearing my path. With a heady mix of guilt, shame, rage and arousal swirling in my gut I get into the waiting car and check my message from my husband.

"*Hey babe, I know you're supposed to be out on a girl's night. I just wanted to call and tell you I love you and miss you. I'll be home in the morning. Don't let Sara get you into any trouble tonight, I won't be around to bail you out. See you soon, Sweetness.*"

Warm lips press against the nape of my neck while strong arms wrap around my body. My brain slowly drifts out of the dream I was having of strong, rough hands holding me down while a dark mysterious stranger devoured my pussy like it was his last meal. "Mmm...you're home early." I turn my face and nuzzle into my husband's neck and inhale his scent.

"Not that early Lo, it's almost noon." Caleb kisses the top of my head and snuggles me into his chest. "You girls have a late night? I don't think you've slept this late since college."

Guilt swirls in my stomach thinking back to the previous night when Drew had given me the best kiss I had in years. "Something like that. I'm sorry I overslept. I would've gotten freshened up for you. Now I have fuzzy teeth and morning breath."

"It's alright, Sweetness, I'm beat. I was planning on

taking a nap anyway. I had to get up at 4am to make it to the airport." I tamp down the disappointment from his brush off and give Caleb a gentle kiss on the mouth.

"Ok babe. You take a nap, and we can have a date night tonight, and you can make it up to me." I shoot him a wink as I slip out of the bedroom, grabbing my phone to text Sara. Aside from my sister Olivia, she is my closest confidant, and the one person I trust with a secret this massive. I have to talk to someone about what happened last night before I let the guilt of it all tear me apart.

> Me: SOS emergency coffee run in an hour. Can you meet me?

> Sara: Uh-oh. Trouble in paradise? Did Caleb not make it back from his trip?

> Me: I'll explain later. Please, I need to be talked off a ledge.

> Sara: K. See you at Brewed Awakening.

An hour later, I'm sitting in an overstuffed easy chair in the back corner of the kitschy coffee shop full of mismatched furniture with sarcastic motivational posters dotting the walls, waiting for Sara to show up. I opt for a chai latte, knowing that caffeine will just ramp up my anxiety to unbearable levels. Last night after leaving the overbearing (albeit sexy) asshole, I fumed the entire ride home. Then spent the entire night in a fitful, disturbed sleep that kept spiraling into pornographic dreams about Drew. I need to clear my conscience fast before I word vomit everything to Caleb and destroy my already fragile marriage.

I spot Sara walking in a few moments later, her eyes finding me right away in our usual corner. She knows when I pick the corner in the very back that I have some very hot tea to spill. She places her order at the counter for her usual half-caf skinny vanilla latte then makes her way over to me.

There is a manic gleam in her crystal blue eyes and a mischievous smirk tugging at her full lips that makes me think she is expecting some juicy gossip. Sara has been my ride or die for the last 15 years since we met in our senior year of high school, when she moved across the street from me after her dad got a new job as the head football coach of our school. She is the main reason why I didn't ditch out of school early and do online classes to finish out the year. High school was not the best years of my life by any stretch of the imagination, but she made it bearable. When I tell her what happened last night, she won't judge me, but she will lose her mind.

"Alright, spill. What's going on? You look like you've seen a ghost vomiting up his little ghostly guts."

"What the hell is that supposed to mean?"

"You look green and pale. Something is seriously wrong with you. Are you pregnant?" Sara's eyes get wide when she glances down at my belly which is sporting its usual round softness and not the telltale pregnancy roundness.

"Fuck off with that shit. I do not need you putting that kind of juju out in the universe right now. My life is already a disaster as it is."

Exasperated, I bury my face in my hands and let the dark purple strands fall like a curtain. After all the manic sex dreams of the sexy, dangerous man from the bar, the absolute last thing I need on my plate are pregnancy rumors. I feel the cushion of the oversized armchair sink next to me as Sara sits and wraps her arm around my shoulders.

"Hey, Lo, what's going on? Talk to me. Did something happen with Caleb? Is everything ok?" Sara pries my hands from my face, forcing me to look at her. "Does he have to go out of town again? Did he cheat on you? Do I need to kick his ass into next Tuesday?"

Despite feeling like my life is beginning to crumble around me I can't help but smile at my friend. "No, but you might need to kick mine. I, umm, might've kissed someone last night that isn't Caleb." I bite my bottom lip to keep it from trembling as the tears that had been threatening to fall finally spill over my lashes. Shocked doesn't even begin to describe the look on Sara's face. Her mouth gapes open like a fish and her eyes almost bug out of their sockets.

She has every right to be surprised. Sara has been around for the entirety of my relationship with Caleb, from our first date in our senior year of college at B.F.U., to our wedding, and everything in between. She was instrumental in getting him to ask me out in the first place, when we were all a part of the college newspaper together. She got sick of me constantly making dirty jokes about how I wanted to ride him like my own personal pony, so she just went straight up to Caleb and told him I had the hots for him. Caleb being Caleb was completely unfazed by her forwardness and did exactly that. He asked me out for a date right then and there. Unbeknownst to us, he had the hots for me too, so her brazenness worked out for the best.

"Wait a goddamn second. Walk that back and start over missy. I know I did not just hear what I thought I heard."

"Well, technically, I was kissed. I didn't do the kissing. At least, not at first. And this is all your fault anyway for ditching me. If you had been there, I would've had a safety buffer between me and the hot-ass Jason Momoa clone who was hitting on me. He kept just saying shit about me being sexy and giving me those bedroom eyes and licking his lips. It was obscene! I tried to be good! When the bartender made the last call, I ordered an Uber and went outside. But he followed me outside and gave me the most panty-destroying kiss I've had in years, then sauntered off looking all tall, dark and deadly." I know I'm rambling. I am talking so fast I can't catch a breath and my face is flushing. The panic is building in my chest, and I am on the verge of losing my shit.

"Calm down, Lo. Deep breaths. I've got you. You said he kissed you? You didn't initiate?" Sara rubs gentle circles on my back pulling me back from the brink of a panic attack. I shake my head at her.

"No, but I shouldn't have been there in the first place. I should've just gone home after you canceled, but he started talking to me and flirting, and for the first time in I don't know how long I felt seen, attractive and wanted. I didn't want to go home and be lonely again, so I stayed and got carried away talking to this guy. Next thing I knew, it was closing time and we had been talking for hours. I knew it was wrong to be on what was basically a date with this guy, so I left. But then he followed me outside and rocked my fucking world with a kiss. Sara, I have to tell Caleb..."

Sara put her fingers to my lips and interrupted me. "I'm going to stop you right there. Nothing good will come if you tell Caleb about this. You did nothing wrong. You chatted with a guy, he got the wrong idea, made a move, you shot him down and left. Right?"

I nod. "But-" She shakes her head. "But nothing. You're never going to see this guy again. It went no further than that. You clearly feel awful about it. If you tell Caleb, it's just going to make things worse. Telling him might alleviate your guilt, but it will break his heart. Do you want to hurt Cal like that?"

I shake my head. "No. I don't. But I just feel awful. I can't stop thinking about the kiss. It felt so good, like he could eat me alive. I haven't felt that kind of passion from Caleb in at least a year."

Biting her bottom lip, Sara nods thoughtfully. "So, get the passion back. Fix things with Caleb. I don't know what's going on with you two, but I know it's fixable. Channel that sexual frustration into seducing your husband and take it out on him."

I think about what she's saying and about my relationship with Caleb. It's not a bad relationship. He's a good husband. But we've been together for 12 years, married for 10 and the last year hasn't been our best. He's out of town constantly, and I'm usually pulling doubles at the hospital now that everyone is bailing out of working in healthcare post-pandemic. We still love each other, but it feels like most of the time we are just two ships passing in the night. I'm lucky if I get laid once a week and the closer I get to 40 the harder that is to handle.

Whoever said women are in their prime in their 30s and 40s wasn't lying. All I want is for my husband to just throw me down on the bed and eat me like his favorite ice cream, but the last time we were intimate, it was a quickie right before he left town. It also felt like we did it because it was something we were supposed to do and not because we couldn't keep our hands off each other. When had we lost that fire? The passion? I couldn't remember the last time we had sex that hadn't felt like just going through the motions.

"Yeah, maybe you have a point. I keep waiting for Cal to make the first move, but life isn't a romance novel.

Maybe I need to take charge and just suck his soul out of his dick to see if that sparks his interest."

"That's my girl. I know you have got to have some tricks up your sleeve from all those spicy books you read. Remind him why he fell in love with you. Make him remember you're the one that's supposed to be riding his dick, not his damn boss."

The sip I've just taken of my chai flies out of my nose as I let out a snort. "Fucking hell Sara, that hurts. Warn a girl next time before you drop the mic like that."

Sara just shoots me a wicked grin before taking a sip of her own latte. "Ok, so what's the plan? How do we get Caleb so fucking turnt out for you he can't keep his hands, mouth and dick out of you?"

"Don't you mean off of me?"

"Out, off, on, hopefully he will be engaging in all of the prepositions by the time you're through with him." Sara's face lights up like a goddamn lightbulb has gone off right over her head. "Ooh, I know! Take him to that new club that just opened, over on Broad."

I crinkle my nose at her. "Allure? Isn't that a swinger's club? I don't know if that would be Caleb's scene."

"What better way to bring the spice back? And make your husband see you as the drop-dead sexy wife you are than having some other dude or lady hit on you right in front of him. There's nothing hotter than a jealous, possessive man. I hear they have private rooms too, so you wouldn't even have to wait until you get home to take advantage of that energy."

I consider her words carefully. I won't lie, the idea of a threesome or even engaging in some sort of new kinky hobby like Shibari had been rattling around in my head for a while now. Maybe just having a drink at a place like Allure will be enough to spark some new ideas in the bedroom and bring us back together.

"Yeah, maybe you're right. We are supposed to go out tonight. I'll make reservations at Mortar and Pestle since it's right down the street from Allure and then suggest a nightcap there." Excitement begins to tingle in my core at the idea of getting Caleb in a place like Allure and finding out what he could be into. I've been wanting to broach the idea of trying new things in bed, but we've been so distant with each other there never seemed to be a good time to bring it up.

"Way ahead of you, sweetie. You've got reservations at 7:30." Sara holds up her phone showing me the OpenTable app with the table reservation she booked for us. "Now get the hell out of here and find something sexy to wear. You've got a husband to seduce."

I give Sara a tight squeeze and kiss on the cheek. "Thank you so much for this. I needed that pep talk more than you know."

"Yeah, yeah, now go. Just text me some eggplant emojis if you get laid. If I don't get at least three eggplants in the middle of the night, I'm going to personally come over and kick his ass in the morning." Excitedly, I gather up my purse and rush out of the coffee shop. A plan is already forming in my mind on how I'm going to seduce my husband tonight.

After my coffee date with Sara, I head home with renewed purpose. Maybe the mysterious Drew was right, and I have been settling for the bare minimum. The bare minimum of attention, affection, and love. That is about to change. I am not letting this marriage go down without a fight.

I get home and find Caleb in our basement home gym working out. I take a moment to stand in the doorway to admire my husband. Caleb has his hands taped up for doing drills with the punching bag and is shirtless with a pair of low-slung gray sweatpants hanging on his hips. His ginger hair is slicked back with sweat, and I can see a slight sheen of sweat glistening in the light dusting of hair on his chest. He isn't as ripped as he had been in college during his days of playing hockey, but I don't mind a bit. I find it easier to feel engulfed by him now that he's a little thicker, a little broader and I feel less self-conscious about my flaws knowing we've both softened up a bit over time. We both started out fit and athletic in college when we met, but time, jobs and comfort in our relationship has taken its toll on both of us.

"Hey handsome," Caleb looks up and catches my reflection in the mirror with his emerald green gaze. He shoots me a grin before he turns around to stalk across the gym to wrap me in his arms.

"There you are. You were gone when I woke up, I thought we were having a date today?" I settle against his chest as I enjoy the warmth of his arms banded around me.

"We are. That's what I was taking care of actually. I met up with Sara and she gave me an idea for a fun date idea tonight. We have reservations for tonight at Mortar and Pestle."

He lets out a low whistle, "Oh it's like that, is it? We're going fancy tonight?"

"Yeah, it's like that. We haven't been on a real date in weeks. We're going to do it right tonight." I reach up and run my hands through his gorgeous copper beard before pulling him down to me for a kiss. I don't care that he's still sweaty from his workout. His musk is intoxicating to me, and I am planning on starting my seduction plan right away.

Caleb cups my jaw with one hand as his tongue gently licks along the seam of my lips seeking entry. I open up easily, relishing in the feel of his kiss as his tongue strokes mine and his teeth nip at my bottom lip. I can't remember the last time we had a solid make out session, so I make a mental note to initiate them more often.

"Mmm...you taste amazing. Like cinnamon. I can't stop kissing you."

I smile against his mouth as I back him up against the wall. "You're going to have to because I have other plans."

I drop to my knees in front of him and give his sweat-pants a hard tug. They slide down his hips easily and his cock bobs free; apparently Caleb is free balling today. I look up at him and train my gaze on his face while I lick my lips. Caleb swallows thickly as he looks down at me on my knees before speaking.

"Fuck, babe. You don't know how hot you look right now." He takes his shaft in hand and gives it a few firm strokes before lightly tapping the head on my lips. "Open up, Sweetness, let me feel that mouth." I do as commanded and open up wide letting my tongue flatten and drag up the underside of his shaft. I swirl it around his thick head, repeating the motion a few more times before I bob down and take his entire length in my mouth. Caleb is blessed. Not in a pornstar way, but definitely in an above-average way. I can take his entire length without gagging, but only just. I swirl my tongue around his shaft as I build a rhythm bobbing up and down. I cup his balls in one hand and give him a firm tug just the way I know he likes while I dig the fingers of my other hand into his ass cheek.

"God, babe...fuck. That feels so good." Caleb has always been a gentle lover. Like right now he is running his fingers through my hair and just barely rocking his hips, letting me control the pace. Gentle isn't what I am after though. I want to make him feral for me. I increase the suction on his dick as I pull back and come off his shaft with an audible pop. I look up at him as I lick my lips before diving in lower and suck one of his balls into my mouth. "Fuuuuuucccckkk..." the groan that leaves him is purely animalistic.

I suck on the other ball before leaning back and looking up at him again. "Cal, I want you to fuck my mouth. I want you to use me until you can't take it anymore and shoot your load down my throat."

His brow creases as he considers my request. "You want me to...what?" I know this request is out of the ordinary for our usual M.O. but there's no putting that horse back in the barn, so I double down.

"I said, I want you to fuck my mouth. Hard. Daddy." I punctuate that last word by grabbing his balls and giving him a firm squeeze.

Caleb only hesitates for a moment before doing as I ask. "Alright then, whatever my baby wants my baby gets." He takes his shaft and taps it against my cheek. "Open up and take my dick, but if I get too rough you let me know, ok?" I nod and before he has a chance to question it I suck the tip back into my mouth, swirling my tongue around dragging another moan from his lips.

Tentatively he gives his hips a thrust and I moan encouragingly as I grip his ass with both hands and pull him in closer. "You like that? You like it when I shove my cock into that pretty mouth of yours?" I nod encouragingly and tighten my grip on his ass. The next thing I know Caleb has my hair wrapped around his hands as his thrusts deepen and become quicker.

"Fuck yes, baby. You take my cock so well. Your mouth is perfect. You're such a good girl taking D-daddy's dick like that." Caleb hesitates a little on calling himself Daddy, but I start to salivate even more with his praise, and I can feel the slickness building in my pussy. His breathing becomes labored, and his thrusts become more erratic. "Lo, I'm gonna come, I'm gon—" Caleb lets out a strangled grunt as his hot load hits the back of my throat. I can feel my nails digging into the firm flesh of his ass and I swallow greedily hoping he senses how much I am enjoying this.

I feel so fucking sexy and powerful right now even if he is the one controlling our movements. It is my mouth and my touch making him lose control and I feel like a goddamn goddess. His grip on my hair loosens as he pulls out of my mouth. I look up at him from under my lashes as I lick my lips. "Thank you, Daddy."

"Shit Lo, come here." Caleb pulls me to standing before crashing his mouth against mine. "I don't know where that came from but damn baby that was amazing. I feel like I need to return the favor."

I nip at his lip as I slip out of his grip. "In due time. We've got to get ready for our date now." I shoot Caleb a wink as I back away. Edging myself hadn't been my original plan, but now the idea of the anticipation building up before I let him make me come sends a spark of excitement shooting down my spine. I want to wait for it because I want to have the most mind-blowing orgasm of our relationship the next time we fuck. "Come on, Daddy. We're all dirty now and need to go get clean."

CHAPTER

THREE

CALEB

TWO HOURS LATER. I'M LEANING AGAINST THE DOOR FRAME IN our bedroom waiting for Eloise to emerge from the bathroom. Since she planned a special date night, I made the effort to dress up from my usual uniform of ripped jeans and 90s Alt Rock band shirts. I'm finishing rolling up the sleeve of my forest green button down (Lo's favorite color on me) when she walks out of the bathroom.

I feel my mouth go dry as I drink her in. She's wearing a sexy black halter dress with a sweetheart neckline that puts her breasts on display before cinching in at her waist and wrapping snugly around her plump ass. Her hair is swept up into some sort of intentionally messy bun with a few tendrils left down to frame her face. My breath catches in my chest when I take in her face. She's biting her lower lip like she's nervous about what I'm going to think. As if I could think she's anything other than perfect. Her normally pale blue eyes that often mimic the color of a glacier have darkened to the color of a stormy sea. I can tell something is going on in her mind that has spurred on this sudden shift in her normally docile personality, but I haven't figured out what it is yet.

"Damn, Sweetness. You look fucking edible. Are you sure we have to go out tonight? I could just feast on you all night." I don't miss the blush that creeps up her freckled cheeks or the way her pupils dilate at my compliment.

"Down boy. We haven't been on a date in ages. I'm going to make you wine and dine me before I let you get in my panties." She walks up to me and runs her fingers through my freshly groomed beard and gives me a quick kiss on the lips.

Wearing heels, she's only a few inches shorter than me so I only have to duck my head a little to meet her mouth. "Then let's get on with it. I want to get you back here as quickly as possible so we can get to dessert."

At Mortar and Pestle, we enjoy a 3-course dinner of mussels in a garlic, white wine broth, hangar steak seared and grilled to perfection served over roasted fingerling potatoes, and roasted wild mushrooms, and a dessert of bread pudding served with a coconut jalapeño sorbet.

As we get deeper into the bottle of Malbec, I can tell Lo is having the time of her life. A twinge of guilt twists in my stomach when I realize just how long it has been since we've connected like this. Harold has been leaning on me more and more to tackle the out-of-town meetings and project bids for the company. I can tell it's wearing on my relationship with Eloise. I make a mental note to talk to him on Monday about pulling back from the travel side of our business and starting to work from home more.

"So, I was thinking there's this new club right down the street that might be worth checking out." Eloise gives me a sultry look as she runs her fingers along the back of my hand.

I take a moment to think about where she could be talking about but draw a blank. "You're not in a hurry to get home for dessert?" I shoot her a wink as I motion for the check from our waiter. "We will just go for a night cap. I've heard some interesting things about this place, and I think you might like it."

Just as we are leaving the restaurant my phone buzzes with a text from one of my work partners.

> Trey: I'm sorry man, it can't be helped. The doctor just put Kara on bedrest for the rest of her pregnancy. She has preeclampsia.

I stop short just outside the door Eloise is trying to lead me through. "Hey, is everything ok?" Eloise grabs my arm, dragging my attention back to her as I still try to process Trey's text message. Before I get a chance to respond my phone starts buzzing again, this time with my boss's face showing up on the caller ID.

"Shit babe, I've got to take this. Will you go in and order me a drink? I'll catch up in just a minute." I see the disappointment flash across her face before she schools her features back into the carefree smile she had been wearing. But now the smile is forced, and I can tell she knows bad news is coming. I give her a quick kiss on the lips and swat on her ass, "Five minutes, I promise." Before she can argue, I answer the call from Harold and take a few steps away to talk in private. I watch out of the corner of my eye as she debates on waiting for me outside for a moment before she heads into the club.

"Harold, It's Saturday night and I'm on a date with my wife. I hope you're not calling for the reason I think you're calling,"

"Sorry, kid. I just spoke to Trey, and he can't go to the Langford site on Monday. I need you to be our site supervisor for this project until Alex gets back from London."

"Harry, are you fucking kidding me? I just got home. Today. I haven't even been home a day. Can't you handle this one?"

"No can do. I'm currently on the beach in Bonaire right now. Last minute anniversary trip with the missus."

"Are you shitting me with this? You're on the goddamn beach and I'm the one that has to pick up the slack?" I run my hand through my hair in exasperation as I attempt to get my anger under control before I get my ass fired for telling off my boss. I pace up and down the sidewalk fighting the urge to throw my phone against the brick wall of Allure.

"Look, it'll only be for a week or two. Alex is almost done with the London project then he can come take over for you. I promise I'll make it up to you when you get back. I know I'm asking a lot, kid, but you're my number one guy and I can't trust the Langford site with just anyone." My irritation grows at Harold's patronizing nickname for me. He fancies himself a father figure to me since my own passed away just before I started working for him right out of college. "I need you for this, Cal. Do an old man a solid and I promise it'll be worth your while."

Grinding my teeth, I growl out a response. "Fine, but this is it. When I get back, we are having a sit down about my role in this company. I'm done with being the default for all the shitty travel assignments and I'm planning on working from home going forward."

"You're the best, kid. I'll have Sonia transfer Trey's airline ticket over to you. Your flight leaves Monday at 8am. She will send you the details tomorrow."

"You owe me one old man." Before he can respond, I hang up and let out a frustrated growl. Eloise is going to be pissed about this. I know in my bones as soon as I tell her this is going to lead to a fight. Things get more tense between us every time I leave town for work, and I know she's tired of it. I'm going to have to find a way to fix my job before it ruins my marriage.

When I step into the club, I scan the room looking for my wife. The lighting is dark and seductive, the music a low pulsing thrum through the speakers. I'm not sure what kind of club this is but it is definitely not like the usual dive bar or brewery we normally frequent. When my eyes find her at the bar, she isn't alone. There is a tall, well-built man with a douchey man-bun piled up on his head standing way too close to her for my liking. "Who the fuck does this discount Aquaman think he is?" I mutter to myself as I begin making my way across the club. After my conversation with Harold, I am in no mood to be cockblocked by some asshole hitting on my wife.

As I approach Eloise the TEMU brand Jason Momoa looks up and catches my eye. I don't miss the sly smirk that tugs at his lips when Lo laughs at something he just said. My returning stare is cold and unwelcoming. When I reach Eloise, I wrap my hands around her shoulders before leaning in to kiss her cheek, not-so-subtly staking my claim.

"Sorry, Sweetness. I had to handle something for Harold." Instead of the heat and lust that had been shining in her eyes all night, Eloise looks up at me with wide eyes, her cheeks a flushed pink like I caught her by surprise. I cut the sub-rate, Conan the Barbarian another look and grudgingly realize he looks a lot more like the Hollywood actor than I originally gave him credit for. Shit, this guy is a stud. I school my features into what I hope is a "totally not jealous but not in the mood for you to crash my date" expression as I take in the stranger trying to flirt with my wife. If this guy thinks he's going to have any luck scoring with her, he's got another think coming.

FOUR

ELOISE

Shit. Fuck, fuck, fuck. Shit... mentally I begin to panic when I feel Caleb come up behind me. Did he just hear what Drew said about being completely incapable of forgetting the taste of my lips? It feels like my heart ceases to beat as I look up at my husband with wide eyes waiting to see the anger or crushing heartbreak that might signal that he heard Drew.

Fortunately, Caleb only looks irritated, not angry or heartbroken enough to have overheard anything. I do feel his fingers tighten on my shoulders in a possessive manner as he studies Drew for a moment. I hold my breath while I wait for either man to speak. One wrong word from Drew, and Caleb will suspect something is up. I can't believe my shitty luck of running into this man two nights in a row at two different bars.

"Hey man, I'm Caleb. This is my wife Eloise you're talking to." Caleb doesn't offer his hand to Drew, only greeting him with a curt nod before picking up the Old-Fashioned I ordered while waiting for his call to end.

"Oh, she's *your* wife? You are a very lucky man to be married to this gorgeous woman." Drew's voice is a deep rumble over my skin as I try desperately not to react to his words. His words are innocent enough, but the way he says them makes them sound anything but. I swallow the lump forming in my throat and interject before they get into a dick measuring contest.

"It was nice meeting you, Drew, but as you can see, I'm in good company for the night. I'm on a date with my husband. Have a nice night." I pray he takes my words for what they are, a dismissal. He takes his time slowly raking his gaze over my body before settling back on my face. He gives me a curt nod before sparing a glance to Caleb.

"I'd be careful leaving her alone in a place like this, man. A woman this gorgeous won't stay alone for very long here." With that, he walks off and takes up a spot on the other end of the bar where another woman is sitting and sipping a drink on her own. Clearly, this is the kind of club where people come to meet and hook up. Maybe I hadn't thought my plan through well before I suggested to Caleb that we come here. Then again, I had wanted to spark some sense of possessiveness and jealousy in him. I just hadn't expected it to be from seeing the man who gave me the best kiss I've had in recent memory. What were the fucking odds?

Clearing his throat, Caleb takes a seat next to me before speaking. "You ok, babe? Was he bothering you?"

He looks at me with an intensity I'm not expecting. My face heats under his scrutiny. To be honest, Drew was bothering me. But not in the way Caleb is asking. Just being near Drew again and feeling his body heat radiate towards me had me all sorts of hot and bothered. Before Caleb had interrupted us, Drew had been looking at me like I was his favorite snack, and he was ready to devour me.

"Oh no. He just saw I was alone and decided to shoot his shot. Obviously, he was barking up the wrong tree." I give Caleb a reassuring smile before remembering why I was sitting alone at the bar in the first place. "So, what was that call all about?" Caleb grimaces at my question and looks away blowing out an exasperated breath before responding. He looks like he wants to do anything but tell me what that call was about.

"Trey's wife has been put on bedrest due to pregnancy complications. Harold was calling to tell me I had to leave Monday to go to the Langford site to cover for him until Alex gets back from London. I'm sorry, Sweetness. I tried to get out of it, but Harold is apparently out of the country now too and I'm the only one he trusts to oversee this project."

A myriad of emotions flow through my mind; crushing disappointment, anger, frustration, concern for Kara and guilt over being mad at Trey for something that is out of his hands. Caleb reaches for my hand, but I pull it away before he makes contact.

"Lo, please, don't be mad. I know you're frustrated,

but I can't leave Harold hanging. He's given me so much at this company. I'm just going to do this trip, and I promise when I get back, I'll talk to him about no more traveling for work."

A derisive snort sneaks out before I can stop it. "Cal, cut the shit. That's what you said before you went to Tacoma and San Diego. I swear, sometimes it feels like you're more married to Harold and this job than you are to me. Did you know last month you were out of town for 20 days? Twenty days I was alone without my husband-missing him and dying a little inside. I don't know how much longer I can do this."

The words leave my mouth before I can even think them through but the hurt that surfaces to the top of the emotional turmoil that I'm feeling is steering this ship at the moment. My hopes of a romantic night sparking the flame of our marriage slips through my fingers. Anguish crosses across Caleb's beautiful face at my words, but before he can say anything I slip out of my seat and step away from his reaching grasp. "I'm going to the bathroom. Can you pay our tab? I'm just ready to go."

I make my way across the dark club, careful to not look at the happy couples dancing sensually near the front of the room, or the ones snuggled together in dark corners clearly enjoying themselves more than I am. In the bath-room, I take a moment to splash water on my face and gather my composure.

Staring at my reflection, I try to decide if I meant what I said about not being able to do this much longer. I love

Caleb. I truly and deeply do, but is it enough if it always feels like I'm in second place for him? Is it worth throwing away over a decade together? Do I deserve to be lonely at night in my bed because he can't stand to disappoint Harold? A knock at the door drags me from my thoughts.

"Sorry, just a moment!" I dry my face and hands quickly and go to unlock the door. Instead of finding a woman waiting her turn, like I expect, Drew is leaning against the door frame looking as tall, dark and dangerous as he did last night. "Shit Drew, what do you think you're doing?" Subconsciously I back away from him and go deeper into the restroom. His gaze sweeps over me once more before landing on my face and he shoots me a concerned look.

"You looked upset. I just wanted to see if you were ok. Doesn't seem like your date with your husband is going so well."

"I'm fine and it's none of your business." I snap out in response. Before I can tell him to leave, he takes two long strides across the room, and he stops directly in front of me. He raises his hand and gently brushes his knuckles along my cheek tucking a loose tendril of my hair behind my ear.

"I thought you said you weren't settling for the bare minimum, Eloise." The way he says my name sends a shiver down my spine and goosebumps erupt along my skin. "That didn't look like a conversation between a couple deliriously in love. It looked like a conversation between a couple barely holding on by a thread."

I close my eyes and take in a deep breath attempting to calm my racing heart, inhaling his spice and citrus with a faint hint of tobacco scent. God, he smells good.

"Please leave me alone." The whisper barely leaves my lips and I'm afraid to open my eyes. I'm not entirely sure if I am strong enough to resist him if he is still looking at me like that. I feel his hand drop away from my face and I immediately miss the contact.

Before I can say anything else, I feel him slip something into my hand as he whispers against my ear, "For when you're ready to stop settling." His lips ghost down the column of my neck before he backs away for good.

I keep my eyes squeezed shut as I will my heart to return to a normal rhythm, listening to his retreating footsteps. I take a few deep breaths before leaving the restroom, hoping nobody noticed a man leaving the women's room. My heart stutters against my chest again when I see Caleb standing at the end of the hall between me and escape. His arms are crossed against his chest and his lips are pressed in a firm line, like he's concentrating on working out a tricky puzzle. Shit, did he see Drew walk out? What am I going to say if he asks?

Inhaling a trembling breath, I hesitantly make my way over to where Caleb is standing, one of his broad shoulders leaning against the wall. I move to walk past him, just desperate to have whatever confrontation outside away from the happy, in love couples in this club. His arm shoots out, blocking my way, and he turns towards me, grabbing my bicep with his other hand, backing me against the wall. He has me caged against the wall with his body as he leans down pressing his forehead against mine.

"Baby, I know you're upset. I get it. I promise I do. I hate doing this to you, to us. I promise you; I will talk to Harold. I'll get him to relieve me of the travel duties and I'll work from home. Don't give up on us, Sweetness. You know you're my world." He reaches up and gently cups my cheek, his thumb caressing away the tears that fall. "Lo, I love you. You're it for me. If I've somehow made you doubt that, then I'm an asshole and I'll do anything to make it up to you. Let's get through this trip and I swear to you I'll fix it. I'll fix everything."

Caleb brushes his lips against mine gently, tentatively as if asking for permission before fully kissing me. My tongue darts out against his lips and I reach my hands up to grab his face pulling him fully against my mouth. My normally sweet, gentle husband kisses me with an almost feral need as his tongue thrusts into my mouth sweeping against my own. His body presses against mine and I can feel his growing erection against my belly. His mouth consumes mine with a heat we haven't shared in such a long time. My teeth nip against his bottom lip as I run my hands up into his hair, tangling my fingers in curls at the nape of his neck. "Fuck baby. I need you." He growls against my lips as he grinds his hips against me. "Let's go home. I need to fuck you and remind you who you belong to."

I nod at his request and pull away just enough to say,

"God, yes. Please Cal. Take me home and fuck me." Caleb takes my hand in his and half leads, half drags me out of the club desperate to get us away from prying eyes. Back at the car my body is buzzing with a need that can't be quenched. Before Caleb has a chance to buckle up, I climb into his lap and start kissing him again. All my heart is telling me is that I need my husband, and I can't wait any longer.

"Babe, what are..." I shush him with a kiss as I reach down between us and undo his belt and open his fly.

"I need you. Now. Please don't make me wait," I plead against his mouth as I reach into his pants and pull out his cock. Caleb lets out a low groan as I give him a few strokes with my hand before I grind my pussy against him. My lace panties are damp with my arousal already and I know it won't take me long to come all over his cock once he's in me. I've been on a knife's edge after the stunt I pulled this afternoon with the blowjob, and I feel like I'm a volcano ready to erupt.

"Lo, we're on the street. Anyone could see us." I can tell his protest is weak, and he's into this as much as I am. The thrill of getting caught sends a pulse of excitement down to my core that rivals the feeling I had when Drew kissed me last night.

"Then let them see." I whisper against his ear as I slide my underwear to the side and notch him at my entrance. I rub the head of his cock against my slick folds one, two, three times before finally sinking down on him, fully seating myself on him. We don't have much room to move so I just start rocking my hips against him, my clit rubbing deliciously against his pelvis, his mouth devouring mine like I'm the air he needs to breathe. The windows begin to fog up from our passion, and I feel giddy, like a high schooler getting it on in their parent's car at the risk of getting caught.

"Yes, baby. Right there. That's it." I'm breathless and incoherent as I grind down on him, Caleb anchoring my hips on his lap with his hands. He lets out a guttural moan as he begins to lose control and starts thrusting up into me. My orgasm builds quickly, and Caleb knows it's coming. He tugs the deep neckline of my dress to the side, freeing my breast, and sucks my nipple into his mouth. "Yes, yes, yes!" I pant breathlessly as I clutch his head against my breast, as my orgasm crests and causes my pussy to clench and flutter, sending Caleb over the edge too. I feel him thicken and his cum pulse inside me as I drop my head onto his shoulder and begin to catch my breath.

"Jesus, Lo. That was amazing." Caleb kisses me gently again, almost reverently. I take a moment to bask in the glow of this moment before climbing off his lap and into my seat. I open the glove box looking for napkins to clean up with, but Caleb shuts it before I can look. "Nu-uh. You're riding home with me inside you. Then I'm going to clean it up properly when we get home."

Fuck, when did my husband become so possessive and dominant? Maybe my plan did work after all. I bite back a smile as I lower my window to let some fresh air into the car and defog the windows. My breath hitches in my chest when I see a dark shadow move against the wall of the alley next to us. Shit, someone did see us. I'm almost ready to point it out to Caleb when the shadow moves into the light, and I see that it's Drew and he has an almost demonic grin on his face. He definitely knows what we were up to and judging by his expression he enjoyed the show. I look away quickly and roll my window back up, deciding against mentioning our audience to Caleb. Maybe Drew will get the picture now and will leave me alone.

Caleb reaches across the middle console and grabs my hand, bringing it to his mouth to place a loving kiss across my knuckles. "I love you, Lo. I'll make sure you come first from now on, I swear it." With that promise we take off down the darkened street and I can't help but wonder if Caleb will keep his word this time or if I'm about to be let down again.

CHAPTER
FIVE

CALEB

"*I don't know how much longer I can do this...*" Eloise's words echo in my mind while I stare at the blueprints in front of me without actually seeing them. It's been four days since I left, and I cannot get the look of frustration and hurt across Lo's face out of my head. Sure, we had the hottest sex we've had in years right after that, but by Monday morning when I left the house, I could tell she was closed off from me again. That, coupled with the fact that we haven't really talked since Tuesday, I feel like my marriage is slipping right through my fingers.

A knock at the door draws me from my thoughts. Ashlyn, one of the lead architects, sticks her head in my makeshift office set up at the worksite. I close out the program on my computer and lean back to greet Ashlyn. "What's up, Ash?"

"A few of the guys and I are going out for dinner. There's a dive bar down the street that supposedly has the best wings in the city, and apparently a killer craft beer selection." I'm a little caught off guard by the mention of dinner and glance at the clock. It reads 7:15. Shit, I didn't realize it had gotten so late. A niggle of worry tugs at my brain when I realize it's been complete radio silence from Eloise all day. That's not normal for us. Even if we don't talk on the phone, we usually exchange a few 'I love you' texts and gifs throughout the day. I open my messaging app and see my last text to her from a few hours ago is still on read with no response.

"Thanks for the invite, Ash, but I'll probably just head back to the hotel."

"Oh no you don't, Caleb. You've been a hermit locked in your hotel room all week. I asked nicely out of politeness but now I'm telling you, you're coming to dinner." Ashlyn flashes me her megawatt smile that lights up her whole face. She's a beautiful girl with a wild mass of dark curls that frames her face like a halo, her skin a gorgeous shade of ebony and eyes so dark, it feels like you could fall into them and never come back out. She also has a reputation for being a woman who knows what she wants and doesn't take no for an answer. Her tenacity is legendary on the work site, and I know from previous experience that I am not going to win this fight.

"Ok fine but give me ten minutes. I'm going to call Lo real quick." Ashlyn shoots me a victorious smile, like she just won the lottery.

"Sure thing, boss. Meet us by the back gate. The bar is

just down at the corner." She tips me a salute before ducking out of my office.

As soon as the door closes, I hit Lo's name on my phone to call her. I just want to check in with her to make sure everything is ok with us. Worry is gnawing a pit in my stomach, telling me something isn't right. She picks up on the 5th ring, right before it rolls over to voicemail.

"Hey, babe. What's up?" She sounds distracted and there is a lot of background noise wherever she is.

"Hey, Sweetness. I was just missing you and wanted to hear your voice. We didn't get to talk last night. I'm sorry I passed out before your shift ended. I tried to stay up for you, but this job is a brutal one. I worked 12 hours yesterday then crashed as soon as I got back to my room. You've been quiet today. Is everything ok?" My ears strain trying to figure out where she is by the background noise on her end.

"Everything is fine, Cal. I was exhausted when I got off work anyway. It was a rough night in the E.D. I took today off to recover; I just couldn't drag myself out of bed this morning. Hey, have you talked to Alex and figured out when he'll be back from London and can relieve you? I miss you so much." Her declaration of missing me soothes some of my frayed nerves but I know what I'm about to say won't make her happy.

"Erm, yeah. I did. He says he'll be leaving London next Friday. I'm here at least until next weekend. I'm sorry, baby. I was really hoping I could get back this weekend."

"Oh...ok." I can feel her disappointment radiating

through the phone. I have to make this up to her somehow before she spirals more into her feelings of being second place.

"I'm going to make it up to you. What do you say when I get back, we take a long weekend and go to that little cabin we spent our first anniversary at? You know, the one up in the Poconos? We can fuck in the hot tub, feed each other strawberries covered in cream, and stay drunk on champagne. Just like we did when we were 25."

"Cal, you better not be making promises you can't keep." Lo's tone is hopeful but cautious. I know she doesn't believe I'll follow through with this plan, so I make it my mission to prove her wrong.

"I'll book it as soon as I get back to my hotel. I'll send you the confirmation email. You better start packing."

"If I remember correctly, I won't need to pack much. There wasn't much need for clothing on that trip." I can hear the smirk in her words, and I bite my bottom lip picturing how amazing she looked in that hot tub, naked and freshly fucked. I hear something like the clatter of glassware on her end.

"Where are you at babe? It's noisy as hell on your end."

"Oh, just meeting Sara for dinner. I'm still waiting for her. You know how she is; she'd be late to her own funeral."

I chuckle, she's not wrong. Sara was Lo's Maid of Honor at our wedding and held our ceremony up by half an hour because she lost one of her shoes between her house and our wedding venue. "Well have fun tonight,

Sweetness. Keep an eye out for that confirmation email. I love you."

"Love you too, babe. Goodnight."

The worry that had been eating at me eases a bit knowing Lo is just meeting Sara for dinner. As I make my way to the meeting spot to find Ashlyn, I pull up the vacation rental app and book the cabin for a long weekend away. Operation "Make my wife fall back in love with me" is now fully underway.

Ashlyn and I walk to the bar together, my mind a little more at ease after making my plan to show Eloise how much I still love her. I glance over at Ashlyn, and she gives me a sly smirk. "You're looking awfully proud of yourself, Ash. Did you win a bet or something?"

"As a matter of fact, I did. I bet the boys I'd be able to get you out for dinner tonight, and they told me there'd be no way because you're a pussy-whipped stick in the mud who never goes out when he's on a job. So now, I get to eat all the free wings I can handle thanks to you." She gives me a playful nudge on the shoulder as my face heats from embarrassment over their impression of me.

"I live to serve. Must be all that pussy-whipping. Always keeps me in line when a pretty lady asks me for a favor." I wink at her, knowing full well she has no problem taking my ribbing.

"I can't say that I blame you, Cal. If I had that waiting for me when I got home, I'd probably stay in my room flicking the bean all night to her pictures." Ashlyn shoots me a salacious wink.

She and Lo have met more than a few times, the first time at a Christmas party hosted by Harold on the company's dime. I caught her flirting with my wife and Eloise eating it right up. If I hadn't stepped in when I did, I'm not entirely sure I'm the one Lo would've gone home with that night, and I can't say that I would've been able to fault her. There is something magnetic about Ashlyn that most women are drawn to, even the straight ones.

"I'll be sure you pass on your regards, Ash." I roll my eyes at her as we step into the bar.

"You do that. Be sure to let her know my offer from Christmas still stands." Ashlyn purrs in my ear and I give her a playful swat on the arm.

"Down girl, that's my wife you're talking about. And what offer are you talking about?" Instead of responding, Ashlyn shoots me a wicked grin and saunters over to the table where several of the engineers and crew members from the site are already sitting. I make a mental note to ask Lo about this mysterious offer to see if I need to worry about playing defense on more than one front.

Ashlyn wasn't kidding when she said she was going to eat all the chicken wings she could handle. It's a few hours later, we are four baskets of chicken wings and several IPAs deep into the night. The rest of the crew have left, leaving me and Ashlyn to settle the tab. Or rather, left me to settle the tab since she won the bet.

"So, what made you decide to come out tonight, Caleb? You are a notorious stick in the mud when you're traveling for work. The guys weren't wrong about that." Ashlyn grins at me as she licks wing sauce from her fingers.

"If you must know, I'm planning on this being my last trip for work. I'm going to talk to Harold when I get back about cutting out the travel and just working at the home office. It's been a huge strain on my marriage, and I think if I don't make a drastic change Lo is going to leave me."

I surprised myself by my confession. The strong beers must be doing a good job of loosening my tongue. It doesn't hurt that Ashlyn and I have a great rapport, and I have confided in her before over personal matters.

"When I started to do this for the company, Harold made it seem like I might be out of town a week here and there a few times a year. Last month I was gone more than I was at home, and it's been like that for a while. Lo has had enough of it and frankly, so have I. It's time to put us first again before our marriage falls apart for good."

Ashlyn nods thoughtfully, taking in my words. She knows what it's like, the constant travel from city to city, job site to job site. But she is in her 20s, unattached, and living for the travel experience. "You're a smart man, Caleb Fitzpatrick. Not many men realize that the job doesn't come first until it's too late. Will old man Jones agree to your demands? You do realize he's been grooming you to take over the company when he retires. That's why he's been pushing you so hard lately."

I shrug as I toss back the rest of my beer. "He'll have to, I'm not asking him, I'm telling him. Lo comes first and he's just going to have to respect that."

Ashlyn has the cheek to snap her fingers and look disappointed at my declaration. "Well damn, I was hoping for an opening to help Lo through her lesbian sexual awakening when she got tired of you. Seems like you're stiffer competition than I realized."

"Better luck next time." I flag down the bartender to pay our tab so we can head back to the hotel.

CHAPTER
SIX

ELOISE

It's Wednesday night at work, and since Caleb is out of town, I offered to pull a double to cover Melanie's shift when she called out this morning. Our department runs in a permanent state of overworked and under-appreciated since the pandemic made people quit the healthcare field in droves. Working through a worldwide health crisis with inadequate PPE, inadequate pay, and watching your patients and co-workers die off like flies will definitely make most seek greener pastures. The only reason I haven't moved on myself is because I went into healthcare to find a career where it feels like I'm making a difference. After a life of menial office jobs, where I mostly spend my days surfing the internet to its very ends, I couldn't take it anymore and said piss off to my degree in English Lit and went back to school. I'm not jaded enough to completely leave healthcare, but I can feel the burnout creeping up on me every double shift I work. I decide if Caleb stops traveling for work, then I will work more sane hours; overtime, incentive, and pay be damned. The stress of basically living at the hospital isn't worth the toll it is taking on my mental health.

It's almost 10pm and I'm on 'til midnight. The E.D. has been popping off all night with drunk frat kids coming in after a brawl at a party on the rowdy side of campus. There was also a multi-vehicle accident on the interstate that resulted in two traumas being called at dinner time. I check the work list and see another patient pop up from the E.D. for an x-ray. I'm the only one working on this side right now, my other two co-workers covering the CT scanners, so I let out an exhausted sigh before printing out the order and trudging off to find my patient in the waiting room.

"Andrew Jameson!"

I call out when I get to the waiting room. Surprisingly, the room appears to be empty for the first time all night. I can only hope that means the rest of my night is going to go better than the last four hours. I refused to tempt fate by thinking of the "Q" word though. "Jameson!" I raise my voice and say the name again as I wander deeper into the waiting room. There are random nooks and crannies where chairs get shoved into, and most patients are usually too drunk, deaf, or zoned out to hear their names being called. Just before I give up, a deep voice that sounds uncomfortably familiar speaks up right behind me from the corner I just walked past.

"I'm right here." My heart lodges in my throat and I

close my eyes for a moment before turning around. There is no fucking way it's him. It's not possible. Why in the hell would fate put him in my path again? Slowly, I turn around, and drag my eyes up from the paper I'm holding. My heart goes from being lodged completely in my throat to falling completely out of my ass when my eyes meet Drew's. He appears to be fighting the urge to smirk when he gives me a very thorough once over before speaking again. "I'm Andrew Jameson." Fuck my life.

"Right, um, yeah Mr. Jameson, if you come back with me, I'll take your x-ray." My professionalism is shot. I'm officially panicking, and I don't know how I'm going to get through this without making it weird or letting him make my panties wet again. Drew, despite having his hand wrapped in a bandage and an ice pack, seems to be completely unfazed. He almost looks amused by my rising panic. I brush past him and just let him follow me back to my department. I give myself a mental pep talk to get through this as quickly as possible, and then consider begging the shift leader to let me leave early.

In the exam room, I motion to the chair I have set up next to the exam table with the detector on it. "So, what brings you in tonight Mr. Jameson? Did you lose a fight against a wall?" I let the sarcastic quip slip as I check his wrist band and position him for the first image.

"I don't know if you're aware, but there was a huge brawl at Maverick's tonight with a bunch of frat bro idiots. I might have got pulled into it and a frat douche might have come in earlier with a broken nose after he met my fist. I cannot confirm or deny anything without speaking to my lawyer first." Drew gives me a lazy shrug as if to say it wasn't the worst part of his night.

"Aren't you a little old to be hanging out in frat bars? Hold still, don't move a muscle." I step back and hit the exposure button before coming back out to rearrange his hand for the next picture.

"To hang, yes. But I was bartending tonight helping my buddy out when half his staff called out with food poisoning." As I move his hand into position, I feel him graze his fingertips against my palm. I glance over at his face to see if it was intentional, and he shoots a wink at me. Fucker. I can't believe he is still this persistent after I tossed the card he gave me and blew him off completely. I rush through the rest of the exam, before I lose my cool completely.

"Ok, I'll take you back to the waiting room," I say with my eyes trained on the computer screen studying the x-rays before sending them to our radiologist on duty. No breaks that I can see, so hopefully that means the doctor will discharge him once the rad gives a negative report. I turn to walk him out of the room and find myself running into an Andrew-sized brick wall. He has me trapped behind the half-wall that separates the controls from the rest of the exam room. Drew is looking down at me with an expression I cannot read, but a chill creeps up my spine from the intense look he is giving me.

"What do you think you're doing? How many times am I going to have to tell you no? Please step back and let me take you back to the waiting room." I try to command him to move out of my way with a lot more bravado than I'm currently feeling. Instead of doing what I ask, Drew cocks his head to the side and studies my face like I'm a puzzle he is trying to work out. He reaches up and brushes the loose tendril of hair behind my ear, mimicking his movements from the club Saturday night.

"You can't tell me you don't feel this. This connection. This magnetism. I can't get you out of my head, Eloise. You are the most stunning woman I've ever seen. I can't forget the taste of you. Why do you think we keep running into each other like this, if not fate?" My breathing grows shallow, and my skin heats up under his touch. He leans down, ghosting his lips over mine before whispering, "You're mine, Eloise. You just don't know it yet."

His words are like a bucket of ice-cold water dousing the flames from his touch. Before I can come up with a response, he is backing away and strolls out the door like he didn't just try to light me on fire and drench my panties at the same time.

Two hours later, I'm dragging my tired bones through the parking lot to my car at the very back corner. Employees are regulated to what we lovingly refer to as the 'back 40' which means we are forced to park a long way from the entrance. Not exactly the safest thing for a woman leaving work at midnight but considering our hospital security guard is every bit of 75 years old and should have retired a decade ago, I tend to skip having him escort me out.

I'm scrolling on my phone checking my text messages for anything from Caleb. We didn't get to talk tonight due to me working late. But like clockwork, I see the string of gifs he sent throughout the day documenting how his day was going. *Confused blonde girl in the car seat* in response to an emergency meeting he was called into this morning, due to someone forgetting to plan for handicap stalls in all the bathrooms. *Ed Bundy from Married with Children* complaining about starving to death at lunch. *Phil Collins smirking from the "Against all Odds" video.* Goddamn it. Now that song is in my head. Neither one of us are big on talking on the phone when he's out of town, but we can have entire conversations in gifs only.

I look up from my phone as I approach my car and see an envelope laying against my windshield. "What the fuck is that?" I spin around scanning the parking lot looking for whoever might have left it. My search is futile, I'm the only one crazy enough to be standing in this pitch-dark parking lot at midnight. I snag the envelope and lock myself in the car before opening it with shaking hands. Inside is a picture. It's dark, grainy and looks like it was taken from a security camera feed. The quality isn't great, so it takes me a minute to realize what I'm looking at. It's a picture of me and Drew kissing outside the bar Saturday night. His hand is clasped possessively in my purple hair and my hands are resting against his chest. From this angle, you can't tell that he's the aggressor initiating the kiss. It just looks like two lovers sharing an intimate moment under a streetlamp. My heart begins to race and a sweat rolls down my back. Did Drew leave this? Did someone else see us on Saturday? Are they going to tell Caleb? Fuck, I can feel the panic clawing its way up my chest.

A knock at my window startles me out of my spiraling thoughts. I shove the photo down into my purse as I look up to see one of the E.D. doctors standing at my door. I roll my window down and greet him in as normal a voice as I can muster. "Hey Dr. E. What's up?"

"I was just going to ask you the same thing, Eloise. I saw you just sitting here and thought maybe your battery needed a jump." Doctor Emory is older, in his mid 50s with a paternal streak a mile wide. He's always looking after his staff as much as he is his patients. I appreciate the hell out of that about him, but right now, all I want to do is get home and crawl under the covers and try to ward off this chill settling in my bones.

"Oh no, I'm good! Sorry, I got sidetracked looking at my phone. I'm heading home now. Thank you for checking on me though, Dr. E., I appreciate it."

"Just be careful, Eloise. I worry about you ladies getting off this late at night. Be aware of your surroundings, ok?" Doctor Emory flashes me a warm smile before backing away towards his car. I give him a little wave as I pull out. Tomorrow, I'll talk to Sara and make a plan to deal with this creepy ass picture left for me.

The next morning, I decided to call out from work and try to work out the mystery of the picture. I have to get this figured out before Caleb gets home and something worse happens. I send Sara a text seeing if she can meet up at Brewed Awakening.

> Me: Emergency coffee run. Now. Brewed Awakening.

> Sara: Another one already? Did you make out with another tall, dark and dangerous stranger? Do I need to put a leash on you?

> Me: I'll explain there, but you're not entirely wrong.

> Sara: WTF *shocked face emoji*

Twenty minutes later, Sara is staring at the picture with a furrowed brow and a worried frown on her face. "Ok, so walk this back for me. Tall, dark and dangerous shows up at Allure when you and Caleb are there, and he not-so-subtly flirts with you in front of your husband. Then you wind up with him as a patient at work last night, where once again he stomps all over your personal boundaries and basically hikes his leg and pisses on you? Then you find this on your windshield when you leave? Am I getting this timeline right?"

"That pretty much sums it up. What should I do?"

Sara's eyes bug out at me like I just asked her if I should go skydiving without a parachute. "Um, go to the police. Obviously. Jesus Lo, you have a stalker!"

Out of all the possibilities that had crossed my mind, Drew being a stalker hadn't occurred to me. "That's crazy. I'm not the kind of girl who gets stalkers. What if it's someone who saw me Friday night and is trying to stir up shit with us? You know his co-worker Tabitha has been sniffing around recently. Just two weeks ago, I stopped by his office for lunch, and I caught her sitting on the edge of his desk in one of those sexy pencil skirts and low-cut blouse combos. Some straight up Mad Men bullshit."

"Lo, I say this with love in my heart. You are a fucking dense bitch. Do you even hear yourself? What is more likely? Option A: Stupid handsome and dangerous-looking stranger who happens to give you the most panty-melting kiss of all time, randomly runs into you three times in one week by chance? Or Option B: Tabitha, the co-worker you didn't even know existed until two weeks ago somehow saw you kissing tall, dark and dangerous, and found the security camera, managed to print out a screen shot from the bar's security camera and then left it on your car at work?"

"Well, when you put it that way, your theory makes a little more sense but what are the police going to do? What am I going to tell them? 'Hi, Mr. Officer, this dude I just met keeps randomly popping up wherever I am. He's devastatingly sexy and keeps ruining my panties. It's bad for my marriage, can you do me a favor and arrest him?'" I shake my head ruefully. "He hasn't done anything illegal. I know how this story goes. The police will shrug their shoulders, tell me to document anything he does that is harassment, be more mindful of my surroundings, but they can't do anything yet without any proof."

Sara blows out a frustrated breath, realizing I have a point. "Ok, fair enough. Then tell Caleb."

I hold up my hand and stop her before she can continue that line of thought. "Absolutely not. He saw Drew at Allure. If I tell him that this guy kissed me and I didn't mention it as soon as it happened, it will devastate him. I'm trying to save my marriage, not drive a stake through its still-beating heart. I just need to make it clearer to Drew that whatever he thinks is between us doesn't exist. I'm not that interesting or attractive. Once he realizes the thrill of the chase isn't enough to break me, he will move on. That's how guys operate. He's just trying to get his dick wet; he'll get bored when he sees I'm really and truly not interested."

I can tell Sara isn't convinced by my reasoning by the nervous way she's chewing on her bottom lip. "I don't like this, Lo. The fact that he left that picture on your car gives me the impression that he is *all* about the chase, and the harder you are to catch the more satisfying it will be for him."

"If it'll make you feel better, I'll get one of those pepper spray keychain things or one of those fancy rape whistle doodads. Caleb has his concealed license, so we have a gun at home if it's needed."

My best friend throws up her hands in defeat. "Fine, but if you wind up on Dateline, I am NOT going to say that you lit up the room when you were around. I'm going to say you died by your own damn stupidity."

I give her an incorrigible grin. "I wouldn't expect anything less. That's why you are my ride or die."

SEVEN

ELOISE

Last night, I decided to test Sara's theory that Andrew is stalking me. I know, it sounds like the dumbest idea ever, but I don't truly think he is. If she's right, then he'll turn up where I am and then I'll know I need to actually go to the police. If I'm right, I just get to drink a few cocktails in peace, and know I don't have a stalker.

I returned to the scene of the crime, The Blind Pig, where we met. I felt guilty lying to Caleb when he called while I was there, but I have to figure this out before he gets back. That means I have less than one week to sort out my Drew mess and set things right. Fortunately, Drew did not turn up last night. I had a beer and some appetizers and split, already feeling better about my situation.

It's Saturday night and I'm getting ready to head into a little speakeasy bar called Stellina. Stellina is a small, intimate bar. There are only a handful of tables, and limited seating at the bar itself. The lighting is low, the music is sexy. It's not meant as a place to hang out, but more of an after-dinner drink before you head home, spot. I chose it because of its small, intimate setting. If Drew does show up, there will be no place for him to hide and watch me from afar. If he is going to show his face, I want to be able to confront him and put a stop to his attention once and for all.

As I walk in, I notice the only seating available is at the bar. I make my way over, casually scoping out the crowd for any familiar faces. It is mostly couples on date nights, with a few single men sitting at the bar that look like they might be in town on business. Nobody that should know me, or Caleb. The picture is still in the back of my mind, and if it was sent from someone other than Drew, I want to be aware of anything I do that might get back to Caleb. I know what it'll look like to someone on the outside who knows us, if they see me going out to bars while Caleb is out of town.

I take my seat at the bar, giving a polite smile to the businessman in the seat next to me. I turn my attention to the bartender and feel my mouth fall open in shock when my eyes meet a very familiar face. Shit, I made a major miscalculation in my plan. Drew is standing right in front of me, leaning against the counter behind him, arms crossed against his chest looking positively delicious in a black button-down shirt with the sleeves rolled up to show off his forearms. A bar towel is tossed casually across his shoulder, his hair up in a messy bun and a wolfish grin spread across his face.

"Well, hello there, darlin'. You just couldn't stay away, could you?" There is mirth dancing in his dark eyes. I can tell he is loving this turn of events. First, he shows up at my place of work, and now I am at his. I debate the option to cut and run before he gets the wrong idea, but this is exactly what I was hoping for isn't it? A chance to confront him and tell him to move on from his interest in me. I take a deep breath, calming my jangling nerves and decide that is exactly what I'll do. I'll have one drink, lay it all out there for him, encourage him to move on and not let him work his panty melting smolder on me. Not today, Satan.

"What do you recommend?" I smile blandly, trying to keep my voice neutral. I will not flirt with him; I will not engage in banter. I am a woman on a mission, and I will not be deterred.

"Depends on what you like. Are you a fruity cocktail kind of woman? More of a smokey bourbon? Do you like bitter or herbal flavors?" Drew leans in closer to me as he speaks, his voice low and melodic. His deep bass shoots straight to my pussy.

"I can give you anything you want. You just have to ask for it." Shit. He didn't get the 'I'm not here to flirt' memo. His stare bores right into my soul and I suddenly feel like I'm in over my head.

"Um...I'll take..." I stutter and glance down at the menu on the bar and quickly tap my finger on a random drink. It doesn't matter, I'm here on business, not to get drunk. "I'll have the Beautiful Dreamer."

Drew nods appreciatively. "Good choice. I created the

recipe for that one myself, just this week. I was inspired by a beautiful woman that I can't seem to get out of my head." He winks at me before turning to collect ingredients for the cocktail. Fuck my life. Is my luck truly this terrible? Or is he just that damn smooth on the fly?

Before I have a chance to spiral, the businessman next to me speaks up. "So do you come here often?"

Is he for real with that opener? I turn and look at him, taking in his appearance. He looks like a complete Chad. Short cropped blonde hair, styled in that 'I was in a frat and went to school for 'business' way' with a chiseled jaw bare of any scruff. He looks like he'd be right at home in the middle of a group of dude bros vying for the affection of some attention-seeking woman on one of those bachelor TV shows. In short, not my type at all.

Before I even respond he speaks again. "I'm Brayden. What's your name, beautiful?" Jesus, this guy is full steam ahead.

"It's 'I'm not interested', thanks though." I turn away from him, driving my point home. The absolute last thing I need right now is one more dick sniffing around my unavailable pussy.

"Oh, come on now, gorgeous. Don't be like that. I'm just trying to be friendly. Toss a guy a bone."

"She said she's not interested. If she has to say it again, I will kick you out on your ass." Drew sets my drink down in front of me before leveling his glare on Brayden. I quirk a brow at him and mutter under my breath.

"Pot, meet kettle." I see him cut his glare back to me,

before returning the full force of it to business douche sitting next to me.

Brayden raises his hands in surrender. "Sorry, my bad man. I'll leave her alone." With a curt nod, Drew turns back to me and waits patiently for me to try my drink. I can tell he's interested in what I'll think of his original creation.

The Beautiful Dreamer is a gorgeous hue of bright red with a lemon zest perched on the rim making the whole thing look like a bright pop of summer. I take a sip and moan appreciatively. It is an herbal gin-based cocktail with hints of lemon and blueberry, and just enough bitters to keep it from being cloyingly sweet. It is delicious and I take another sip before saying so to Drew. "This is amazing. Do you make up most of your own cocktail recipes?"

Drew grins at me like I just told him he'd be taking me home tonight. "Most of them, but my staff have a few of their own creations on the menu too. We have monthly collaboration meetings to come up with new seasonal cocktails."

"Your staff?" I perk up at this bit of info. If he's the manager of this place, then maybe he will listen to what I have to say without causing a scene. I can get in and out quickly without drama.

"Stellina is my place. My baby." Drew sweeps his hand across the bar, grinning like a proud papa.

"Hey boss! I need a keg change, please!" A pretty, petite blonde comes up from the other end of the bar with a foamy, half full beer. "The Belgian just kicked. Do you mind taking a break from flirting with the customers to do some work?" She shoves the beer at him and shoots me a cheeky grin. I return her grin, appreciating the fact that his employees feel comfortable enough to give Drew a hard time. Surely, he wouldn't have that level of rapport with his employees if he was a total creeper.

"Remind me again why I keep you around, Lisbeth?" Drew levels a mock serious look at his pint-sized dynamo of an employee.

"Because I rake in the big tips and keep the lonely businessmen coming back for more." She turns on her heel and sashays back to the other end of the bar to finish filling the other beers.

"I'll be right back. Don't go anywhere darlin'." I watch Drew saunter away, the black dress shirt stretched tight against his broad shoulders. It should be criminal for someone to be that cocky, and good looking. I take the reprieve from Drew's intensity to refortify my defenses. I will not waiver from my mission.

There is a thump on the floor next to my feet and I look down, finding my purse has slipped off the hook under the bar. Corporate Ken doll notices it too but does not offer to pick it up for me. He just gives me a derisive eye roll and returns to his beer. *Yup, definitely not my type at all*, I think as I slide off my stool to retrieve my purse.

When I pop back up, Reality-TV-bachelor-wanna-be Brayden is grinning like he has a secret. I decide I'm going to finish my drink, put Mr. Andrew Jameson in his place, and go home. I don't want to linger long enough for either one of them to decide to try their luck again. I finish my drink just as Drew returns from the back. "Can I get you another, darlin'? Looks like you're in need of more." I groan internally, why does everything this man says have to sound like an innuendo?

"Actually, I'm all set. I don't need anything more." I level a pointed look in his direction as I pull out cash to pay for my drink. "Look, I don't know if you left that picture on my car the other night, but I just need you to know that whatever you think is going on between us, isn't. This is the last time you're going to see me, Drew. Thanks for the amazing drink and I wish you well on your future endeavors."

Out of the corner of my eye, I see Brayden throw a twenty down on the bar top, chuckling to himself as he waltzes out. I'm sure seeing me shoot down Drew so thoroughly after dismissing him, has made his night. A dark shadow passes over Drew's face and I can tell he is clenching his jaw, biting back some sort of retort. I don't give him the chance though, slipping off my stool and walking out of Stellina, and out of his life for good.

As I walk outside into the sultry summer air, a wave of dizziness sweeps over me. I lean against the brick wall of the building, waiting for it to pass. A wave of nausea rolls through my gut, and I squeeze my eyes shut, willing it to go away. What the fuck is going on? Am I having an adrenaline crash after confronting Drew? Low blood sugar? Something feels wrong.

"Hey, are you ok?" A large hand clamps down on my

shoulder more firmly than necessary. I look up to see Business Douche Brayden leering down at me with a manic gleam in his eyes. I try to shove his arm away, but my limbs suddenly feel like they're made from lead.

"I'm fine. Leave me alone," I try to respond but it comes out more like, "I'm funnnn, leave m'lone." Panic starts to rise in my chest when I realize something is most definitely, terribly wrong. I try to pull out of his grip, but that just results in me stumbling into the wall and scraping my elbow on the brick. My vision is starting to darken at the edges, and I know if I don't get away from him something awful is going to happen.

"Hey, I'm going to help you. Don't worry, beautiful. I'll get you somewhere safe." A warm hand cups my cheek and tilts my head back. I'm unable to protest, but I hear a dark rumble of thunder come up from behind us that sounds an awful like Andrew.

"The hell you will, you fucking rapist." Suddenly, the punishing grip Brayden had on my shoulder is gone, and I'm sliding down to the ground unable to support myself any longer. Just before I pass out completely, I see Brayden's limp form collapse onto the ground next to me and I feel strong, warm arms wrap around me, lifting me from the ground. "I've got you darlin'. You're safe now."

The next morning, sunlight streams in through the high windows of the bedroom I'm in. I try to throw my arm over my face to block out the light, but a heavy weight is keeping my arms pinned down. There is a jackhammer in my head, and I desperately do not want to open my eyes to figure out what the hell is going on. Warm breath tickles my neck and the realization that I am not in my bed at home, alone, slams into me like a freight train.

"What the fuck..." I open my eyes to take in my surroundings. I appear to be in a bright, airy, loft style apartment with exposed beams in the ceiling and windows that go all the way up. Carefully I turn my head to the right to try to figure out who has me pinned down in the bed. Ice water runs through my veins when I see Drew staring at me, his face inches from me, a look of concern etched onto his features. "Drew...why are we in bed together?" I can feel the panic in my voice. "Oh god... what happened last night?"

Drew raises his arm from its resting place across my body and gently sweeps my hair out of my face. "Nothing that you didn't want to happen, Eloise. I made sure of that." My heart seizes in my chest as I take in his rumpled, shirtless appearance. No, no, no, no...quickly I sit up, causing a riotous explosion to go off in my head. I look down at myself and see I'm still wearing the same dress I had on last night. I can feel my bra digging into my back, so I know it is still in place, as is my underwear.

"Oh god, I think I'm going to be sick." I moan. Drew leaps into action, jumping off the bed and bringing me a small trash can to puke in. He rubs my back gently and I have just enough presence of mind to see he is wearing some gray sweatpants that do nothing to hide the weapon between his thighs. It's not much better than being naked, but it's something. I retch into the trash can, feeling like I've been run over by a Mack truck.

"I think that cocksucker roofied you. One of my regulars came and got me when they saw him leering over a girl outside who looked out of it. When I got there, you were barely standing upright, and he looked like he was getting ready to take you somewhere. I knocked his fucking lights out and brought you up to my place to keep an eye on you. I figured you probably didn't want to have to explain to your husband how you managed to get roofied while at a bar all alone when he's out of town." Drew brings a glass of cool water to my lips, and I drink it greedily.

"But why were you in bed with me?" I rasp out, my throat feeling like it has razor blades in it.

"To make sure you didn't get sick in your sleep. I didn't want you to be on your back if that happened. I promise you; I was a perfect gentleman all night." He is clenching his jaw again, like he's offended by my insinuation that he would've taken advantage of me. I nod, then immediately regret the motion as it sets off another round of jackhammering in my skull. "Here, take these and drink more water." He hands me some painkillers and I take them gratefully from him.

"I need to get home. Thank you for saving me, but I

can't be here." I attempt to swing my legs out of bed, but he presses a gentle but firm hand on my shoulder.

"You're not going anywhere like this. I want you to rest, eat and then shower. If you feel up to it after that I'll take you home, or to the police station if you want. But I want to make sure you're ok first." His tone brooks no arguments, so I lay back on the pillow and close my eyes again. He's not wrong. I don't think I could handle getting home in my current condition anyway. I just pray that Caleb doesn't try to call me or check my location on our phone plan, until I get out of here. I don't even know where I am, and I'd have no way to explain why I'm downtown on a Sunday morning instead of at home in bed.

Sometime later, the bright morning sun that had been streaming in through the windows has lessened in intensity, and it looks like it might be afternoon now. Thanks to the painkillers, I can open my eyes now without setting off the jackhammer in my head. The smell of frying bacon has me sitting up in bed and my stomach grumbling. I can hear the clatter of dishes in the kitchen and the smooth bluesy sound of Nathaniel Rateliff and the Night Sweats pouring out of speakers throughout the whole apartment. Before heading out into the kitchen, I make a stop in the ensuite bathroom. I take in my appearance in the mirror. My makeup is smudged, my hair looks like a raccoon tried to braid it, and a bruise that looks suspiciously like fingerprints is forming on my left shoulder. I do my business, scrub the makeup from my face, steal some of Drew's mouthwash and attempt to tame the rat's nest on my head. I still look like fresh hell, but at least I look slightly less zombified.

As I enter the open plan living and/kitchen area I spy Drew plating us a feast of eggs, bacon, toast, fruit and yogurt. "Rise and shine, princess. How are you feeling?" He gives me a thorough once over that feels a lot like an inquisition with his eyes. Much to my chagrin, he is still only wearing those gray sweatpants that do absolutely nothing to draw attention away from his dick.

"Ugh, don't call me that." I grumble as I sit down and immediately start inhaling the food in front of me. I can't help the near sexual moan that leaves my mouth when the salty bacon hits my tongue. "God I'm hungry." I mumble as I chew, hoping that between the puking and my unladylike behavior he'll be so completely turned off by me that he'll be eager to be rid of me.

Drew quirks a brow at me and lets out a low chuckle. "Fair enough, you definitely aren't a princess, judging by the way you're stuffing your face right now." I flip him the bird as I chug some of the juice he poured for me. "Now, now, that's no way to treat your knight in shining armor. I defended your honor last night, not once, but twice. You wound me." He grabs his chest playfully like I've shot him straight through the heart.

"Knight in shining armor, or kidnapper? I don't remember you asking me if you could bring me back to your villainous lair when you quote, unquote, rescued me." I level a hard stare at him as I tear into the toast on my plate viciously. Who knew being roofied would make me so ravenous? Then, I glance at the clock behind him on the stove and see that it reads 2:15pm. Well, that explains why I'm so damn hungry.

"Like I said before, I didn't think you wanted to explain to your husband how you got roofied. I got to you before he was able to do anything, so I figured it would be safe enough to let you sleep it off here. If I was wrong, I apologize. Just say the word and I'll take you to the hospital." He levels his own no nonsense glare back at me, knowing he is right. I don't want to explain this to Caleb. Why does it feel like instead of getting out of this mess, I keep finding ways to dig myself in deeper?

"Look, Drew, I appreciate what you did for me last night. I do. I also really fucking appreciate this food right now, but this can't keep happening. We can't keep doing this." Drew walks around the kitchen island and turns me around on the stool to face him, caging me in with his arms.

"Let's get something straight darlin', you're the one that showed up in MY bar last night. I was minding my own business working in my own goddamn bar and you waltzed in looking like a sex personified and then had the nerve to tell me to leave you alone. You came to me. You found me, again. If you don't want this to keep happening then you better start practicing what you preach, buttercup."

Before I can bite out a response, Drew slams his mouth on mine, plunging his tongue inside, taking no prisoners. One fist is gripping the back of my head, hair tangled tightly in his fingers. The other grips my jaw, forcing my mouth to open wide so he can plunder me with his tongue and take what he deems as his. I can feel my control over this situation rapidly slipping away as he uses his knee to shove my legs apart so he can further invade my space. Mentally, I'm screaming. Physically, my body is lighting up like a Roman candle. This man's touch is electric, and I need to get the hell away from him.

I feel his hand drop away from my face and land on my thigh. As it travels up and under my skirt, the shock of his touch there, absolutely where it shouldn't be, snaps me out of the lust-filled haze he is trying to drag me into. I manage to get my hands between us, and I shove at his chest as forcefully as I can. "What part of 'this isn't happening' do you not get?" I snap, giving him another hard shove, so I can duck away from him and get some breathing room.

"What part of 'you are mine', do you not get, darlin'?" He stalks towards me slowly, like a lion hunting a gazelle. I eye my purse on the counter and snatch it as I back towards what I assume is the front door. "I don't think for one second that you wound up in my orbit by accident. Not after last night. I know you think you love your husband, but I can tell, he's not enough for you. You want more. You need more. You need to be owned. And I am going to own you. You're not ready for it yet, but you will be soon." His gaze is molten, and I feel it like flames licking across my skin. Now I'm not so sure that Business Douche Brayden was the biggest predator last night.

"You've lost your goddamn mind. Go take a flying leap." I jerk open the door and bolt out of it before he has a chance to stop me. I rush down the stairs, out onto the street, barefoot and hoping like hell my car is still where I left it. I am in way over my head, and I need to get home and regroup so I can figure out my next move.

When I get home, I head straight to the shower, eager to wash the guilt and shame from last night and this morning from my skin. I can't even begin to fathom how things went so sideways last night, but I am beyond angry at myself for getting into that position and for letting Drew put his mouth on me again. I should have bolted as soon as I was functional enough to walk. Clearly reason is not going to be the way I get through to this man.

I strip down in the bathroom, tossing last night's clothes into the hamper. I take a good long look at myself in the mirror, trying to recognize the woman standing in front of me. It feels like I'm losing control of my life; my marriage is slowly starting to slip through my fingers like sand on the shore being washed away by the waves. I take a closer look at the bruises on my shoulders, wondering how I'm going to explain that to Caleb if they aren't gone before he gets home. Just before I turn to step into the shower, I notice something that causes a ball of ice to form in my gut: more fingerprint-like bruises on my inner thighs. A chill crawls across my skin as I step towards the mirror for a closer look.

"No, no, no...no....," In a panic, I wet a towel and wipe it along my thigh trying to wash the purple smudges away, but they don't go anywhere. Terrified of what else I might discover but needing to know, I shove two fingers up my vagina to check for any suspicious moistness or soreness. Nothing hurts and it doesn't feel like anyone has come inside of me, but would I truly know if he had used a condom? Did Business Douche Brayden get more handsy than I remember?

I try to breathe through my rising panic attack and think logically. All my clothes were still in place when I woke up this morning, underwear included. I couldn't remember anything from last night after Brayden approached me outside of the bar. I remember the sudden wave of dizziness, leaning against the wall and a strong hand on my shoulder. Maybe he got another grope in before Drew stepped in and decked him. That has to be what happened. I would know if I was raped. Surely, I would know...right?

I keep repeating that mantra in my head as I shower and scour everything that happened last night from my skin. To believe anything else will result in a full mental breakdown, and I will not allow that to happen. After my shower, I decide the last thing I need right now is to be alone. I consider calling Sara but I'm not ready for her lecture, so I dial my sister, Olivia, instead. She answers after three rings, the sound of squealing, happy children in the background.

"Hey Sissy, what's up?" She sounds happy, and maybe a little harried from chasing her three rug rats around.

"Not much, I was just wondering if you and the kids wanted to come over for dinner? I'm flying solo, Caleb is out of town. I've got a lasagna prepped and plenty of wine."

I try to sound laid back and casual and not like I desperately need my big sister to lean on. Olivia pretends to consider my offer, but I know she will come, nothing will get her out of the house faster than not having to make dinner. She could easily qualify for one of the Worst Cooks of America type TV shows and she knows it. If she wants something homemade, she comes knocking on my door.

"Weeelllll, Micah is out tonight for fantasy baseball nerd stuff. I suppose I could bring the kids over. Do you have any plain spaghetti to make butter noodles for Rowan? You know he won't eat anything that has touched a vegetable. I'm honestly shocked he's made it this long without succumbing to scurvy."

"Oh, come on, if you can make it to your teen years on a solid diet of pizza and macaroni and cheese before discovering not all vegetables are poisonous, I'm sure Ro will be fine. Just slip him some Flintstone vitamins on the reg. I'm pretty sure that's how mom kept you alive."

Olivia lets out a very unladylike snort. "And God bless

her for it. The fact that I willingly eat tomatoes now as an adult is the only thing that keeps me from completely despairing over this kid's diet. Do you mind eating early? I've got to get the kids in bed by 7:30."

"No prob, sis. I just have to throw the lasagna in the oven. Come on over and we will hang out while it bakes." Relief washes over me after I hang up with my sister. Aside from Sara, she is my best friend, my rock. I can count on her to help me through these issues with Caleb and to offer some much-needed perspective. She and Micah were high school sweethearts and have been rock solid for almost 20 years. If any couple gives me a reason to believe in love, it's them.

An hour later, Olivia and I are drinking chilled Moscato on my back deck while the kids play with the sprinkler in the yard. She and the kids come over often enough that I try to keep enough fun toys around for them to play with. Rowan, the 8-year-old, is leading the twins, Poppy and June, through some sort of convoluted game of Follow the Leader that involves several makeshift obstacles that take the kids through the stream of the sprinkler. Poppy and June are four and think that the sun rises and sets on Rowan. He's a decent big brother too. What he lacks in ability to eat adventurously, he more than makes up for in willingness to take care of his little sisters.

"So, how's Caleb?" Olivia shoots me a sidelong look that says she knows I've got something to get off my chest. We're only a year and a half apart in age and have always been able to tell when something is eating at the other. I should've known she'd figure it out as soon as I called her to invite her over.

"Cal's good. Working a lot. Traveling a lot..." I trail off, trying to think of what to say. She saves me the trouble by cutting straight to the heart of the matter.

"And how are you doing with that? You think I haven't noticed how often we get invited over for dinner? Not that I'm complaining, I'm glad someone inherited Dad's cooking ability, but what used to be a monthly thing is almost a weekly thing now. He's gone a lot, isn't he?" I see her give me a pitying look, but I refuse to acknowledge it.

"Honestly, it's been hard. What was supposed to be a week here and there a few times a year has turned into more of a 60/40 split of travel versus being home. I don't know how much longer I can deal with it, Liv. Caleb swears he's going to talk to Harold and make a change, but he's told me that before and it never happened. I love him, but I don't want to spend my life waiting for him to come home. I don't want to feel like I'm missing out on life with him when he's not here. How are we ever going to have kids if he's always gone? I'm not trying to raise them by myself. I'm not that strong."

Olivia nods and takes a sip of her wine before responding. She's always been like that. She takes information in, mulls it over, considers the options before voicing her opinion. She is level-headed, a mighty oak that won't sway in a storm of emotion. My emotions blow through me like a hurricane.

It's why I'm prone to panic attacks. I get swept up in the storm of worst-case scenarios and need someone like Olivia or Sara to bring me back to Earth. I'm also prone to following my whims and getting lost in fantasies. It's why I like reading so much; it gives me a safe outlet to fall into when my mind wants to get swept away on some grand adventure when life becomes stale or difficult.

This is exactly why I'm in the situation I'm in now. I got caught up in the thrill of having some tall, dark and dangerous stranger flirt with me. Instead of going home and burying my nose in a book like a good married wife, I enjoyed an evening of what if and now my life is falling apart all around me.

"Did you know Micah and I separated for a month about a year after Ro was born?" I nearly choke on my wine at her words.

"Excuse me? What? No, you didn't, I would have known that." I say incredulously.

Olivia rolls her eyes at me. "Not if I didn't want you to. This was when he was trying to get his business off the ground. He was working 13-14 hour days, never home to help with the baby. I'd had enough of being second fiddle to his job, so I gave him the Come to Jesus talk and told him to choose. Me, or the business."

"Clearly he chose you…" I interject, but she holds up her hand.

"Spoiler alert, there is a happily ever after, but it didn't start that way. He was pissed. He thought I was trying to undermine what he was trying to build. He thought he was doing what was necessary to provide for us. He watched his mom struggle, working two jobs after his dad bounced, and he swore he wouldn't be a deadbeat father and that I would never have to work two jobs to care for our kids. " Olivia pauses, taking a deep, steadying breath before continuing.

"What he didn't realize was by working so much, he was abandoning us in a different way. So, I told him to get out and find a hotel. If he wasn't going to be around, then I wasn't going to clean up his messes or do his laundry and be a warm body for him to hold when it was convenient for him."

I can feel my mouth gaping open like a fish. I am completely dumbfounded by my sister's revelation. I try to think back to the time she is referring to, trying to look for clues I might have missed. I didn't see her as much when Rowan was a baby, but I always chalked it up to her being committed to the nap, feed, and play routine that all new moms seem to fall into. "So, what happened?"

"It took a few weeks, but Micah finally realized that providing for your family isn't just about money. It's about time. It's about sharing the load. It's about being there in the moment when your baby takes his first steps or says his first words. It's about being there to help with bath time and bedtime. It's about letting your wife nap after she's been up all-night cluster nursing. Living in a hotel room for a month was his actual Come to Jesus Moment. He came home, we got into couples therapy and he hired someone else to help with the business. Things have been so much better since then. Not perfect mind you, but good. We are happy now."

I ponder her words, wondering if this is what Caleb and I need. A Come to Jesus Moment that will make him realize what he's missing out on. "Are you saying I need to give Caleb an ultimatum?"

"I'm not saying that, but I am saying if it does come to that, don't lose hope. Sometimes it takes losing everything you have to make you realize what's most important in this life."

The timer for the oven goes off, and I go inside to get the lasagna out of the oven, wondering exactly how far I'm willing to go to prove to Caleb that what's most important in our life is us, our bond, our marriage.

Later that night, I'm lying in bed, trying to forget the events of last night by reading the 5th book of an epic romantasy series by my favorite author. It's the spiciest book of the series, and during an epic 'feast' at a dining room table I find myself missing my husband in a very particular way. Just as I think about snaking my hand into my panties an idea occurs to me. I grab my phone and hit the FaceTime button for Caleb's contact. He answers after a few rings, looking adorably sleep rumpled in his hotel bed. "Hey Sweetness, what's up?"

"Oh nothing, I was just missing my husband. I want to see you but if you're sleeping, I can let you go…" I tease him in what I hope is a sultry voice. I'm desperately hoping he will pick up what I'm not saying and play along with me. That has his attention. I watch him as he sits up fully in bed and switches on the bedside lamp.

"Don't ever let it be said that I'm a man that denies his wife of her needs. I'm here Sweetness. How can I be of service?" He quirks his brow and his full lips turn up in a cocky grin.

"Oh, I just wanted to tell you about this new book I'm reading. It's so interesting and it made me think of you…" Caleb knows what kind of books I read. He fully supports my spicy reading habit, as he gets to reap the benefits when he's around. This is the first time I've decided to call him on a work trip for the sole purpose of phone sex, but he doesn't look like he minds a bit.

"Is that so? What is happening in this book of yours that made you think of me?" I see his arm moving and he angles his phone so I can get a better view of his bare chest and face.

"Well, the hot as fuck fae warrior with wings decided he was hungry and the only thing he wanted to feast on is the pussy of the woman that hates him. It's fucking hot as hell, enemies to lovers hate fucking, and I'm so wet right now. I wish I had your face between my legs to help relieve this ache." As I detail the scene for

Caleb, I slip my hand into my panties and begin to stroke my clit.

Caleb tuts disapprovingly, "Maybe you shouldn't read such spicy books when I'm not there to help you relieve the tension. If I were there, I'd be able to bury my face right into that sweet cunt of yours while you read me the play-by-play of exactly how to reenact that scene." He bites his bottom lip as he lets out a low groan. I can see the rhythmic movement of his right arm just off to the side and I know exactly what he's doing.

"God babe, I miss your tongue. I wish you were here licking my pussy and sucking on my clit. I want to ride your face so bad right now." A low moan slips out as I stroke my clit faster, building a rhythm that matches his. We stare at each other through the phone, getting lost in chasing our pleasure, fully absorbed by watching the other's lust build and build. My breathing grows shallow as I get closer to my release, and I tip my head back and close my eyes.

"Nu-uh, Sweetness. Eyes on me. Watch me when you come. I want to see the look in your eyes when you come all over your fingers and then I want to watch you lick them clean." Caleb's dirty words tip me over the edge, and I explode all over my fingers.

"Oh, God, baby...come with me. I want to hear you come. Please." My plea comes out in a breathy whisper as I do as he asked and bring my wet fingers, covered in my release, to my lips. I suck them into my mouth one by one, maintaining eye contact with him as he furiously strokes his cock to his own release.

"Lo, Jesus...so fucking hot...fuck." Caleb lets out a low groan as he throws his head back and comes all over his stomach. A few seconds pass as we both stare at one another with sleepy, satisfied grins on our faces. "Now I know I'm going to have sweet dreams tonight." The grin he gives me is boyish and sweet and reminds me so much of the man I fell in love with in college.

"Same, babe, same. Please hurry home to me. I need you next to me in our bed every night."

"I know Sweetness. I'm working on it. I'll be home soon. Now get some sleep. I love you."

"Love you too, babe. Goodnight." We hang up and I turn off the bedside lamp. With the orgasm leaving me relaxed and sleepy, I'm able to finally drift off into a dreamless sleep, far away from the drama of last night.

CHAPTER

NINE

ELOISE

It's Monday evening, almost time for my shift to be over at the hospital. It's been a busy day full of cases in the operating room, a busy E.D. with a full waiting room and at least two callouts from my co-workers. I've been asked if I'd be willing to stay and help cover the evening shift, but after my run-in last week with Drew at work, I'm hesitant to stay any later than necessary. My mind is still a spiraling mess of anxiety from the events over the weekend, and I barely made it through the workday while holding onto my composure. Caleb will be home in a week and I'm still no closer to having the Drew situation handled. I need to nip this shit in the bud before he gets home.

I haven't told Sara about Saturday night. I'm still burning from the shame of getting myself into such a stupid situation, and I know her advice will either be to go to the police or tell Caleb. Neither of which I am willing to resort to just yet. Going to the police will result in Caleb finding out and shit hitting the fan. I'm still delusionally optimistic that I can get this situation under control without throwing a live grenade into my marriage. As unhappy and unsatisfied as I've been with Caleb's job requiring so much of his time, I'm still not willing to let our marriage go without a fight. I'm not a quitter and if Caleb follows through on his promise to talk to Harold, then we still have plenty to fight for.

On my way home Caleb calls me. I answer over my car's Bluetooth, excited to hear from him, hoping he's got good news about his return trip home. "Hey babe, are you calling me with good news?"

"I am, actually." He replies and I can hear the smile in his voice. "I heard from Alex; his flight is booked for Friday morning. I've got my flight booked for Sunday morning. After he and I sit down and go over everything about the Langford project, and I hand it off to him, I'll be heading straight to the airport."

I let out a sigh of relief. "Thank God. I was worried he'd get held up in London and not be able to come back Friday. I was ready to just come to you in Nashville if that was the case."

"No need, Sweetness. I'll be home in a week, and a week after that we are taking a long romantic getaway to that cozy little cabin in the mountains to celebrate my telling Harold to shove this travel business where the sun doesn't shine."

"Mmm, babe, that's the sexiest thing you've ever

said…" I let out a flirty purr, hoping to keep his eye on the prize.

Caleb lets out a low, sexy chuckle. "Even sexier than when I told you to lick your come off your fingers last night? Damn. Who knew all I had to do to get you hot was to talk shit about Harold?"

I'm laughing at his joke as I pull into our driveway. "Just imagine how hot and bothered I'll be when you come and tell me you'll be working from the home office full time. I'll ride your cock so hard you'll see stars."

I make my way up the front steps to our adorable Craftsman home built in the 1920s. We bought it when we got married and fixed it up ourselves, trying to keep as many of the original details and built-ins true to the era as possible, while adding a modern twist. The front door is a happy turquoise blue that never fails to make my heart smile when I come home. As I reach the top step, I spy a long, white box resting on our Snoop Dogg welcome mat that was a gift won during an especially rousing game of Dirty Santa.

"Oh Cal, did you send me flowers? You shouldn't have!" I recognize the logo from one of the local flower shops as I scoop up the box and carry it inside, cradling my phone between my ear and my shoulder.

"Flowers? What are you talking about–" Caleb's response gets cut off as I lose my grip on the phone, and it drops to the rug.

"Shoot." I pick up my phone and see that the call was hung up in the drop. I hit Caleb's name to call him back as

I lift open the lid to the box of flowers, expecting to see my favorites, like ranunculus or peonies. Instead, a dozen long stem blood red roses are in the box with a white card.

"Hey, what happened? What were you saying about what I shouldn't have done?" Caleb's voice comes through the phone as I stare at the roses dumbly.

I know in my gut these flowers are not from my husband. Only once in our relationship has Caleb given me roses. It was shortly after we had started dating, and while the gesture was sweet, I let him know that roses were some of my least favorite flowers, and if he wants to buy me flowers, he should get something less cliche. He took that advice to heart, and every time he buys me flowers now, it's something different and unique.

"Huh, what? Sorry, I dropped the phone. Oh, um, I think someone misdelivered a package." I stumbled over the lie, hoping Caleb buys it. If these flowers are from who I think they're from, I do not want to open that can of worms while I'm on the phone with him. "Yeah, actually I think these were meant for the house next door. Can I call you back later so I can take these over?" Fortunately, Caleb buys my lie.

"Yeah, sure babe. We'll talk later. I need to go over some plans that were revised late today anyway. I love you."

"Love you too Cal. Talk soon."

I hang up the phone and stare at the envelope like it's a coiled rattlesnake ready to strike. I take a deep breath and steel my nerves before snatching it up and ripping open the flap. Instead of a card there is only a Polaroid picture that falls out. It is a picture of me laying in a bed that is not my own. It has to be taken from Saturday night. I'm lying in the strange bed, looking peacefully asleep; my bare shoulders peeking out above the duvet, giving the impression that I'm naked under the covers. My dress from Saturday night was strapless so you can't see any sign of it. It's taken from an intimate angle, perhaps from someone laying on the other pillow facing me. In the white space at the bottom of the picture there is a message written. "This is where you belong. See you soon, D."

My knees turn to jelly, and I lean over and hold myself up on the wall before I collapse into the floor. My heart is thundering in my chest, as several thoughts occur to me at once. One, Drew took pictures of me in his bed. How many? What will he do with them? Will he send them to Caleb? Two, he knows where I live. Three, he is not going to be getting over this obsession. I am severely out of my depth now with being able to deal with him on my own, but I have no idea who to turn to.

Nausea roils in my stomach as a wave of panic consumes me. Just before I completely lose myself to a breakdown, I realize my front door is still wide open. I stumble over to it, slamming it shut and locking it. I slide down with my back to the door and bury my face in my hands as I let the feeling of completely losing control of my life wash over me.

TEN

CALEB

I'm sitting at my desk, packing up my computer and revised plans I need to go over before the morning. It's almost 8pm and I've had enough of the office for the day. I'm going to finish going over everything in my hotel room with a beer, instead of sitting in this miserable little trailer. I'm mentally counting down the days until I get to fly home. I know a lot of people love being on the road and seeing new places, but the long hours prevent me from seeing much of any city that I work in. Coupled with the fact that I'm married and missing my wife, traveling for work is a less than stellar experience for me. I've been mentally preparing for the conversation I'll be having with Harold in a week to tell him just that. I'm hoping that our conversation will go smoothly. I'm not above threatening to leave if I need to, but I hope it doesn't come to that.

Just as I finish packing up, a knock at the door draws my attention and I see Ashlyn poke her head in. "Hey Ash, you trying to con another free dinner out of me?" I shoot her a grin as I walk towards her. "You might be in luck. I'm just leaving and I'm starving." Instead of responding with some sort of playful banter or sarcastic remark, Ashlyn looks nervous. Almost like she has bad news to share.

"Well, I was stopping by to see if you could talk, and the office probably isn't the best place for this kind of conversation." Ashlyn's tone is somber, and she immediately has my attention.

"Is everything ok?" I put a hand on her shoulder and lean down to look her in the eye. She's biting her lower lip and looks like someone just kicked her puppy.

"Let's get out of here and we'll talk." Her words aren't reassuring at all, but I follow Ashlyn as she heads back out the door. I lock up and follow her to the same bar down the block that we had dinner at the other night. We grab a corner booth and place an order for some beers. When the waitress walks away, I turn to Ashlyn.

"Alright, shoot. Tell me what's going on. Someone get fired? If you tell me Alex got fired and that I'm stuck here, we are going to have a problem."

"How's Eloise? Are you guys doing ok?" Ashlyn looks at me with concern etched across her features. Her brows are furrowed into a worried crease, and she reaches across the table to grab my hand. Her sudden shift in attitude has me thrown for a loop.

"Um, Lo is good. I talked to her a few hours ago. I was going to call her when I got back to the hotel. Why are you asking about Lo?" Just then the waitress returns with our beers. Ashlyn leans back and shoots her wary smile, waiting until she leaves before continuing.

"Alright Caleb, I want to preface this by saying I'm not trying to start shit. But something came to my attention, and I want to talk to you about it before someone else brings it to you. I know all too well how the office rumor mill operates and I want to get ahead of this before it gets out of control." Ashlyn looks serious, but she also looks like she's really worried about something.

Unable to handle the suspense, I snap. "Get to the point, Ash. Why are you asking me about Eloise?"

She pulls out her phone and taps on it a few times before sliding it over to me. "Tabitha sent me this picture today. She took it Saturday night. She said she thought she saw Eloise outside of Stellina and she snapped this picture." Ashlyn points at her phone and I pick it up to get a better look. It's a picture of Eloise; I'd recognize her hair and tattoos anywhere. She's leaned back against a brick wall, looking up, and a tall, blonde man, I don't recognize, is leaning over her. One of his hands is gripping her shoulder, the other is cupping her chin, lifting her face towards his, and his face is just inches from hers. I can't see much of either of their expressions, the photo is a little out of focus and looks like it was taken by someone trying to be stealthy.

I'm unable to say anything. It feels like a pit has opened up beneath me and I'm falling into it. My lungs constrict as I forget to breathe for a moment, while I stare at another man with his hands on my wife.

Ashlyn continues on, filling in the blanks of the questions that are forming in my mind that I can't give a voice to. "Tabby was heading into the Italian restaurant next door when she snapped this, so she didn't actually see what was going on. This may be nothing to worry about at all, but I know how Tabitha has been sniffing around you at the office and I wanted to talk to you about it before she got her claws out. She said they were both gone when she came back out about 10 minutes later. Did you happen to talk to Lo Saturday night? Any friends she might have been out with?"

I shake my head dumbly, racking my brain trying to remember when I talked to Lo on Saturday. We had talked earlier in the day while she was out for a walk. She had mentioned maybe seeing her sister sometime that weekend but said nothing about going out that night. Normally Lo is a homebody who lives to stay in and read when she's left to her own devices.

"She didn't mention going out. I don't recognize that guy as anyone we know. Why the fuck are his hands on her? Why is she letting someone touch her like that?" I gasp out as I squeeze Ashlyn's phone in my hand, my grip so tight my knuckles turn white.

"I'm going to just go ahead and take this back before you hulk out and crush my phone." Ashlyn snatches her phone out of my grasp and takes my hand in hers. "Look at me, Cal. Don't freak out yet. There could be a perfectly innocent explanation for this, and I want us to figure it out before Tabitha starts some shit. I know you and I know Lo;

this doesn't seem right to me. That's why I brought it straight to you." Ashlyn's voice is low and calm, like she's trying to soothe a lost child.

Lost is exactly how I feel right now. I know things haven't been the best between us, but never in my wildest dreams did I think Lo would step out on me. Not Lo; She has too much integrity for that. If she were that unhappy, she would ask me for a divorce. But then what other explanation could there be for that picture?

"It looks like he's about to kiss her! What kind of innocent explanation could there be for him to be leaning down in her face like that?" Tears sting the back of my eyes. I close them and take a deep breath, desperate to calm this panic rising in my chest. This can't be what it looks like. I can't be too late in saving our marriage.

"Hey, hey. Like I said, that's what we are going to figure out." Ashlyn scoots out of her side of the booth and comes to sit next to me. She slings an arm around my waist and rests her head on my shoulder. "We will get to the bottom of this, Cal. Don't worry. Did you talk to her Sunday? Did she mention anything then?"

"We talked Sunday night, but everything seemed fine on her end. But um, we didn't really talk about anything like that..." My cheeks heat as I remember the intense phone sex we had Sunday night.

Ashlyn gives me a knowing look and smirks. "Say no more fam. But that's good. If she's playing hide the sausage with someone else, then surely, she wouldn't be trying to get into your virtual pants. That's a move a dude would pull. Women don't like to ride multiple disco sticks in a short amount of time."

I let out a derisive snort at Ashlyn's euphemism. "Clearly you don't read the same books Lo reads. And how would you know, you don't ride any disco sticks." Ashlyn just rolls her eyes at me like I'm the village idiot.

"My point exactly. The devil's eggplant isn't worth the trouble it brings, and any woman smart enough knows to not put more than one on her plate at a time. Eloise is a smart woman. Besides, she told me you're the last man she'll ever date." She shoots me a wink as she takes a large swallow of beer.

"Fuck you, Ash. Stop trying to steal my wife. You sure you're not trying to stir up shit?" I drink down half of my beer in one go. Ash's joking around is working wonders to settle my jangling nerves. She's right, Lo isn't the kind of woman that would mess around behind my back. I have to trust in that until I can unravel this mystery.

Ashlyn motions to the waitress to bring us another round. "I promise you Cal, I solemnly swear I am not trying to steal your wife. I prefer my women to come to me of their own free will. Now I know you are going to stress out about this, but I wouldn't bring it up to her until you get home. I don't think fighting about something that you know nothing about is going to help matters. Give Lo a chance to tell you what's going on face to face. You love her too much to not give her the opportunity to look you in the eye when you ask her if she's cheating on you."

The waitress returns and deposits two fresh beers in

front of us. "Now let's get drunk and Sherlock the shit out of this little mystery so it doesn't have to come to that."

Later that night I'm lying in bed in the hotel room staring at the picture. I made Ashlyn forward it to me, so I could have it on hand on the off-chance Lo denies going anywhere Saturday. Ashlyn is of the opinion it's just some guy that tried to shoot his shot at my 'hot ass wife' and he likely got shot down. In my heart I want that to be true so hard it hurts, but there is still a gnawing pit of worry in my stomach that won't go away.

Just as I get ready to shut off my phone and go to sleep a little notification pops up from our video doorbell alerting me to activity on our front porch. I switch over to the app but when I pull up the camera feed nothing is happening. While in the app a thought occurs to me; I pull up the activity log to see the recent alerts. I scroll back to Saturday, feeling slightly like a sleaze as I spy on Eloise's comings and goings. Saturday around 7 p.m. I see a clip of her walking out the front door. She's wearing a strapless black dress that showcases her tattoos on her arms and across her back. Her hair is piled up in a messy bun and she definitely looks like she's heading out for a night on the town. Maybe she did go out with Sara and just forgot to mention it.

Curious to see what time she made it home, I look at

the log again, and the pit that had threatened to swallow me up back at the bar opens up again when I see the next notification isn't until Sunday afternoon. I click on the clip to watch Lo walk up the front porch, barefoot, carrying her shoes, and still wearing last night's dress. Her hair is down, a tangled mess, and it looks like she's been crying when I see a glimpse of her face. She looks like she's making the walk of shame, and ice settles into my veins as I realize there is something going on that she isn't telling me about.

CHAPTER

ELEVEN

ELOISE

Tuesday morning, I trudge into Brewed Awakening before my shift at the hospital. I barely slept the previous night, anxiety nightmares plaguing me anytime I got remotely close to dozing off. After locking the house up tight and tossing the roses into the trash bin, I shut myself in my bedroom to have a full-on mental breakdown. I forgot to call Caleb back in my panicked state and I hope that he was too caught up with work to notice.

"Next!" The barista behind the counter calls me up to the register.

"Large, iced coffee please, cream and sugar. Add a shot of espresso." The barista doesn't even raise a brow at my order. It's stronger than my usual but I'm sure it is par for the course for a coffee shop that caters to med students and residents that frequently pull all-nighters. I pay for my drink and step to the side still lost in thought, mulling over how I am going to deal with my Andrew Jameson problem. Sara's suggestion to go to the police certainly has some merit, but I'm not entirely convinced Drew has done enough that they would actually get involved. Sending me flowers and saving me from date rape are hardly grounds for issuing a restraining order. Dismissing the idea, I google where to buy pepper spray instead, making a mental note to pick some up after my shift.

"Large, iced coffee with a shot of espresso!" The barista calls out my drink order and places it on the counter. Still scrolling through my phone absently trying to find the closest sporting goods store, I grab my coffee and turn to leave, heading out the door. My exit is stopped short just outside when I abruptly run into a broad chest in a suit jacket. I narrowly miss spilling my coffee all over the man I just ran into.

"Shit, sorry." I stutter out as I take a step back and look up at the poor schmuck in my way. The hairs on the back of my neck stand up when my eyes meet Business Douche Brayden's steely gray gaze. He is looking at me with an expression I can't get a read on. He looks confused, maybe a little concerned and more than a little mad. He reaches out to grab my arm but I back away. "Don't touch me, dickbag. I know what you did to me."

"Look lady, I don't know what you think I did, but I was trying to help you." Brayden's tone is condescending and not even a little apologetic. It's then I noticed the black eye and yellowish bruise coloring his right cheek. That must be the souvenir Drew gave him when he rescued me. He takes another step towards me like he wants to talk quietly but I slip past him and walk backwards down the sidewalk not taking my eyes off him.

"Stay the fuck away from me. I swear to God if you come near me again, I'll go to the cops." My voice waivers and I'm sure I'm full of shit. He knows it too. He looks me up and down and lets out a derisive snort.

"Ok, sure lady. It's your funeral. Good luck with that crazy bartender boyfriend of yours." Brayden storms into the coffee shop.

As soon as the door closes behind him, I run to my car and lock myself in. My hands are shaking and the tiredness that had me dragging my feet has been expelled by the adrenaline of running into the man who slipped me a roofie. Just as I calm down enough to drive into work my phone chimes with a text alert. It's from a number I don't recognize. I put the car back into park and open the message.

> Unknown: I need to see you again. I can't stop thinking about your body pressed against mine.

Attached to the text is a picture. It's another close-up picture of me asleep in Drew's bed. Only this time I am turned on my side and my face appears to be laying on his chest. My hair is partially obscuring my face, but I can make out the tattoo on his bare chest and the lower half of his face in the top of the picture. Fuck my life. He took a goddamn selfie of us cuddling in his bed while I was passed out cold. I let out a scream of frustration and bang my fist into the steering wheel. The car horn beeps and an older lady walking by with a small yappy dog shoots me a nasty look. I give her a sheepish wave and turn my attention back to my phone.

> Me: This isn't happening. Lose my number.

> Unknown: Oh, it's happening. Meet me tonight. My bar at 9.

> Me: Fuck all the way off Drew. I said no.

The response I get to that is a screenshot of Caleb's contact information. Shit, he must have gotten into my phone when I was at his place Saturday night. It's probably how he got my address too. My hands begin to shake again and my skin goes clammy. The implication that he could very easily send that picture to Caleb isn't lost on me.

> Unknown: You weren't saying no Saturday night. I distinctly remember you begging for more. You're lucky I'm such a gentleman. The smell of your soaking wet pussy in my bed was almost impossible to resist. I don't think Brayden would have been so gentle with you.

> Me: Please don't do this.

> Unknown: Eloise, I'm not asking you, I'm telling you. You owe me one. I'll see you at 9.

"Fuuuuuuuuuuuuuuccckkkk!" I let out a frustrated scream as I chuck my phone across the car. The fucker is blackmailing me, and he knows it. I stew over my predicament as I put the car into drive and head into work, hoping I work out a solution to getting out of this meeting by the time my shift is over.

That night after work, I find myself at the local sporting goods store staring at the pepper spray and self-defense keychains. I had no idea there would be so many options to choose from. There are a variety of weapons to choose from including knives, stun guns, batons and something called a kubotan that looks like a very dangerous butt plug. I'm lost in my thoughts mulling over the options when a gruff voice interrupts me.

"You need some help, miss?" Startled, I look up to see an older man with a bushy gray beard and kind eyes looking at me from behind the counter. His arms are covered in old school Sailor Jerry style tattoos, and he is missing a few teeth. I notice he also has a very prominent bone frog tattoo on his forearm that is usually associated with Navy Seals. Good, if anyone can explain these options to me, Navy Seal Santa should be able to do the job just fine.

"Um, yeah. I need something for protection. I'm um... having some difficulty with an ex-boyfriend." I don't know why I feel the need to lie or come up with some sort of back story, but the words fall out of my mouth before I can stop myself.

"You looking to kill to protect yourself or just hurt them enough to get away?" The look he gives me is all business and I notice the guns in the cabinet a few feet to the left of us. I know for sure I'm not up for killing so I respond that I'm interested in the second option.

"I just want to be able to give him a very firm no if he keeps refusing to listen to my words. I was thinking about a stun gun or some pepper spray? Also, something discreet that I can carry without being obvious."

"I've got exactly what you need, sweetheart." Over the next twenty minutes Bad Ass Santa describes the options available and I wind up purchasing pepper spray (for distance), a small stun gun for closer range, and one of the dangerous looking butt plugs that can also be used to break car windows in an emergency. All small enough to fit into a clutch and black so they don't stand out. He even takes the time to demonstrate how to use each one and what to do if I get pepper spray in my face by accident. I still don't feel good about meeting with Drew later, but if push comes to shove, maybe I can get my point across with a little zappy zap to the nuts.

When I get home my phone rings with an incoming FaceTime call from Caleb. I quickly stow away my purchases before answering him. "Hey babe. What's up?"

"Just calling to check in on my wife. How was work?" Caleb smiles at me, but it doesn't quite reach his eyes. His tone is pensive and somewhat melancholy. This doesn't feel like the same man I just spoke to yesterday. In the back of my mind panic starts to rise that maybe Drew has already reached out to Caleb.

"Work was fine. How was your day? You look stressed." I bite my lower lip, hoping he isn't going to mention any mysterious messages he might have received.

"It's fine, just wrapping up what I can before Alex gets here. I just miss you. I know you must be so lonely while I'm gone. Have you been staying busy? Visiting with Sara or Olivia?" His line of questioning sends an uncomfortable squirm of suspicion through my gut. Does he know? What does he know? Or is he just chatting?

"I- uh, yeah. I saw Olivia on Sunday. You know that. Might see if Sara wants to get drinks tomorrow night since it's been a while since I've seen her. I'll probably just heat up some leftovers for dinner and call it an early night. I'm beat." The lie tastes bitter on my tongue. I don't like lying to Caleb, but I am telling myself one way or another, after tonight Drew will get the picture that I am not interested in him. An expression flickers across Caleb's face for a second, but he banishes it with a smile before I can make out what it is.

"Sounds like a good plan, Sweetness. God, I miss you. I

can't wait until I get home and can show you exactly how much." His words are sweet, but the tone behind them is anything but. It almost sounds like he is talking about punishing me, not making love to me. My greedy pussy isn't entirely opposed to the idea either. I just pray he doesn't know exactly how much punishment I actually deserve.

"Are you threatening me with a good time, Mr. Fitzpatrick?" I give him a saucy wink, hoping some blatant flirtation will distract him from his line of questioning.

"Oh, it's more than a threat, Sweetness. It's a promise." His voice is a low growl that I've never heard come from my sweet, mild-mannered husband before. My body flushes at his possessive tone. Before I get a chance to respond, a text notification pops up on my screen from Drew.

> Unknown: T-minus 60 minutes, Eloise.
> Don't keep me waiting, darlin'.

The reminder of my meeting with Drew tonight effectively kills the heat building in my core. "I-, I can't wait for you to s-show me…" I stammer out lamely. I've got to come up with an excuse to get off the call so I can meet with Drew. Caleb saves me the trouble when he glances off his screen for a moment then draws his attention back to his phone.

"Hey babe, I gotta go. Ashlyn and I are going out to dinner tonight. Call me later if you don't pass out too early."

Relieved, I nod my agreement. "Sure thing, tell Ash I said hi. Love you."

"Love you too, Sweetness. Have a good night."

After we hang up, I go upstairs to take a quick shower and mentally prepare for this reckoning with Drew. I keep telling myself if I say "no" enough he will finally get the picture. I run through a million speeches in my head as I get dressed, my nerves getting no less jittery as I rehearse all the ways I can tell him to fuck off.

At 8:45, when I can't stall any longer, I grab my black clutch, which is currently housing my pepper spray keychain and small stun gun and head out the front door, locking up behind me. I inhale a deep calming breath before descending the front steps.

"Here goes nothing. Get this shit over with, Lo." I mutter under my breath and head off to the lion's den.

TWELVE

I'm sitting in my hotel room, downing my third beer as I watch the video footage of Eloise leaving our house after she told me she'd be staying in. This is the 5th or 6th time I've watched the footage, not entirely able to reconcile with the fact that my wife had lied to me. I hadn't planned on spying on her through our video doorbell, but her cagey attitude on the phone had raised my suspicions enough that I had to check the notification that popped up on my phone. She left shortly after our call ended, looking dressed up to go out, carrying a small black clutch.

"Where the fuck are you going, Lo?" I take another sip of my beer as I pull up her contact in my phone. My thumb hovers over the "Find my friend" option, I hesitate, debating on if I want to sink to this level of tracking her whereabouts. We've always shared our location with each other as a safety measure, but I couldn't remember the last time I actually pulled hers up to check on where she was.

Is this too much of an invasion of her privacy? Is my trust in her broken enough to do this? Is my checking up on her more unforgivable than her lying to me about her plans?

I take another long pull from my beer as I consider my options. Am I really the one breaking trust by checking her location after she told me she'd be staying in? She's already lied to me once by not admitting that she went out Saturday night. I decide to give her one more chance and hit the call button instead of tracking her location. If she answers and is up front about being out, then clearly, I have nothing to worry about. The phone rings. And rings. And rings. Eventually the ringing clicks over to her voice-mail. *"Hey you've reached, Eloise. You know what to do."*

Dread pools in the pit of my stomach as I hang up the call without leaving a message. I tap on the "Find my friend" button and pull up the map of her location. Her little dot is in the heart of downtown Birch Falls, at Stellina; the same bar she was spotted at Saturday night.

Something cracks in my chest as I toss my phone across the room and open my 4th beer in an attempt to drown out the intrusive thoughts. Thoughts of her lying. Thoughts of her cheating. Thoughts of another man's hands on her body; lips on hers. "Fuck, Lo, why?" Something wet slides down my cheek and I rub it away, realizing I'm crying. I didn't realize our problems had gotten so big, and now I don't know if saving my marriage is even possible.

THIRTEEN

I'M STANDING OUTSIDE OF STELLINA, NERVOUSLY SHIFTING FROM foot to foot, trying to work up the courage to go inside. The bar looks dark, like it isn't even open. The windows from the street are tinted so it's hard to tell for sure if anyone else is inside. Suddenly, a large warm body is pressed up against my back. Drew places his hands on my shoulders and leans in to whisper in my ear.

"You came for me. Good girl." His voice is a dark rumble of thunder that sends shivers down my spine. I hate that my body still reacts to him, even when my mind is screaming that he is all wrong. He places a gentle kiss on my neck, right on my pulse point, before guiding me through the door to the bar with his arm wrapped possessively around my waist.

The bar is empty, apparently closed to all other patrons for the night. The lighting is even dimmer than it was Saturday night, and one bar height table is set in the middle of the room with a candle flickering and a rose in a vase. Drew guides me to the table, firmly pushing me into my seat before crowding into my space in front of me. He lifts my chin up, so I'm forced to look him in the eye as he studies my expression.

"You don't have to be scared, darlin'. I'm just trying to make sure you see what's out there, waiting for you. What you deserve." He brushes his lips against mine, in the briefest hint of a kiss before pulling away. He goes behind the bar and starts mixing some drinks. I take a moment to breathe in deeply, attempting to calm my nerves and work up the courage to do what I need to do.

"Look, Drew. I'm only here to say-" He cuts me off with a raised finger.

"Don't say anything more, darlin'. You and I are going to have a drink and a little chat. But you are going to listen to me first." His tone is commanding and dangerous, brooking no argument. I have to play my cards right and hope I can talk some sense into him. The more I argue with him the more possessive he seems to become. I nod meekly and start studying my wedding rings on my left hand, wondering how much longer I'll be able to keep wearing them.

Drew comes back and sets a light-colored drink with a very faint purple hue to it in front of me. "What's this?" I ask without looking at him. I eye the cocktail warily. After the roofie incident with Brayden, I haven't had any alcohol to drink.

"An Honest Mistake. A gin and tonic with lavender

syrup, fresh lime, and mint." He brushes a lock of my hair behind my ear before lifting my chin again, forcing me to meet his gaze. He studies me for a very long, intense moment, almost as if he's memorizing my features. He brings the drink to my lips, and I don't have a choice but to take a sip, otherwise I'll wind up wearing it.

The cocktail is herbal, slightly floral, slightly minty and just sweet enough to cut the bitterness of the gin. He doesn't stop until half the drink is gone. He sets the glass down and leans in to kiss me, one hand cupped around my neck to keep me from pulling away.

His kiss is possessive and dominant. He isn't asking for anything with this kiss, he is taking what he thinks is his. I let him kiss me, hoping if I give him just enough to keep him calm, I'll be able to reason with him. I know I'm playing a dangerous game, but I know I need to keep him from getting angry. I don't want him to reach out to Caleb with any damning pictures out of spite. If I can talk him down and reason with him, maybe he will let me go willingly.

Drew pulls away after thoroughly plundering my mouth with his tongue and sits across from me. I study my drink, trying to hide from his probing gaze. It feels like the man could literally undress me with his eyes. I feel exposed and raw in his presence.

"Eloise, here is what's going to happen. You are going to leave your husband, and I am going to show you exactly how a queen deserves to be treated." My eyes snap up to meet his. I don't know what I was expecting from him, but this clear demand to leave my husband wasn't it.

"Um, Drew, no. I can't...I don't want to. I love my husband. Look, I came here to tell you that this isn't happening." My heart is racing, and I feel heat rushing up my chest and cheeks, the early signs of an impending panic attack.

Drew grabs my hand in his, gripping it to the point of being slightly painful. "Eloise, you're not hearing me. I'm giving you the chance to do this on your own, however you see fit. You're not meant for him. He doesn't deserve you. A man that lets a gorgeous woman like you troll bars while he's working, doesn't deserve to come home to your sweet pussy or those gorgeous, delicious, kissable lips. He doesn't get to claim you as his when he doesn't even care where you are. Did he even notice you didn't come home Saturday night? Does he even care that his wife was almost taken advantage of?"

I jerk my hand from his and hop off the bar stool I'm sitting on. I back away slowly, holding my hands up placatingly. "Of course, he doesn't know. I didn't tell him! He would care if I told him, but I'm not trying to blow up my marriage, Drew. You're not hearing me. I *don't* want to leave my husband. I'm sorry if you got the wrong impression that first night, but you have to understand. I'm not leaving Caleb. I love him." My whole body is shivering like I'm cold. Another sign of the looming panic attack. I have got to get this situation under control before I lose it entirely.

Drew gets up from his seat and stalks towards me. I keep backing up until I hit the wall and can't go any further. I realize then, I've made a mistake as I spy my clutch holding my self-defense weapons at the table. Way to go, dumbass, I mentally chastise myself. He cages me in with arms pressed against the wall on either side of my head.

He leans down to speak directly into my ear. "Darlin', this is going to go one of two ways. Either you leave your husband on your own terms, or I do it for you. Do you think those pictures I sent you were the most damning thing from Saturday night? Do you not remember begging to ride my cock when we got back to my apartment? You were rubbing up on me like a goddamn cat in heat. Your pussy was dripping for me, and you were begging me to fuck that sweet, tight hole of yours."

It feels like the floor has gone out from under me. My vision blackens on the edges as I realize I forgot to breathe during his tirade. "Y-you said y-you w-were a gentle-man..." I stammer out, desperately racking my brain trying to remember if there is any truth to his words. The entire night after I walked out of Stellina is a gaping black hole in my memory.

"I was. I didn't fuck you Eloise, even after you begged me so prettily. But I didn't want to just leave you hanging like that, baby girl. So, I tasted that delicious cunt of yours until you came all over my face and passed out. You are my new favorite flavor." He licks up the side of my neck until he reaches my ear. He bites down on the lobe as he wraps his other hand around my neck. "Do you want to see? Do you want to see how good I made you feel? I recorded it."

Oh god. No. This is worse than I thought. I feel the hot wetness of tears spilling down my cheeks. Drew nuzzles his face against mine and licks a path up my cheeks, cleaning them up. My heart feels like it's been thrown into a blender and nausea is roiling in my gut. I believe him. I believe every word he says, and I know I have fucked up beyond belief. My marriage is over. My life is over as I know it. There is no way I can come back from this. Caleb will never forgive me. "Please...please don't do this." I beg in barely more than a whisper. The fight has gone out of me because I know Drew isn't going to let me go. I'm his now, whether I want it or not.

"I'll give you one week to figure it out, darlin'. One week to break your husband's heart in whatever way you see fit. Then you come to me. If you don't, I'll send him, and everyone else in your contact list, that video of you riding my face until you soak me and then I'll come to you. I promise you; I'm going to make you forget all about him when it's all over with. You won't even remember his name. It's up to you how badly you want his heart to be broken." He kisses me again, gently this time, almost reverently on the corners of my mouth. "You are mine now, and I take care of what's mine."

FOURTEEN

ELOISE

I SIT IN MY CAR, A TREMBLING MESS, SOBS WRACKING MY BODY. Drew's threats echoing clearly in my mind as I try to work a way out of this mess. Before he let me leave, he told me that I was not to confide in anyone about what was going on and if I didn't leave my husband by the time my week was up, he was going to take matters into his own hands. He made me watch the video of him going down on me. The visual of his large palms spreading my thighs open while he feasted on me is seared into my brain. In the video I absolutely do seem to be into the way he is worshiping my pussy, but I have no recollection at all of any of it happening. Putting the car into drive, I head home, desperate and terrified that my whole life as I know it is about to be over.

By the time I get home, it is well past midnight. I drove around aimlessly for a couple of hours just trying to clear my mind, trying to purge the guilt and shame clinging to me like a second skin. I don't feel worthy of being in my own home or sleeping in the bed I'm supposed to be sharing with my husband.

Instead, I change into some comfy sweats and grab a blanket to cuddle up with on the couch with a bottle of wine. I shoot a text off to my supervisor claiming to have a stomach bug and letting her know I won't be in to work in the morning. I know I am absolutely not in the state of mind to be caring for patients and my number one priority has to be getting out of this mess. I see a missed call from Caleb in my notifications from when I was with Drew. He didn't leave a message and I don't have the courage to call him now. I don't think there is any way I can speak to him without breaking down entirely. I polish off the bottle of wine, instead, and pass out in a blissfully, dream-free drunken slumber.

The next morning a loud banging at my front door draws me from sleep. Thanks to the wine I finished off by myself it feels like there is a jack hammer going to work in my brain. I sit up, only to hang my head between my knees as the hangover from hell crushes my skull. Fucking red wine. I know better than to get drunk off of it. The tannins always leave me with a splitting headache and dry mouth. A pained moan escapes my lips as I attempt to open my eyes and figure out who the hell has the nerve to be knocking at my door.

"Open up, Lo! I know you're in there. Your car is in the driveway!" Sara's voice comes through the front door as she pounds on it again.

"Calm your tits, I'm coming!" I shout, and wince immediately at the pain that shoots through my skull. Slowly, I get myself off the couch and make it to the front door to let my best friend in. She's standing there, wearing her running gear, coated in a light sheen of sweat that makes her look like she's glowing. Only Sara could look this good, this early in the morning, after a run.

"Why are you here?" I step to the side as Sara barges into my home, like she lives here too.

"Girl, you look like shit. Did you get run over by a train?" She crinkles her nose as she takes in my disheveled appearance. If I look anything like how I feel, then her reaction is completely warranted.

"Bottle of Merlot, more like." I grumble as I push past her to go into the kitchen. I fill up a glass of water and chug it down while she studies me with a worried frown on her face.

"What's going on, Lo? Aren't you supposed to be at work and not hungover in the middle of the week? Is everything ok with Caleb?"

I chug down a second glass of water and dig around in the cabinet until I find some painkillers to take for the skull-splitting headache, before answering her. "Things are not ok, Sara. Not even a little ok." My voice cracks on that last word, and the tears I thought I had run out of last night spill out again. My shoulders slump and I wrap my arms around my middle and begin to sob in earnest again. I feel Sara wrap her arms around me, she strokes my hair and makes comforting sounds, as I bury my face in her shoulder and let the stress and grief of my marriage falling apart wash over me.

"Ssh, ssh. It's ok. Tell me what happened. I thought things were improving with you and Caleb?" She pats my back and lets me sob on her shoulder.

"I can't do it...I can't save it. It's over." My knees give out and we both slide down to the floor. Sara refuses to let me go, holding me as tight as she can. She doesn't prod or ask questions. She just holds me together and lets me have my breakdown. As my best friend she always knows exactly what I need and when I need it. She knows what I really need to do right now is let go. I have to spiral to the bottom before I can get back up again.

We stayed like that for what felt like hours. Me pouring my heartbreak out, Sara holding me and soothing me to the best of her ability. She doesn't push me or ask questions. She knows I'll open up when I'm ready. "Sara, I can't stay..." I begin to tell her what's truly wrong, but Drew's words echo in my mind before I get the rest of the sentence out. *"You're mine now."*

"It's over. I'm leaving Caleb." There is no feeling in my voice. No emotion. The words taste bitter in my mouth. Sara pulls back and looks me dead in the eye.

"Bullshit. You were just fighting for your marriage a

few days ago. What could've happened since the last time we talked? He's not even back yet, did you guys have a fight? Did you run into tall, dark and deadly again? Lo, this isn't making any sense to me. Make it make sense." She stares into my soul as she waits for my response. I know I can't lie to her. Sara has always been able to call me out on my bullshit. I decide to go with a partial truth and hope she buys it.

"Yeah, um, I ran into him again. He's the one I want." The words sound as hollow as I feel inside. Sara isn't buying it either.

"Again, I call bullshit. Lo, what the fuck is going on. You are crying like someone died, not like a woman who has found a new love of her life. Please tell me what is going on. I want to help. I'm worried about you."

I shake my head, denial on my tongue. "The only thing that is going on is my marriage is over Sara. I fucked up and now it's done. When Caleb gets back, I'm leaving him. It's just how it has to be." I loosen myself from her hold and stand up, keeping my back to her. I'm not ready to do this yet. I thought I'd have a few more days to come up with a plan but Sara finding me in the midst of a breakdown is making it impossible to keep up with the lie.

"Look, I appreciate your concern, but I really just need some time alone to work through this. Can you just go for now? I'll call you later." My tone is cold, and I know I'm being hurtful to one of the people who love me more than almost anything. Sara would understand if I told her but I'm too paranoid that Drew will find out and send the video to Caleb. I can't take that chance. I won't let Drew destroy Caleb like that. If I must end my marriage, I want it to be on my terms and with as little heartbreak as possible. If there is any way I can protect Caleb's heart, I have to try.

"Yeah, sure, Lo. Take whatever time you need. But please know, whatever this is, you don't have to go through it alone." She comes up behind me and gives me a tight hug and kisses my temple. "I'm here for you, please talk to me before you do something you can't take back." I keep my back to her as I listen to her walk out the front door. I grab another glass of water and trudge back into the living room to collapse on the couch to sleep off the last of my hangover. Between the wine and the crying, I feel as physically rung out as I do emotionally. I close my eyes and fall into a fitful sleep, praying a solution will come to me in my dreams before I have to go through with Drew's demands.

My phone is ringing, and Caleb's face pops up on the screen. I let it ring out and go to voicemail. He's called me twice today, and twice yesterday; I've ignored every call. I can't talk to him. I won't be able to hear his voice and act like everything is completely normal. I sent him a message claiming to be sick, and it's not a complete lie. I've been so stressed out I haven't been able to keep any food down since I woke up hungover yesterday. I called out of work again today. I know I'm on the verge of getting a disciplinary action for my absences, but I can't bring myself to care. Sara has sent me a few texts checking in, and Drew has sent two messages with more pictures of Saturday night, and a still from the security camera in his bar from our meeting. He's got himself a hefty portfolio of damning evidence of my infidelity and he's not above reminding me of it.

The way I look at it, every option is terrible. If I try to tell Caleb the truth, he'll probably hate me or not believe me, especially if Drew sends him the video. I can claim I was drugged until I'm blue in the face, but there is nothing in that video that backs up my story. If I don't leave Caleb and Drew sends him the video, he will definitely hate me. That leaves me leaving him, willingly. That is the only option that allows me a small bit of control over the narrative, a way to break his heart without completely shattering him. I can claim it's related to work, or we've grown apart. Something amicable that won't lead to him despising me. It'll hurt like hell, but I can't live with the thought of him hating me. My only hope is if we split on good terms, maybe there will be a way to salvage our relationship once Drew grows bored of me, if he ever does.

A text comes through on my phone from Caleb.

Caleb: How are you, Sweetness? I'm worried you won't answer your phone. Can you please call me when you're able? I miss you, Lo.

Caleb: Should I text Liv or Sara to come by and check on you? Have them bring you some dinner?

Caleb: If you don't call me back in an hour, I'm going to tell them to come check on you.

I let out a weary sigh, knowing he will make good on that threat. I reply in text, still unable to make myself talk to him.

Me: Sorry. This stomach flu is kicking my ass. If I'm not puking, I'm sleeping. Don't have them come by, I don't want them to catch it. I'll be ok. I've got Gatorade and crackers. Love you.

Just for good measure I send him a GIF of Liz Lemon leaning over a toilet. I pray it injects enough normalcy into my response that he will drop the issue. A knock at the door makes my heart stop. I hope he didn't already call in the calvary. I am absolutely in no state to deal with Sara or Olivia and their questions. I get up and peek through the side window only to see the absolute last person I want at my house standing on the other side of the door. Drew.

"Open up darlin'. I know you're home." His tone is light, sweet and indulgent, like he isn't currently black-mailing me into leaving my husband.

"You can't be here. Please leave." I plead through the still closed door, my eyes closed tight against the flood of tears threatening to break free.

"Eloise don't make me ask again. I'm just coming by to

check on you. I want to make sure you are ok." Drew's tone is a combination of soothing and patronizing, like he's chiding me as if I'm a young child. Sighing, I relent and open the door a crack. He immediately reaches through, pushing it open the rest of the way, and leans against the frame preventing me from closing it on him.

"That's my good girl." He gives me a dark smile as he brushes knuckles against my cheek. He leans in to kiss me, and I lean back before he makes contact.

"Why are you here Drew? You can't be here! My week isn't over. This isn't the agreement we made." I take a step back and he follows me into the house. Shit, this is bad. I can't have him inside my house. Fuck. I hold up my hands, begging him to stop.

"Please, don't come any further. Drew I don't know why you are doing this but please, don't come into the house I share with my husband. It's too much." Surprisingly he listens to my request and steps back, leaning one shoulder against the doorframe.

"You haven't been to work. I was worried about you, baby girl. Just coming by to check on your well-being and making sure you haven't gone AWOL on me." His words sound concerned, but the look he gives me is anything but. He scorches me with his intense gaze as he takes in my disheveled appearance. My hair is in a messy top knot, and I'm wearing one of Caleb's t-shirts paired with leggings. When he realizes that I'm wearing one of Caleb's shirts, a sneer crosses his face.

"Darlin', you need to take care of yourself. Why don't

you clean up and I'll take you to dinner?" I ignore his command and focus on something else he said.

"How do you know I haven't been to work, Drew?" My heart is racing, which seems to be its natural state when he is around, invading my space, stealing my ability to think rationally.

His smile completely unnerves me. It's almost like he's mocking me now. "I keep tabs on what is mine, Eloise. Surely you don't think I haven't been watching out for you, while you're all alone in this house?"

His words send ice water cascading through my veins. "How long have you been keeping tabs on me?" The words barely come out in a whisper, as I take in their implication. Sara was right. He has been stalking me. But for how long? His answering grin is positively feral.

"Long enough to know everything about you, darlin'. Your wants, your needs, your darkest desires…I know you in every way that matters but for one, Sweetness. That will come soon enough." His mocking use of Caleb's nickname sends a sharp pain straight through my heart. I back up another step and bump against the table in the hallway. The clutch I carried the other night with the pepper spray and stun gun is right by my hand. Without thinking I reach in and pull out the first thing my hand touches, the small cylinder of pepper spray.

"Drew, you need to fucking leave now. You gave me a week and I am taking it. You said you would let me do this my way. I swear to fucking God if you don't leave now you are going to get a face full of spicy pepper jizz." My voice sounds much stronger than I feel right now. My hand holding the pepper spray is shaking violently, but I am not going to back down. I will not let this man into my home.

Drew tosses his hands up in a placating gesture. "Fair enough, I'm a man of my word, Eloise. You'll have your week as long as you are following my rules." The meaning behind his words is clear. He will follow through on his threat if I don't do what he asks. My aim with the pepper spray waivers briefly and he takes the opportunity to step in again and grabs my wrist, pulling me flush against his body. He crashes his mouth against mine for a possessive, demanding kiss. He forces his tongue into my mouth as he crushes my body against his. I can't get away from him, no matter how hard I shove against him. With one last harsh bite on my bottom lip, he pulls away and steps back outside.

"I'll be seeing you soon, darlin'." With that he jogs down the steps and hops into a black SUV with tinted windows. Once I have control over my faculties again, I slam the door shut, and lock it before rushing into the bathroom to get sick.

CHAPTER

FIFTEEN

CALEB

It's Thursday afternoon, and I'm pacing in my office completely unfocused on anything, other than the fact that my wife may be cheating on me and I haven't talked to her in more than a day. I tried calling her last night and today, but she isn't answering my calls. She sent one text simply saying she wasn't feeling well and sleeping a lot. No other explanation or communication. I've checked her location on my phone, and she hasn't left the house since returning late Tuesday night. I watched for the notification on our doorbell obsessively until she got home after midnight. I feel like a creep for spying on her, but her radio silence and lies about her whereabouts have me on edge. The only notification I've gotten from the doorbell since Tuesday night was Sara making an unexpected visit yesterday morning.

I decide to send her a text under the guise of being a concerned spouse. I'll offer to have her sister Liv, or Sara come check on her if she doesn't respond. I need to hear from her. This level of radio silence isn't normal in our relationship, and I have to know she's ok. Her response is another brush off excuse about being sick and she rejects the offer for help. I don't feel any better, but at least I know she's checking her phone.

A few minutes later a notification for the doorbell pops up on my phone. I open the app to see if it is Lo leaving the house again, but I am surprised to find a man banging on the door. A familiar, dark haired, knock off Jason Momoa. "What the fuck..." I hit the button to listen to the audio of him talking.

"Open up darlin'. I know you're home."

Lo's response is muffled, like she's talking through the door.

"You can't be here. Please leave."

I'm torn between hitting the button to talk and tell him to fuck off myself, but his next words stop me cold.

"Eloise don't make me ask again. I'm just coming by to check on you. I want to make sure you are ok."

The sound of the door opening comes through, and he steps forward, out of the line of sight of the camera. I hear one last bone chilling phrase before the audio and video cut off

"That's my good girl."

What the ever-loving fuck is going on with my wife? I stare at my phone in dismay, not fully able to believe what I just witnessed. This was not the man in the picture with her in front of the bar. I would know that asshole anywhere after studying that photo for countless hours. This is the man I caught flirting with her at Allure. Dread pools in my stomach as I consider the possibility that she could be cheating on me with more than one man.

Ten minutes later the doorbell app notifies me of the mystery man's departure. He strolls off our front porch with a jaunty step like he doesn't have a care in the world. The doorbell camera can see the street well enough that I can see the black SUV he is driving. I call Eloise again; this attempt goes straight to voicemail. I leave a message this time.

"Hey, Sweetness. I...um...I'm just calling to check on you. I need to talk to you. Please call me back. This can't wait." I almost tell her I love her but stop myself. I can't bring myself to utter those words after hearing another man call her a good girl. I end the call and start searching for flight options to get home as soon as possible. Whatever this shit is, I am not waiting until Sunday to figure it out.

CHAPTER
SIXTEEN

ELOISE

It's Friday afternoon, in the middle of my shift at the hospital. I volunteered to spend my whole day holed up in the O.R. in an attempt to avoid my co-workers and manager. In the operating room I can hide my haggard appearance behind a surgical mask and keep to myself. I'm not expected to interact with anyone if I don't want to, and I can stay in my head mulling over my problem as much as I need to, as long as I hit the exposure button every time the doctor tells me to.

Right now, I'm in a total hip replacement operation, but we are nearing the end of the procedure. I'm dreading returning to the department. I know my manager has been looking for me all day to speak to me about my absences, but it just isn't a problem that's high on my list to deal with at the moment. Currently, guilt is eating me alive over the fact that I still haven't called my husband. I know the longer I wait, the more questions he is going to have, but nausea churns in my gut and I break down every time I think of calling him.

"Alright, X-ray, we're done. Good work." Dr. Nolen's dismissal brings me out of my daze.

"Do you need me for anything else today, doctor?" I ask, hoping there is at least one more case I can do, to finish out my day.

"Nah, we're done for the day. "He pulls off his sterile gown and tosses it in the trash as he strolls past me. Guess I'll be having that meeting with my boss today, after all. I sigh as I pull out my machine and start cleaning it up and shutting it down. After I roll my C-Arm out of the operating room and down into the storage closet I head back to the X-ray department, readying myself to face the music.

"Hey, Lo! You have a delivery!" One of the front desk secretaries calls out to me as I walk by. I turn to see her pointing to a large vase of roses on her desk. "You should've seen the delivery guy. He was a total hottie. Looked like that Khal Drogo guy from the dragon show. Caleb is so sweet to send you flowers, what's the special occasion?"

I can feel the color drain from my face. Those flowers aren't from Caleb, and that wasn't a delivery guy. It was fucking Drew keeping an eye on me. "Oh, um, I guess he's just missing me since he's out of town this week. He knows I was upset that he had to leave again so soon." The lie spills out easily. I don't want my co-workers to have any reason to gossip about the state of my marriage. I'm struggling enough keeping my shit together as is, I cannot handle any questions about my relationship, here too. I snatch up the vase and take it to the break room to open the card in private. It is another picture of me in Drew's bed. With the words *"This is where you belong."* scrawled across the bottom.

"This fucking guy." I move to throw the flowers away, but my manager comes through the door before I make it to the trash can.

"Oh, Lo! There you are! I've been looking for you all day. You got a minute to talk? Ooh, pretty flowers. Those from the hubby? Is he in the doghouse for something?" I bite back the snarky comment I'd like to make about it being none of her fucking business. Might as well not dig the hole I'm in any deeper.

"Yeah, sure Diane, just let me put these in my locker." I pocket the picture and shove the flowers into my locker unceremoniously. I don't even worry if it seems careless to stuff them in there with my other stuff. They're not making it out of this hospital if I have anything to do with it. Judging by the puzzled look on Diane's face, I'm not giving the flowers the care she thinks they deserve.

I follow Diane to her office, fully aware of why she wants to talk. I've missed three days of work in the last week and a half since Drew came into my life. I'm on the verge of a write up, I'm sure of it. "Look, Diane. I know this is about me calling out. I couldn't help it; I had the stomach flu." Diane shakes her head, cutting me off before I fully launch into my defense.

"Actually, Eloise. There's something else I wanted to

talk to you about. We received a complaint from a patient that you took care of last weekend when you were working the night shift and I wanted to get your side of the story." I have absolutely no idea what she could be referring to. I didn't have any unpleasant patients last week, so I shrug helplessly.

"Um, sure, I don't remember having any tough patients, but I'll try to help."

"Well, it's not exactly from an angry patient. Do you remember taking x-rays on Andrew Jameson last Wednesday?" My stunned silence must be all the confirmation she needs since she presses on. "There was an anonymous complaint that you were inappropriately flirting with him while he was in your care. You know inappropriate behavior towards patients is not tolerated here at Birch Falls Memorial."

"Diane, I don't know what you're talking about. I would never, ever flirt with a patient. I'm married. Happily. I...I don't know what to say. You know me better than this." I'm flustered and I can feel my cheeks heating from embarrassment and confusion. Did someone see Andrew talking to me that night? I thought the door to the room was still closed, but maybe it hadn't been? Did someone get the wrong idea when he was the one being inappropriate with me?

"Look, that patient was drunk or something, he was a little too friendly towards me, but I promise, I was nothing but professional towards him."

"I believe you, Lo, but we do have to follow up on all

complaints made of this nature. So, someone will be contacting the patient to get his side of the story. I'm sure it'll back your version up, but I had to ask you and give you a heads up that we will be looking into this matter." I nod dumbly as I process what she is saying. Someone from work will be talking to Drew. What will he tell them? Will he tell the truth or throw me under the bus?

"I understand...is that all? It's um...time for me to go home." I stand and start backing towards the door.

"Of course, Lo. I'll follow up with you about this when we get in touch with him. I'm sure it's a misunderstanding." Diane starts shuffling papers on her desk and I give her a quick wave before ducking out of her office.

On my way out of the hospital I decide to stop by the Medical Care Unit and leave the flowers with an older patient named Helen who has been admitted for the last three months. She has dementia but is sweet as a button. Helen rarely gets visitors, so I leave her the roses to brighten her day.

On the drive home, I debate my options for dealing with Drew. I consider calling him to see if he will be on my side when my work contacts him, but I feel like asking for his help is just going to be another opportunity for him to blackmail me. When I get home, I'm no closer to a decision. I'm so lost in thought when I walk through the front door, I don't realize I'm not alone right away. I'm staring down at my phone, biting my bottom lip as I weigh my options, when the sound of someone clearing their throat pulls me from my thoughts. I look up, so startled I almost drop my phone, and see Caleb standing in front of me. There are dark circles under his red rimmed eyes, and his hair is mussed, like he's been running his fingers through it constantly. He looks like he's been going through the same hell I've been living, and I know at that moment that my time is up.

"Lo...what is going on? Why have you been avoiding me?" His voice is low, and raspy. Like he's lost it after a long night of screaming, and my heart shatters because I know I did that. I put that miserable, heartbroken look on his face, and I know I'm about to make it worse.

CHAPTER
SEVENTEEN
CALEB

Eloise stands in front of me frozen in place with a shocked and terrified expression on her color-drained face. It is clear she wasn't expecting me and I'm the last person she wants to see. She doesn't approach me; she doesn't run up to give me a hug or kiss or do anything a wife missing her husband might do after being apart for nearly two weeks. She stays rooted to the spot right in front of the door, looking every bit like she wants to run away.

I repeat my question as calmly as possible, but I know my voice is harsh and on edge. I haven't slept in nearly 24 hours and spent the morning flying back, with an extra-long layover in Charlotte thanks to a weather delay, just to get here today. "Lo, what is going on? Why are you avoiding me?" I take a step towards her, but she tenses up, so I step back again. I'm not trying to scare her off before I get the answers I'm looking for.

"Lo, I know something is up. I need you to talk to me. If you don't tell me what is happening, I can only assume the worst. Who is he?" My voice cracks on the last word as I plead with my wife to tell me the truth.

Eloise shakes her head frantically, tears spilling from her eyes. "He? There is no he. I don't know what you're talking about, Caleb." She won't look me in the eye as the lies spill from her lips. She's staring at her hands as she nervously picks at her cuticles, a tic she has when her anxiety is spiking.

"Eloise, look at me. Don't lie to me, Sweetness." I slowly step up to her so I can tip her chin up gently and force her to meet my gaze. I know whatever she's not telling me I'm not going to like, but I have to get her to talk to me. "Tell me the truth." I stare at her face, trying to read the truth that she won't speak out loud. Her eyes shimmer with tears and her bottom lip quivers as she finally looks me in the eye. Whatever she sees in my expression finally cracks the emotional wall she is trying to hide behind and she crumples into me, sobbing.

"Caleb, I fucked up...I ruined it. I ruined everything." Eloise sobs as I wrap my arms around her trembling body, holding her against me as tightly as I can, terrified this might be the last time I ever get to hold her like this. Whatever she is getting ready to tell me is going to change our relationship permanently, I have no doubt of it. I steel myself for the blow that is coming.

"I'm so sorry. It was never supposed to happen. I don't know how it happened. I never wanted to hurt you." She hiccups against my chest as her tears soak into my rumpled t-shirt. She clings to me like I'm her life raft in the middle of an ocean and the only thing preventing her from drowning. We stay like that for what seems an eternity, holding on to each other and our relationship as we know it desperately, knowing once we pull apart everything is going to change.

Eventually, Eloise pulls herself away from me and makes her way over to the couch. She sits, keeping her gaze trained on the floor. I remain standing, my hands stuffed into my pockets so she can't see how badly they're shaking. A long silence stretches between us as I wait for her to find her words. My patience begins to wear thin when she doesn't start talking, so I prod her.

"I know there is someone else. More than one someone actually." That gets her attention. Her head snaps up, shock showing across her beautiful features.

"What are you talking about? There is not more than one someone!" Her eyes dart back and forth looking around the room like she's waiting for someone else to pop out of the woodwork and scream 'Got ya!'

"Don't fucking lie to me, Lo! Cut the shit. I saw the picture of you with some asshole outside of a bar. I saw that fucking douche canoe from the club come to MY goddamn front door! I HEARD HIM CALL YOU, MY WIFE, 'BABY GIRL'!" I'm yelling at her now, every shred of understanding and calm I had been desperately holding on to, completely evaporates.

The guilt stricken look on her face is all the confirmation I need. "You saw him? Here?" She gasps, completely horrified I already know so much. I give her a terse nod, but don't say anything else. I'm waiting for her to decide if she is going to come clean. Realization dawns on her face. "The doorbell..." I nod again and she lets out a defeated sigh.

She takes a long time to gather her courage to speak again. The urge to rage and start breaking shit becomes almost unbearable. The thought of that fuckstain putting his hands on my wife makes me want to scream.

"I never meant for anything to happen...I didn't want anything to happen...it just...did." Her words are barely a whisper as she begins her confession. I bite back the urge to make a snide retort about her accidentally tripping and falling on his dick.

"Lo, I'm only going to ask this one time. Did you cheat on me? Are you sleeping with him?" The last part comes out as little more than a whisper. I'm barely able to give voice to my biggest fear.

"No. I didn't sleep with him." Her voice is surprisingly firm and resolute with that answer. She looks me straight in the eye when she says it, so I believe her.

"Then what happened? Explain this to me because my brain is going to a very dark place, right now."

Eloise takes a deep breath, and I find myself unable to breathe on my own. "I...um well, have run into him a few times. And he's been pursuing me. At first, I shut him down, but he kept turning up, and making me feel... special." She hesitates on the word special, like it tastes bitter on her tongue. "The picture of the other guy you saw, um, he was at Drew's bar Saturday night, when I was there, and I think he roofied me. When I walked out, he followed me and grabbed me. Drew stopped him before anything happened and knocked him out. I think...it's all very hazy. Then he took me to his place to keep an eye on me until the effects of the roofie wore off."

I feel sick. The thought of my wife being roofied and almost being taken advantage of nearly takes me to my knees. Whatever relief I feel about her being rescued by this Drew character is quickly quelled by the thought that she spent the night with him in an inebriated state. "Are you sure he just looked after you? If you don't remember anything then how can you be sure?" I'm not even sure how it's possible, but she goes paler at my question, like I hit the nail on the head.

"Um, he took care of me. Gave me water...pain meds; fed me breakfast. I didn't feel like I had been assaulted..." She stammers out her reply and I know there is more she isn't telling me. "He's given me a lot to think about, Cal. I was going to talk to you when you got home. I think...I think we need some time apart." Tears are silently streaming down her face and my heart cracks wide open at her request.

"Lo...you can't mean that. Things were fine when I left! Things were fine up until Saturday night. What aren't you telling me?" I reach out to grab her, but she leans away from my touch.

"Things aren't fine, Caleb. Not now. Maybe they

haven't been for a while. I'm going to pack a bag and go stay somewhere else. I think I just need some time to figure stuff out." She stands up and walks towards the stairs that lead up to our room. "I don't want to hurt you, Caleb. I've never wanted to hurt you. But I'm afraid that's all I'll do now." I'm rooted to my spot on the floor unable to bring myself to go to her. My brain is still trying to process this revelation that things aren't ok; that things are way more fucked up than I knew. I'm still standing in the same place when she comes back down a few minutes later with an overnight bag slung over her shoulder.

"Where are you going? Are you going to him?" I rasp out, stopping her as she reaches the door.

She shakes her head, looking at me with as much heartbreak etched on her face as I know I have on mine. "No...I don't know where I'm going, but I'm not going to him. I just need some time. I love you."

With that she walks out the front door, taking my heart with her.

PART TWO
EVERLONG

CHAPTER
EIGHTEEN
ELOISE

I DRIVE AN HOUR OUTSIDE OF TOWN, TO A LITTLE SCENIC RETRO 1960's-style motel, nestled right off the parkway that winds its way through the nearby mountains. Caleb and I have stayed here before on little weekend staycations. It's quiet, surrounded by hiking trails and has a gorgeous view of the sunrise over the mountains. I had considered calling Sara or Olivia to see if I could come stay with them, but I wasn't lying to Caleb when I said I needed some time to think about things. I hadn't been ready to confront Caleb about any of the shit going on and I wasn't prepared at all for him to know anything about Drew, or apparently Brayden. My hope to have been able to control the narrative slipped right through my fingers when Caleb said he had seen Drew on the doorbell camera.

After checking into my room, I toss my bag on the bed and flop down burying my face in the pillow. It doesn't take long for exhaustion from all the stress to claim me, and soon I find myself drifting off into a fitful sleep. I have dreams of Caleb walking in on me with Drew in our bed. In it, Caleb just stands and watches while Drew brings me to orgasm over and over again with his tongue and fingers, while Drew tells him, "This is how you treat a Queen." In the dream I keep trying to apologize to Caleb, to tell him that I don't want this, but every time the words reach the tip of my tongue another orgasm takes over, stealing them. Drew never relents, lashing at my clit with his tongue while his fingers plunge deep into my cunt, hitting my g spot over and over. In the dream Caleb never moves, never says a word, only looks at me with a heartbroken and defeated expression.

The chirp of a text notification from my phone drags me from the dream. I sit up, feeling confused and more than a little aroused. It takes a few moments for me to come back to reality and get my bearings. Shame sweeps over me as I feel slick wetness between my thighs. Apparently, the orgasms in the dream were real. I dig my phone out of my purse and check to see who is texting me. In my heart I am hoping it is Caleb asking me to come home, even though I have no right to wish for such a thing. The clock on my phone reads that it is a little past 10:00 p.m. I must've been out for a few hours. I guess the stress from losing a marriage is more exhausting than one would think.

I see a few missed texts from Drew and one from Caleb. I ignore the ones from Drew and open Caleb's first.

> Caleb: Can you let me know you're ok? I know we have shit to work out, but I need to know you are safe.

My heart melts a little, knowing even after everything that happened, Caleb doesn't hate me. At least not yet.

> Me: I'm fine. Staying in that little motel off the parkway. Alone. I'm sorry for everything. I just need time to figure some things out. You probably do too.

I take a deep breath and steel myself for opening Drew's messages. Dread pools in my gut, wondering if he knows Caleb is home already. If he's going to up the timeline on me and demand I come back to him.

> Drew: Where did you go, darlin'? You're not at home. Looks like hubby is, though.

> Drew: He doesn't look very happy. I can see him pacing in front of the window. Did you tell him the truth about us? About how good I make you feel?

> Drew: Eloise, if you don't talk to me, I might have to go ask him where our Sweetness ran off to. I don't really feel like getting into a fight, but I will if I need to in order to find you.

Rage courses through me as I read his threat. This

fucking guy. Where does he get off? Why the fuck does he even think this is going to lead to some kind of happily ever after for him and me?

> Me: I fucking did what you asked. I left. Now leave me the fuck alone while I grieve my marriage you ruined.

The little typing bubble pops up almost immediately, like he was waiting for my response.

> Drew: Good girl. Come see me tomorrow. We can celebrate.

Celebrate? Is this guy smoking something? How does he think this is going to go? I toss my phone to the side and head to the bathroom to clean up before I climb back into bed. Once I'm back under the covers I decide to see if I can dig up any information on a one Mr. Andrew Jameson of Birch Falls. He seems to know an awful lot about me, but aside from his name, where he works, and his favorite Cohen Brothers' movie, I know nothing about him.

I start out by looking him up on social media. I check the usual sites, but nothing comes up for him. His name is common enough that I get plenty of hits for various Andrew Jamesons across the country, but none here in Birch Falls. I look up the page for Stellina next, to see if it might have a profile linked to him. There are a few professional looking photos of him behind the bar doing various bartending stunts, and schmoozing with customers, but nothing of use. It looks like he opened Stellina about 2 years ago, and it's been a success since day one. Under each picture are dozens of comments from women and men alike making puns about being thirsty and ready to be *'served'* by him. It seems like he isn't lacking in attention. Why in the hell is he so focused on me?

I switch to looking him up on a search engine, typing in various combinations of his name and location. There are a few news articles from when he first opened Stellina, one of them mentioning that he went to school at my alma mater. That's interesting...I change up my search terms and try looking him up from his time in college. That's when I finally hit pay dirt.

I find a police report about a domestic disturbance involving him and what seems to have been his girlfriend at the time. There is a picture of his mug shot, his dark hair short and spiky, face bare from any facial hair, a slight smirk playing on his full lips. His soulless dark eyes staring straight into the camera like he doesn't have a care in the world. The article doesn't specify what exactly the disturbance was, but it does have the name of the woman involved. Cassidy Grainger. That name tickles my brain in a familiar way, so I look her up next. What I find sends a cold chill down my spine.

Cassidy Grainger was a young college co-ed that went missing her senior year at Birch Falls University. She was a couple of years older than me, so we didn't cross paths, but I remember when she went missing. She had failed to return to her apartment after an off-campus party one night, and her roommate reported her missing a day after that. There were search parties all through the woods surrounding campus and they even sent divers into the river and the swimming hole near the falls. Her body was never found, and a suspect never named in her case. It went cold about a year after. The circumstances of her disappearance are tragic, but it is her picture that has me shivering beneath my covers. Her long blonde hair is the same honey gold mine naturally is when I haven't dyed it. Her eyes are a light glacier blue, similar to my own and she has a heart shaped face with rosy cheeks a lot like mine. She was shorter than me, a bit more petite but our builds are similar in that we both have shapely curves in the right places.

In the article there is a link to a memorial page for her. I click on it and scroll through all of the messages from her friends and loved ones wishing her happy birthday every year, reminiscing about fun times in her life, and how much she is missed. One message in particular catches my eye. It is from an A. James, no profile picture, and it only says "You'll always be mine, darlin'. No matter how long we are apart." There is no doubt in my mind that message is from Drew. Fuck a duck. Is he obsessed with me because I remind him of an old girlfriend? Is this something I can use to reason with him? Was he involved in her disappearance? My mind is racing as I consider all the possibilities this new information opens up.

The next morning, after a very restless night full of dreams about missing girls and non-consensual orgasms while my husband watched on, I decide to take a hike on one of the trails surrounding the motel. My mind keeps turning over the new information I learned about Cassidy Grainger. I keep coming up with two possibilities, both disturbing, but one a lot more bone chilling than the other.

The first is that Drew and Cassidy were in a relationship when she went missing, and he is still grieving her and thinks I remind him of his lost love. Crazy, but a kind of crazy I might be able to work with.

The second is the much scarier option. Drew and Cassidy were in a relationship, he was involved in her disappearance, and now he's obsessed with me. I keep trying to brush this option off as a product of binge-watching that stalker show on Netflix but I'm not stupid enough to dismiss it entirely.

The hike through the woods does little to calm my nerves or clear my mind. I didn't bring my phone with me so I could avoid the temptation to check for calls or texts from Caleb, but in my hyper paranoid state, every rustle of leaves or snap of a branch nearly sends me jumping out of my skin. After only the first mile I turn back, giving up on the idea of Mother Nature providing any clarity to my situation.

As I approach the motel from the trees, I notice a familiar looking black SUV with tinted windows parked next to my little Subaru. "Surely not...there's no fucking way." I slow my steps and duck behind a tree to watch for a moment to see if Drew is the one in the SUV. Unfortunately, thanks to the tinted windows, I can't see if anyone is actually in the vehicle. "Fuck a duck." I mutter as I step away from my hiding spot. I can't hide in the woods forever, so I might as well face the music. I purposely ignore the SUV as I approach my room, manifesting the Drew-less energy I want in the world.

The manifestation must work because I make it into my room without incident. I turn the deadbolt and shove the heavy armchair in front of the door for good measure. It might be overkill, but I've watched enough crime shows to know how flimsy the exterior motel doors are. I check my phone, hoping for some message from Caleb, but it is complete radio silence from him. I know I don't deserve to hear from him. I broke his heart and shattered our marriage. I deserve his silence, but that doesn't make it hurt any less. Sighing, I gather my clothes and go take a shower to prepare myself for facing Drew.

CHAPTER

NINETEEN

CALEB

After watching Eloise walk out our front door, taking my heart with her, I completely lose it. In a fit of frustration and rage I knock everything off the hall table and upend the table itself. The lamp that had been sitting on the table, shatters as it hits the hardwood floor. Eloise's little black clutch skitters across the floor and the contents spill out. Disgusted with myself for letting my temper take control, I force myself to leave before I do anymore damage to the home we made together.

Unsure of where to go, or what to do, I choose the most cliche option and find myself at a bar ready to drown my sorrows. A healthy way to deal with my emotions over my crumbling marriage? Absolutely not. But right now, the only thing I want to do is numb the pain away.

"You look like a man whose wife just left him. What'll it be?" The bartender in front of me is a gruff older Hispanic man with slicked back black hair, a face pockmarked with scars and a lively glint in his eyes. He reminds me of a less scary Danny Trejo, but no less capable of taking out the trash when necessary. His forearms are huge and covered in tattoos that seem like they might be military related.

"Jack and Coke, hold the Coke." The misery in my voice confirms he was spot on in his guess. The bartender nods and steps away to pour my drink. He returns a moment later with a double of Jack Daniels and a large glass of ice water. I quirk a brow at the water when he sets it down in front of me.

"I don't like sloppy drunks in my bar. I'm getting too old to be carrying heavy asses like yourself out the door. I'll let you take the edge off, and if you want to talk, I've been known to be a good listener. But I'm not going to over serve you and send you back out into the world drunk and angry. Name's Sal, by the way." He raps his knuckles against the bar and walks off to serve a newcomer that just walked in.

"Thanks Sal." I mutter into my drink before downing half of it in one swallow. He's not wrong. I am angry. So, fucking angry. Angry at Eloise for not giving me the chance to fix things. Angry at myself for letting this chasm open up between us. Angry at Drew for wiggling his way between us and putting doubt into my wife's mind. I close my eyes and try to take a calming breath before I spiral even more out of control. I think back to when I first saw him talking to her at the club weeks ago. Was that the first time they met? Had I interrupted something more than an innocent conversation? Eloise confirming she's seen him several times sheds new light on the way he continued flirting with her even after I introduced myself.

I toss back the rest of the whiskey and motion to Sal to pour me another. He comes over, shaking his head like a disappointed father, but pours me another double. "So, what's your story kid?"

"My wife needs space. Apparently, she's met someone and now she has a lot to 'think about'."

Sal gives me an understanding nod as he wipes down glasses from the dishwasher. "You kids been married long?"

"Ten years. Been together for 12. Things have been good up until this last year. I've had to travel for work a lot and be away from Lo. She hasn't been a fan of it." I know I'm giving a very brief synopsis of our problems, but honestly until a couple of weeks ago I hadn't realized just how unhappy Lo was with the situation. I thought we could tough it out a little longer. I thought she loved me.

"Ahh, you put the job before your wife. She wasn't your number one priority. I'll tell you a secret; you can't take a good woman for granted for too long. No matter how long she's been with you. A woman you want to keep, knows she's worth keeping and will not settle for playing second fiddle. You may love her, and she may love you, but if you don't love her in the way she needs, someone else will. Sounds like she found a volunteer, too."

"It's more complicated than that, Sal." I snap out a defensive retort, not willing to take all the blame in this situation. "My boss needed me to handle a lot for him in the company. He's grooming me to take over for him when he retires. I told her it was temporary, and I was going to stop traveling so much."

"Ok, but did you, or did you not make your wife a lower priority than your job?" His words are slow and measured, almost like how a therapist would talk. He spears me with an unrelenting stare as he waits for them to sink in.

I can't deny he's nailed the crux of the matter. "Yeah, I did...but-"

"No buts about it kid." He cuts off my defense before I can spout out more bullshit about it being for the good of our future. "Your wife becomes your number one the day you marry her. Nothing else comes close. You cherish her, love her, and make her feel like she's your world. Her love is a flower that must be watered and tended to otherwise it will wither and die, or someone else will come along and pluck it right from your hands, without you even noticing."

He's not wrong and I have no response to his lecture. He glances down the bar and nods at the customer at the end waving him down. Before he walks off, he offers up another gem. "If you still want her, prove to her that she's the most important thing in your life, no matter her indiscretions. If you can't do that or don't want her then let someone else love her. A marriage requires both parties to be all in at all times." With that he walks away to tend to his other customers. I finish my drink and toss a twenty on the bar before heading back home.

When I get home, I send Lo a text checking in on her, just to assure myself that she's somewhere safe. I'm considering Sal's advice, trying to figure out if I can forgive her indiscretions, and if I can offer her the love she deserves. Am I enough? Can I be?

I trudge up the stairs and get ready for bed. Her response comes through as I'm brushing my teeth. I'm surprised to find out she's at a motel and not staying with her sister or Sara. I guess she's not ready to let the rest of the world in on our problems. When I get to the bed, I start to rummage through the nightstand to find Lo's stash of CBD gummies she keeps on hand for sleep, knowing I'm going to need the assist if I want any sleep at all.

I stop my search short though when I see a picture of her poking out from between the pages of the fantasy novel she's been reading. I pull it out and take in the image of her asleep in an unfamiliar bed with her bare shoulders peeking out from under a black comforter. There is a message scrawled across the bottom of the picture. *"This is where you belong. See you soon, D."* I crumple the photo in my fist and let out a pained scream as the realization that she lied about sleeping with him washes over me.

The next morning, a loud banging at the door draws me from my extremely restless night of dreams. Visions of the long haired, tattooed stranger thrusting into my wife and making her come repeatedly plagued my dreams. I glance at the clock on the nightstand and see it's only a little after eight in the morning.

"Who the fuck is banging on my door?" Slowly I sit up and try to shake off the hangover from the whiskey. I should've drunk the water Sal offered. Fucking rookie mistake. Another loud bang gets my attention and I stumble downstairs to see who is at my front door. "Coming! Calm your tits!" I jerk the door open and let out a near feral growl when I see who is on the other side.

"What the fuck are you doing at my home, asshole?" The fucker doesn't even have the decency to look ashamed to see me. Drew offers up a fake apologetic smile and holds up his hands in a placating manner.

"I know Lo had a rough day at work yesterday, I was just coming by to check on her and see how she's doing. She didn't mention you were home."

A rough day at work? What the fuck is he on about? How does he know anything about her workday? My mind is spinning over the implication that he knows something I don't. "You have no business coming anywhere near my wife. Fuck off before I kick your ass." My voice is full of venom as I raise up to my full height and meet his gaze. He's a few inches taller than me, but I'm not worried about not being able to take him. I played hockey for over half my life and can hold my own in a fight on and off the ice. I will not let this asshole intrude on my territory.

"I'll go wherever Eloise needs me, Caleb. Someone needs to be around looking after her." Before I realize what I'm doing, I step up to him and shove him hard in the chest. Unfortunately, he's a huge fucker and only takes a small step back.

"STAY AWAY FROM MY WIFE." I shove him again, forcing him to retreat another step. He chuckles as he relents and starts back down the stairs.

"Is she still your wife? Where is she, Caleb? I don't see her car here. She's not coming up behind you, telling me to leave. Seems to me, she's already left you. Sorry, 'bout your luck man. I'll take good care of her." With that Drew turns on his heel and saunters down the sidewalk towards his vehicle. Rage courses through my veins like a hurricane, and it takes every bit of self-control I possess to not chase after him and beat him to a bloody pulp. As I watch him leave, his words repeat on a loop in my head. *"Is she still your wife?"* I can honestly say that I don't know the answer to that question.

CHAPTER
TWENTY

ELOISE

After my shower, I spend some more time looking into the Cassidy Grainger disappearance. I'm hoping to find some information that might give me more of an idea of how worried I need to be about Drew being a potential murderer. Unfortunately, her case was declared cold about five years ago by the local police department. All leads had been exhausted and no new tips were rolling in. I find some old news clips on YouTube and Drew is even interviewed in a couple of them. He seems suitably distressed over the disappearance of his girlfriend, he even headed up several volunteer search parties, but I've listened to enough true crime podcasts to know that is no badge of innocence. Many killers stay close to the investigation under some false sense of security that they won't be caught.

I do find a website that is updated semi-regularly devoted to Cassidy's case. It seems to be run by her sister who makes posts asking for tips every couple of months. My heart aches for this poor woman still trying to solve her sister's disappearance. I decide to take a chance and email her asking if she's still in town and if I can meet up with her. As obsessive as Drew is with me, I can't help but wonder if he was the same way with his former girlfriend. Maybe my experience with him will help her connect some dots on her sister's case.

A knock at the door startles me from my thoughts. My heart feels like it seizes up in my chest until I hear the soft voice of the housekeeper. "Housekeeping! I need to turn over the room!" I look at the clock and realize I've stayed an hour past checkout time. I open the door a crack and poke my head out.

"Oh, um, sorry. I was actually hoping I could rent the room another night. I'll just run down to the front desk." The housekeeper shakes her head adamantly.

"I'm sorry ma'am. We are all booked up. The rooms are all rented, and I need to clean this one." I glance dubiously at the nearly empty parking lot.

"Are you sure? I haven't seen hardly anyone here since last night."

"We have a wedding party coming for a sunrise wedding in the morning. They booked up the whole motel." Well shit, there goes my fortress of solitude. I was planning on hiding out here while I sift through the debris of my ruined marriage.

"Um, ok. I'll just be a minute and I'll be out of your hair. Sorry for overstaying." I think she can tell I'm barely holding on by a thread by the way my voice waivers. She gives me a soft smile and assures me that I can take my time.

"I'll go clean the room next door. Take your time, darlin'. It doesn't look like you trashed the place. It won't take me long to turn it over." The use of the endearment sends a shiver down my spine.

"Um, thanks…" I pause for a moment trying to spot her name tag.

"Rosalie. It's no trouble dear." She pats my shoulder and moves on down to the next room.

"Thanks, Rosalie." I say anyway before retreating back inside to pack up the few belongings I brought with me. Looks like I'll be finding a new place to crash for the night.

Later, I find myself back in Birch Falls walking into Brewed Awakening, looking for some caffeine to help me power through this epically shitty day. Apparently, there is some sort of major softball tournament happening on campus this weekend, so all of the local hotels are booked up. I'm not completely without options. I know I could call Sara or Olivia and they would gladly open their homes to me, but the thought of having to answer their questions or deal with their pity makes my stomach squirm.

I'm standing in line, staring blankly at the menu boards listing the specialty coffee drinks, when I feel a warm, hard body press against my back. I tense up and for the briefest of seconds let my mind hope that it is Caleb. But when two tattooed hands donned in silver rings and leather cuffs grasp my shoulders, I know it isn't him. Drew leans in next to my ear and inhales my scent.

"There you are. I've been looking all over for you, darlin'." His grip on my upper arms is bruising, his voice a low admonishment. "I even stopped by your house to check on you this morning."

The person in front of me finishes placing his order and steps out of the way. Drew walks me forward to the counter. I find myself completely unable to form coherent words as I process what he just told me. He stopped by my house. He *stopped* by *my house.* Oh god...*he stopped by my house.* My house, where my husband is. Drew orders us two iced coffees and steers me off to the side where there is a couch to sit on. He sits down and pulls me down, practically in his lap. I try to squirm out of his hold to get some space, but he keeps one arm wrapped around my shoulders while placing the other hand possessively on my inner thigh.

My posture is stiff, and I'm not entirely sure I remember how to breathe. Is this why I haven't heard from Caleb today? Because of Drew? What did he say to Caleb? "W-why did you g-go to my house?" I hate how my voice wavers. I can hear how close I am to breaking. This man is insidious. He's an oily black monster with tentacles, worming his way into my life and ripping it apart.

"I wanted to come check on you. I got a call from your

work last night. Sounded like you were in some trouble there. I thought maybe you might've gone back home this morning instead of coming to me like you were supposed to." His words are innocent enough, but I can't help but pick up the undercurrent of a threat in them. "Your husband wasn't very happy to see me, but I take care of what's mine, regardless of who is in the way." He whispers the last words in my ear, causing goosebumps to rise up all over my body. I can't figure out what part of his mind-fuckery to deal with first. That he spoke to someone at work, or that he talked to my husband.

"I told you I needed time. Why the fuck would you go to my home? I did what you fucking wanted. I broke my husband's heart and ripped mine out in the process." I practically spit the words at him and desperately try to lean away from him again.

Out of the corner of my eye I see the waitress approach with our orders. Drew flashes her a dazzling smile, like he isn't actively in the process of ruining my life. She blushes under his attention as she drops off our drinks. "Thanks sweetheart." He says with a wink as she backs away.

Once she turns away his focus swings back to me and I can feel the anger radiating off him. He studies me for a long moment, as if deciding his next course of action. I'm completely caught off guard when he leans in and presses a gentle kiss to my lips. I'm too stunned to do anything but let him kiss me. He pulls back just enough to talk, but I can feel his lips brush against mine as they move. "I know you feel like everything is falling apart all around you, darlin', but I promise you, this is what's supposed to happen. You and I are inevitable. You'll realize that soon enough."

He pulls back and grabs our coffees. He hands me mine and waits for me to take a drink, like a gentleman. I eye him warily over the beverage, suspicious of everything he does now. "Aren't you going to ask me about the phone call from your work?" Fuck. I had almost forgotten about that. "Seems, someone had placed an anonymous complaint about your behavior towards me when I was there, and they called me looking for my side of the story." He leans back from me, giving me a few inches of personal space. I scoot back to the corner of the couch trying to escape his touch.

"I know why they called you. What did you tell them? Did you tell them the truth?" I pray he's decent enough to not have lied about our interaction and cost me my job.

He gives me a reassuring smile and runs his fingers through my hair. "Of course, I did. I told them you were professional and provided excellent care. But I did mention it was surprising to see you turn up in my bar just a few nights later looking for me. The woman from HR was very interested to hear that. Tell me, Eloise, do you often make it a habit to stalk your patients to their place of work?"

I rear back like I've been slapped. "That's not what happened, and you know it!"

His brows furrow and his lips turn down in a frown like he's concerned for my sanity. "Isn't it? I seem to remember you turning up in *my* bar just three nights after treating me as your patient. I never told you where I worked, but I'm sure your hospital has my place of work on file."

"That was a coincidence! I didn't know you worked there! You showed up at *my* place of work first!" I am flustered and feel like I'm starting to lose my grip on reality. All the words he says are technically true, but it isn't the truth.

"Darlin', you work in one of two hospitals in town. Where else was I supposed to go to get my hand checked out after that bar fight? Look don't worry your pretty little head about it. I told them everything was fine, and no matter what I'll take care of you. I've got you. I won't let anything ever hurt you again." The look in his eyes when he says the last part sends a cold chill down my spine. Is he talking about me, or is he talking about Cassidy?

"Come on, darlin'. Let's get out of here." He stands and grabs my hand, giving me a tug, pulling me to my feet before I have a chance to protest. He leads me out of the coffee shop, not letting go of my hand. When we reach the sidewalk, we nearly crash into a couple heading into the cafe. I slam into Drew's back and nearly lose my balance before he tucks me in his side and wraps his arm around my shoulder.

"Lo??"

"Sara?" I look up and see my best friend staring at me in shock. Her husband is next to her, with little Liam perched on his hip. Derrick cuts a wary glance towards

Drew and then looks at me, confusion written across his face. I can see in his hazel green eyes he's trying to figure out if he's just run into something he isn't supposed to know about. Sara is giving me a much more worried look, like she just caught me shooting up meth, I can see her getting ready to stage an intervention right here on the sidewalk. Shit, this can't get any worse.

"Who's...your friend, Lo?" Sara asks me while staring daggers at Drew. She's not going to let this slide. She knows he's the reason I was having a total mental breakdown on my kitchen floor. Her hackles are up and she's ready to defend my honor. Drew interjects before I can say anything.

"I'm Drew. You're the lovely Sara, right?" He turns on the charm like a switch and offers his hand to her. Her eyes narrow in suspicion as she pointedly ignores his proffered hand. He takes it back and sticks it in his pocket and gives her 'aw shucks' shrug and smile, like he knows he's an interloper in our group. "I've heard so much about you from Lo. Any friend of hers is a friend of mine." What the fuck is he talking about? I look up at him trying to figure out what game he is playing. He turns his attention to Derrick and Liam, giving Derrick a bro nod and Liam a smile. "Hey little man, nice to meet you." He offers Liam a fist bump, but because Liam is a smart kid and knows evil when he sees it, he buries his face in Derrick's shoulder instead.

"Lo, can we talk for a minute?" Sara reaches out for my hand to pull me out of Drew's hold. I move to follow her, but Drew's hand on my shoulder tightens to a painful grip and he angles me slightly away from her.

"Actually, we are running late for our date. We've got time sensitive plans. We were just leaving. It was nice meeting you all. I'm sure we will be seeing more of each other." He flashes that patented panty dropping smile of his and turns us both, so we are walking away from my lifeline, leaving Sara and Derrick in a wake of confusion. I look back over my shoulder and see her and Derrick with their heads close together talking in hushed whispers. She's gesturing wildly like she's threatening to run after me, and he is clearly telling her to mind her business.

"Drew, let me go. I'm not going anywhere with you. Fuck. Why are you doing this?" I try to tug out of his hold but it's impossible. He keeps leading me down the sidewalk away from my car. "I said, stop! I've had enough of your shit." I try my hardest to stop following him but he's too strong. When we reach the opening of an alley, he turns us into it and slams me against the wall out of sight from Sara and Derrick who are still arguing in front of Brewed Awakening.

"Eloise. Do I need to remind you that I haven't sent your husband the video of me feasting on that delicious pussy of yours as a courtesy? Keep testing me and I'll send it to him and then we won't have to worry about any possibility of him forgiving you in the future. I'm trying to be a nice guy and not tell your husband what a dirty little slut you are for me, but if you keep pushing my buttons, I'll make sure he feels the full depth of your betrayal."

He cages me against the brick wall, one arm planted next to my head, the other hand not so gently wrapped around my neck. With his body pressed against mine, I can feel the bulge of his erection pushing into my belly. My stomach turns as I realize he's turned on by this. I feel tears silently track down my cheeks and my body trembles under his touch.

"Oh darlin', don't cry. This is all for the best." He nuzzles his rough beard against my cheek before he licks up the path left by my tears. "I told you, I'm always going to take care of you." With that he shoves off the wall and pulls me along with him back out onto the sidewalk. I let him tug me along, suddenly and completely without the will to fight anymore.

Tucked safely under Drew's arm, he leads me to where my car is parked around the corner. I go along willingly now, the tension and fight that had me wound up, completely absent now after his little reminder of what we've shared. My arms hang limply by my side, and my eyes are cast down to the ground, because I'm afraid to finally look up and acknowledge my new reality.

"Come on darlin', get in." He opens the passenger door and gently pushes me in by the nape of my neck. He pulls out the seat belt and reaches across, buckling me in. He leans in way too closely and inhales my scent before pulling away. "God, baby, you smell like heaven. I can't wait until my sheets smell like you again." He plants a kiss on the corner of my mouth before backing up and closing the door.

He quickly rounds the front of the car and hops in. He takes only the briefest moment to buckle in and check oncoming traffic before pulling away. He must think I might be planning on running if given the chance.

After driving for a few minutes, I finally speak up to ask, "Where are we going?" He glances at me out of the corner of his eye while I stare blankly out of the passenger window.

He reaches over and takes my small hand in his and gives it what I assume is supposed to be a reassuring squeeze. "It's a surprise, darlin'." I don't hold his hand back, but I don't pull away either. I'm scared to incite any more of his anger until I figure out a new game plan for dealing with him. He just smiles at me like we have all the time in the world to work through our 'difficulties'.

CHAPTER
TWENTY-ONE
CALEB

I'M STANDING IN MY LIVING ROOM, STARING AT THE DESTRUCTION I left in my wake last night in my fit of rage. The entryway table is knocked over, everything that had been on it scattered across the floor. A broken flower vase litters the ground and Eloise's black date night clutch is tipped over; its contents spilled out. I move to start cleaning up but stop short when I see the little black cylinder and black rectangle that had fallen out of Eloise's clutch. I crouch down to pick them up and realize it's a stun gun and a can of pepper spray.

Not once, in the entirety of our relationship, have I known Eloise to carry any kind of personal protection. She has never walked through this world with any fear in her heart, even when I started leaving town frequently for work. I offered to buy her something to keep her safe when I was gone and make me feel better when I'm not around to protect her, but she blew me off saying - *"Cal, baby, we live in the safest city in the state. I'm not worried. Besides, knowing my luck I'll probably just wind up spraying myself with pepper spray and I don't want to die with my eyes on fire."*

The memory of her playfully dismissing my concern haunts me now and I wonder what possibly could have made her afraid enough to finally buy something for protection. Then the cold realization that she's now out there alone, without this protection, dawns on me and my stomach plummets.

"Fuck. Lo." I drop the items and frantically pull out my phone so I can call her and make sure she's ok. No matter what is happening now between us, she's still the love of my life and I have to know that she's ok. I hit the dial button on her contact and listen to her number ring. And ring. And ring. Then her voicemail picks up. *"Hey you've reached, Eloise. You know what to do."*

"Lo, um, it's me. I'm just checking up on you...I...uh, I'm worried. Can you come home? Or at least call me so we can talk? Please? We can work this out. Come home to me, Sweetness."

I end the call and decide to call Sara instead. Lo tells Sara everything and I'm sure she's got to know more than Lo has told me. Sara surprisingly picks up on the first ring, almost as if she was expecting my call.

"Hey, Caleb. I was just going to call you. We need to talk." She sounds worried, and I know deep in my gut if she's worried something is seriously wrong.

"Yeah, Sara, we do. I need you to tell me what is going

on with my wife. She left me last night and I think you know why." Sara's sharp intake of breath tells me that apparently, she didn't know that bit of news.

She curses under her breath. "Damnit, Lo." Then louder, as if she remembers she's on the phone she says to me, "I'm coming over. I'll be there in 20."

While I wait for Sara, I quickly clean up the mess I made, making sure to sweep up all the broken pieces of glass. Just as I'm putting the table back in its original location, she waltzes through my front door not even bothering to knock. "Sure, Sara, come on in. Mi casa es su casa." Sara just rolls her eyes and ignores my sarcastic greeting.

"Yeah, I know Cal. That's why I walked in. Your home is practically my home. Always has been, always will be." She walks past me and makes a beeline to our liquor cabinet and pulls out the Jameson and two rocks glasses.

"Bit early in the day for drinking, isn't it?" Truth be told, after last night I'm not entirely sure I'm ready for more whiskey yet. I haven't completely gotten over my hangover from this morning. She ignores me again as she pours two healthy measures in each glass.

"Trust me, you'll want a drink for this. Come, sit." She makes her way to the couch and curls up on one end, tucking her feet under her like she always does. I've never seen her sit like a normal human being in all of the years that I've known her. She's always sitting on her feet or slinging a leg over the armrest or even twisted up like a pretzel. I don't know how she does it. My knees stopped bending like that five years ago. She pats the cushion next to her and motions for me to come sit next to her. I relent and plop down beside her and accept the offered beverage.

"Alright, spill. What the fuck is going on with my wife. I know you know something. When I left things were fine. We were working shit out. Then suddenly she's spending nights out away from home and this fucking Jason Momoa knock off starts coming around my house, sniffing around my wife. Is she cheating on me? I need to know Sara. Please don't lie for her."

"Shit, ok so you know about TDD. Ok, that's good. I won't be betraying her by telling you." She takes another sip of her whiskey, summoning her courage to continue on.

My brow furrows, "TDD?"

"Tall, dark and dangerous. The nickname she gave him."

"Sara, focus. Start from the beginning." I take a sip of the whiskey, steeling myself for whatever information Sara is getting ready to dump on me.

"Ok, so the night I was supposed to meet her for drinks at The Blind Pig, you were still out of town. I bailed on her, but she decided to stay out and have a drink anyway before heading home. Apparently, he was there, sitting next to her and started chatting her up. She said they talked for a few hours, had a couple of drinks and then she left. But when she was waiting outside for her Uber he came out and kissed her."

"HE WHAT-" Sara puts her hand over my mouth and shuts me up.

"She called me the next morning, asked to meet up and she confessed everything over coffee. She was distraught, Cal. She couldn't believe she let things get that far and she felt so guilty. She was going to tell you and I talked her out of it thinking it was just a one-off thing and she'd never see this dude again. She told me things have been hard with you being out of town a lot and she was feeling lonely and neglected. I told her to focus her energy on reigniting the spark in your marriage instead."

It feels like my emotions have been thrown into a washer on the spin cycle and I can't keep track of what I'm feeling. Incredulity, betrayal, anger, guilt, and soul crushing heartbreak.

Sara continues on. "She made a plan to have a fancy date night with you, and work on things between you two."

I think back to when she got home from her coffee date and gave me the best head of my life, then the date we went on that night that ended in explosive public sex. "He was there that night, when we went to Allure. I had to take a call and she went inside before me. I found him talking to her when I came inside. I thought he was just some douche hitting on my wife."

Nausea swirls in my gut when I realize she knew exactly who he was, and he had already had his lips on her. Had he kissed her again before I came in? Were they making plans to meet up again? Was her fight about my work just a way to open the door for him to swoop in?

Sara places her hand under my chin, forcing me to look up and meet her gaze. "Stop, Caleb, I see you're spiraling. It's not what you think. Yes, he was there but she was just as surprised as you. She didn't want to see him."

"But-" I interject, but Sara shushes me again.

"Listen to me. I'm telling you everything I know. So anyway, you left again, and this dude shows up at her work one night when she's pulling a double. He flirted while she took x-rays of his hand. She sent him packing but that night when she left there was a picture of a screen grab from the security feed from The Blind Pig showing them kissing." At this point I've finished off my drink and grab the bottle of Jameson and pour another splash in my glass. I am completely overwhelmed by the information coming from Sara.

"How do you know all of this?" I stare at her incredulously.

"Best friend. Duh. She made me meet her for an emergency freak out after that encounter. I tried to get her to go to the police because I was getting major stalker vibes from this douche canoe, but she insisted it wouldn't do any good and that she didn't want you to know and freak out over the kiss. She thought she could handle it by just shutting him down if he turned up again. Wednesday morning when I was out for a walk, I noticed her car in the driveway. I came up to check on her and she was a mess,

Cal. She was hungover and having a complete mental breakdown, sobbing because she 'ruined things'. She just kept saying she fucked up. She said she had to leave you."

My heart seizes in my chest, and I forget how to breathe. My mind is fitting the puzzle pieces together. Lo's story about the roofie, and Sara seeing her completely wrecked and distraught after that...my mind can only conjure up two possibilities and they both make me want to vomit. Either she's lying about the roofie to cover up sleeping around on me, or she was drugged, and he raped her, and she thinks it's her fault. Sara's hand grasps mine, dragging my attention from my spiraling thoughts.

"Cal, I think something bad happened. I think something bad is still happening. I saw them. Together. Today. She looked like a fucking ghost, and he had his arm wrapped around her like he was afraid she was going to run away. I couldn't even get her alone to talk to her. She barely said two words to me before he marched her down the sidewalk away from me."

"She's with him?! Now?" I jump up from my seat on the couch and start pacing, dragging my hands through my hair. "Fuck. Sara! This guy is bad news. I found pepper spray and a stun gun she bought. I think she's afraid of him. Why the fuck didn't she go to the police after the roofie?"

Now it's Sara's turn to be surprised. "Roofie? He roofied her?" She jumps up and stops me in my tracks forcing me to face her. Shit, she doesn't know that part. I quickly recount how I came home early to confront Lo about Drew being at our house; the story Lo told me about the guy at the bar slipping her a roofie and Drew coming to her *rescue*. And how Lo asked for some time to figure things out because things haven't been right between us.

Sara's face visibly pales, and she sits back down on the couch and buries her face in her hands. "Fuck! I knew something was off. I should've just fucking grabbed her and made her stay with me. I could tell she didn't want to be around him. Caleb, I'm so sorry." Sara looks up at me, tears shimmering in her blue eyes.

I sit down next to her and put my arm around her while I fight back my own tears. "Sara...do you think she..." the words are stuck in my throat. I can't give voice to my deepest fear.

"No Caleb, stop that. She didn't want this. She loves you. I know that in my soul, and you know it too. We need to find her before he does something worse."

TWENTY-TWO

DREW DRIVES US OUT OF TOWN BACK INTO THE MOUNTAINS. IN my mind I know I've probably done the dumbest thing possible by coming along with him but I'm not entirely sure what other option I had. Every time I turn around there he is, like some fucked up gravitational pull keeps drawing us together. Maybe he's right, maybe this is inevitable. Maybe in my subconscious I do want this. I am the one that went looking for him. He's not wrong about that. Fuck, have I self-sabotaged my marriage and relationship with Caleb without even realizing it? A pathetic little whimper escapes as I clench my eyes shut and try to fight the urge to cry in front of him. I feel him wrap his hand around the back of my neck giving me a gentle, almost reassuring squeeze.

"Don't cry, darlin'. I told you, I'm going to take care of you. I know you don't believe me yet, but this is a good thing. I'm going to make you so happy." His thumb rubs gentle circles on my pulse point while the rest of his fingers gently knead away the tension in my neck.

My phone starts ringing. The sound is muffled since it's currently tucked away in my back pocket. I reach back to grab it but Drew beats me to it and slips the phone out of my pocket. He glances at the screen and we both see that it's Caleb calling. "We don't need any interruptions where we are going. You can get back to him later." Without even asking he shuts off my phone and tosses it into the backseat.

With that he turns off the main road and onto a smaller unpaved gravel road. We are at least 30 minutes outside of town in a section of the mountains where a lot of cabins have been built to support the tourist economy. Birch Falls gets a lot of leaf peepers in the fall to take in the gorgeous colors of the mountains when the leaves change. Summer isn't usually the busiest season for the area but with all the hiking trails and the nearby waterfalls the town does decent tourism business year-round. I watch, taking in the scenery as we climb higher into the mountains. The driveways that mark various cabins and campsites are numerous to start with but soon start becoming more and more sparse the higher up we get. Eventually the road dead ends close to the top with a spectacular view of the valley below.

Drew turns off the car and gets out. He comes around to my side and opens my door for me. I let him help me out and he guides me to the small cozy cabin off to the side overlooking the valley. It's rustic but seems to be well maintained, built out of a hearty Eastern Pine wood. It has two stories with a peaked roof and a balcony that seems like it hangs right off the edge of the mountain.

"Is this your place?" I ask as he unlocks the front door and opens it with a grand gesture. I walk into the modestly appointed cabin. It has an open floor plan with floor to ceiling windows that lead out to the deck with a spectacular view. There's a fireplace with an overstuffed couch in front of it. A small kitchen with an island separating the two spaces. Shelves line the opposite wall full of books and a few pictures and knickknacks. A spiral staircase in the center of the room leads to a loft where the bed is tucked away.

"Welcome to my sanctuary. It's the Jameson Family cabin. It's been in our family for at least 100 years now." Drew takes me by the hand and leads me to the French doors set in the middle of all the windows looking out over the mountains. We walk out onto the balcony to take in the view. He cages me in from behind and places his hands on mine on the railing. My heart is racing so hard it feels like it might explode right out of my chest.

"Why did you bring me here?" My voice wavers when I ask the question. Everything feels wrong. I shouldn't have come with him. What if he doesn't let me leave? Is Caleb thinking I'm a whore really worse than whatever this is? Drew plants a kiss against my neck and wraps his arms around me.

"I thought this would be the perfect place for you to really get to know me. Just you and me with no interruptions. Just give me a chance, Eloise. Let me prove to you how good it can be with me." He spins me around and cups my face in his large palms. He leans down and presses his forehead to mine and breathes in my scent. "I know you're scared, darlin'. These are big changes happening for you. But we are going to get through them together."

"Drew, you can't keep me here. I have a life. I have a job. I still have a husband. Whatever you think is going to happen here, can't. I'm not ready for this. I...I'm still processing." I try to keep my tone calm and placating. I don't want to set him off again, not here when I'm alone with him in the middle of nowhere. I need to buy some time to reason with him and at least make him see what he's doing is crazy. I need to talk him into letting me go willingly. There's no way I'm getting out of here if he doesn't want me to leave.

"You can have all the time you need to process, darlin'. I can take care of you so all we have is time." He wraps his arms around me again, pressing me against his hard chest. He drops a kiss on my head and runs his fingers through my hair like I'm a wild animal he's trying to soothe. I change to a different tactic; it seems the more I push him away the harder he holds on.

"You'll take me back tomorrow, right? I do have to go to work Monday. I could lose my job if I don't show again... I like my job, Drew. Please don't let me lose that too." I'm hoping if he senses I'm willing to stay for one night he will think he's winning the battle. I've got to keep him thinking he's winning me over. If he believes I'm coming around maybe he will loosen up and give me a chance to get away.

He lets out an amused chuckle before responding with a very unconvincing, "Sure, darlin'." He wraps my hair around his fist and tilts my head back so I'm looking up at him. The look he's giving me can only be described as possession. He's looking at me like he wants to own my entire soul. Before I can protest, he crashes his mouth into mine and uses his other hand to pry my jaw open to let his tongue enter my mouth. He devours me with his kiss, and I force my body to stay pliant and accommodating. I have to make him believe this kiss. I have to get him to let his guard down. I let the kiss continue for a few more seconds before I pull back and push against his chest, separating us.

"Um, do you have anything to drink? I think I could use some wine. Or liquor. The last couple of days have been a lot to process." To my relief he nods and steps further back, giving me enough space to finally feel like I can breathe again. I follow him back into the house and reach into my back pocket out of habit to check my phone before remembering it's shut off and still in Drew's car. Shit. I need to get it back in case I get a chance to call for help. I glance around to see if the car keys are laying on the counter, but I don't see them.

While he busies himself with making us some drinks I wander over to the bookshelves and take in the glimpses of Drew's life on display. He's big into the classics apparently. Or at least someone in his family was. There are a few framed pictures scattered on the shelves. Several seem to be Drew as a young boy with his mom and dad, but one picture in particular catches my attention. It's college age Drew standing next to a pretty young blonde tucked into his side. They're both wearing B.F.U. sweatshirts and are flashing huge smiles at the camera. I don't know why but I'm surprised by how happy he and Cassidy look together in this picture. I take a chance and ask him about the photo, hoping I can get him to open up. Maybe if I can make him realize how not like her I am he will get over this infatuation with me.

"Who's this?" I hold up the picture and show it to him. He glances up at it in the middle of mixing up the cocktail he's working on. He stops suddenly and comes up to me before I even have a chance to put the photo back on the shelf.

"Nobody you need to worry about, darlin'." He takes the framed photo from my hand and puts it back, exactly where it had been before. Okay, so this is a sensitive subject for him. I need to tread carefully.

"She's pretty. Old college girlfriend?" I say conversationally as I follow him over to the island and take a seat on one of the bar stools.

"Yes, but she's been out of the picture for a long time. Now drop it." The set of his jaw clenching lets me know I'm treading in dangerous waters, so I back off and don't ask any more questions. I accept the drink he offers me and take a sip. It's spicy, citrusy and reminds me of the beach.

"Dark and stormy?" I question as I take another sip. He nods in confirmation as he walks around to my side of the island and invades my space again. Before he can lean in and kiss me again, I hold my palm up and push against his chest. "I said I need time, Drew. You want me to get to know you, so start talking. Convince me why blowing up my marriage of ten years to be with you was a good idea." I shoot him a droll look, hoping he takes the bait. The smile he gives me in return is nothing short of dazzling. Damn, it's not fair for someone this beautiful to be such an awful human being.

"Gladly." With that he pulls me over to the overstuffed couch and gets us settled in all snug and comfortable in an attempt to lull me into some sort of cozy, relaxed state while he makes his argument. All I want to do is keep him focused on talking and nothing more, but it doesn't take long before my eyelids start feeling heavy and a warm flushed feeling takes over my body. Drew is playing with my hair, and I feel myself melting into his touch. I nuzzle my face into his shoulder, and I feel him take my still half full drink from my hand.

My body starts to feel like it's humming or buzzing. Like there's an itch under my skin I can't scratch. I feel his hot mouth caress my neck and I let out a low hum of pleasure at his touch. "That's it, darlin'. Let me make you feel good." His low rumble in my ear sends a jolt of arousal straight to my pussy. Deep in my consciousness I know something is wrong, but I can feel my body squirming against his, seeking friction and release from this desperate ache building inside.

He pulls me into his lap and tugs my shirt off. His mouth finds my nipple through the thin lacy bralette I'm wearing, and he sucks the pebbled nub drawing another low moan out of me. "Oh god...more." I plead as I grind down on his erection. He switches to my other breast, giving it the same worshipful attention while his hands undo the button and zipper on my jeans. Caleb's face flashes in my mind for a moment causing me to halt my movements. My brain tries to bring it back into focus, to come out of the fog but his hand slips inside the front of my jeans finding my slick wetness. He slides a finger inside of me as his thumb begins to circle my clit and any reasonable thought I almost had a grasp on flies out of my mind as my body responds to the overwhelming pleasure he sends crashing through me. I feel him tug my bra down so he can bite and suck on my breasts unhindered as I ride his hand, searching for the release my body is desperate to feel.

"That's it baby girl. Use me. Ride my hand and come all over my fingers. I want to taste you." He slips another finger inside me and pushes harder on my clit. I grind down harder on him and feel an animalistic scream of ecstasy rip out of my body as I come, my core clenching down on his hand and my arms banding around his head keeping him latched to my nipple as I ride out the orgasm. I collapse against him, feeling wrung out and boneless. He kisses his way up my chest, nipping, sucking and licking until he makes it to my mouth. I whimper against his mouth as I feel him remove his hand from my pussy, the aftershocks of the orgasm still fluttering through me.

"Taste yourself for me. See how good I made you feel." He sucks on one of his fingers before forcing me to take the other into my mouth. The flushed feeling of arousal doesn't dissipate with the release from the orgasm. Instead, I find myself feeling the need to come build up again.

"More...I need more." I plead as my body begins seeking friction again. Drew pulls me away from him and I whimper at the loss of his heat. We aren't apart for long though. He picks me up once he's standing and makes his way up the staircase to the bedroom loft. Once we make it to the bed, he tosses me onto it like I weigh nothing. Before I can react, he jerks off my pants and underwear and buries his face in my pussy. He laps up the arousal from my first orgasm like it's his favorite flavor of ice cream. He alternates between plunging his tongue deep into my cunt, fucking me with it, and pulling back to lick and suck on my clit. When I'm a desperate needy mess, squirming and trying to grind my pussy down on his face he pulls back completely leaving me on edge and feeling bereft. "No...don't stop." I look at him through hooded eyes for the first time since this animalistic need to fuck came over me. He looms over me, looking every bit like a dark god, a manic smile spread across his face. He jerks down his own pants and climbs on top of me, nestling himself between my thighs.

"I'm going to make you mine now, Sweetness. After this, there's no going back." The use of my pet name triggers a memory of Caleb's face to come to the forefront but before I can say no, he sinks into me and bites down on the juncture of my neck and shoulder. I let out a gasp at the pain of the intrusion as he begins to rut into me with powerful thrusts, while sucking and biting on my neck until it bruises. Tears spring to my eyes as I picture my husband's face while he pinches my nipple, coaxing another orgasm from my body before he roars out and unleashes his own climax.

The last conscious thought I have before passing out is that he's right. There is no going back now.

TWENTY-THREE

I try calling Eloise again, while Sara watches me from the couch. I'm pacing, running my hand through my hair as once again my call goes straight to voicemail. "FUCK! I think her phone is off. It won't even ring now." I kick the coffee table and it crashes into the wall. Pain ricochets up my leg, but I ignore it in favor of grabbing the bottle of Jameson and taking a swing straight from it. Sara looks up at me with wide fearful eyes as she gnaws on her thumb. Once we realized how dangerous this situation was, we both started trying to get in touch with Lo, neither of us having any success.

"Cal, sit. Take a breath. We need to think about this rationally. Does she share her location with you?" Sara tugs on the bottle in my hand and sets it off to the side.

"She does but will that work if her phone is off?" I'm already pulling up her location on my phone desperate to see if it works.

"It might at least give us her last location." Sara offers hopefully. I hold my breath as I wait for Lo's last location to pop up. Her icon appears on the road leading out of town into the area known for vacation cabin rentals, last updated an hour ago.

"Look. He took her out of town where all the cabin rentals are. Do you think he's got a place on the mountain?" Sara bites her lower lip as her brows form a V as she studies the screen.

"Maybe? But there are dozens of cabins and campgrounds in that area. I don't know how we'd figure out which one they're at. I think we need to get the police involved, Caleb." She places a reassuring hand on my arm, drawing my attention away from the phone screen. I stare at her dumbly for a moment as I take in her words. Something cracks inside my chest as I realize the implication of her words,

"Do you think he's a danger to her?" I rasp, barely holding on to my composure by a thread.

"I don't know if she's in danger, but I do know she doesn't want to be with him. That's enough for me to want to go to the police. We need to call and file a report." I swallow thickly and nod, desperately trying to hold on to my composure. I dial the local police number and wait for someone to answer. Sara doesn't let go of my other hand and gives it a reassuring squeeze.

"Birch Falls Police Department. How can I direct your call?" An overly friendly voice picks up after a few rings.

"Um, I need to file a missing person's report." My voice

comes out in a hoarse whisper and Sara nudges me, signaling that I need to speak up.

"Let me connect you to an officer who can take your statement. Hold please."

"This is Officer Randall. Who am I speaking to?" A gruff older man's voice comes through the line.

"Caleb Fitzpatrick."

"I understand you need to file a missing person's report? Who is missing and how long have they been gone?" I put the call on speaker so Sara can help me give the details from when she last saw Lo.

"My wife, Eloise Fitzpatrick. She went to stay in a hotel last night and today she isn't answering her phone. It's turned off I think..."

"So, the last time she was seen was last night?" Officer Randall asks, I can hear him typing in the background, hopefully taking notes.

Sara chimes in, "No, I saw her this afternoon. Just a couple of hours ago. She was with a man I believe has been stalking her."

"Who is speaking now?" Randall asks.

"Sara Cunningham. I'm Eloise's friend. I'm here with her husband Caleb."

"Sara, did she seem like she was distressed or in danger in any way? Did you notice any bruising or injuries on her?" More typing in the background from Officer Randall.

"Not exactly, um, she was quiet. She didn't really get to say anything to us. The man she was with did all the talking. She looked upset though. I didn't see any physical injuries on her."

I chime in now, to hopefully fill in the gaps. "When I came home last night from a work trip, Eloise was upset and distraught. She claimed she needed some time away because she's not sure about our marriage. But things were fine the last time we spoke on the phone. This isn't like her, and she mentioned she had been roofied at a bar last weekend. I'm worried this is the man that roofied her. He's been showing up at my house and pursuing my wife."

"Are you sure she's not with this man willingly? It sounds like a marital dispute to me." The officer is now sounding dubious about our claim. I clench the phone so hard my knuckles start to turn white.

"I'm sure, Officer Randall. This is not normal behavior for my wife." The words come out in a harsh bite as I feel the frayed tether holding my temper back start to unravel.

"Ok, I am just covering my bases. Look, I'm going to send someone out to take a complete statement. If you have any recent pictures of her it would be good to give it to the officer that comes out. What is your address?"

I rattle off my address and Officer Randall promises to have a squad car out to us in the next half hour. I hang up not entirely convinced that the officer believes my wife is missing and not just out gallivanting with a new beau. I stare helplessly at Sara and shake my head. "I don't know if he believes us."

Thirty minutes later a knock sounds at the door. I open it to find a young female officer. She looks like she's barely out of the academy and I'm not entirely sure she's old enough to be doing this line of work. Great, the veteran officer sent a rookie to take my report because he doesn't believe me. I clench my teeth so hard it feels like they might crack.

"Hello, Mr. Fitzpatrick? I'm Officer Roberts, I'm here to take your statement. I understand you think your wife is missing and possibly in danger?" She looks at me with a studious expression. There is no doubt in her eyes and her voice is serious and tinged with just enough concern to make me think she is taking me seriously. I step to the side and motion for her to come in. We all take a seat in the living room so I can tell her everything I know.

"Yeah, um, there's this guy. His name is Drew and he's been coming around a lot lately, harassing my wife. Sara says Eloise even had a picture left on her car one night after she got off work at the hospital. He had been there that night as a patient." I run through the entire timeline of events as I understand them, with Sara chiming in with what she knew. Officer Roberts didn't stop taking notes the entire time we spoke and asked pertinent questions to clarify details that she deemed important.

"Do you know anything else about this Drew? Last name? Where he works or lives?"

"Umm..." I wrack my brain trying to come up with more information they can use to track him down. "I think he was at the bar Stellina the night she said she was roofied. Lo said he took her up to his place to let her sleep it off and she made it sound like he might live in an apartment in the same building."

"That's good information, Mr. Fitzpatrick. I'll get in touch with the bar to see if they have records of him working there. We are going to find your wife, I promise. I'm going to check into him some more. You said the last known whereabouts of your wife was in town?"

"Yeah, I saw her with Drew outside of Brewed Awakening. But they left right after that." Sara chimes in. "Caleb tried to find her with her phone location, but the last location was updated a couple of hours ago outside of town near where all the cabin rentals are."

"Can I see that on a map, Mr. Fitzpatrick?" Officer Roberts asks me. I nod and pull up Eloise's Find my Friend location on my phone and see that it still hasn't updated since the last time I checked. Officer Roberts nods and takes a picture of it with her phone.

"Yeah, there are a lot of cabins in that area. Once I have his name hopefully, we can contact the rental companies and property owners to see if he might be renting one. I'll keep you updated on the case, Mr. Fitzpatrick. We will find her. I promise." Officer Roberts places her hand on my shoulder and gives it a reassuring squeeze. Before she leaves, I give her a few recent pictures of Eloise to use for the report.

"Call me if she gets in touch or if you think of anything else important. Here's my card with my direct number. You can call me any time, day or night." I take her card and give her a tight smile as she starts back down the steps to the street. Before she gets too far, she turns around and says, "We'll find her, Caleb. I know you think Officer Randall sent you the rookie just to get you off his back, but I'm good at my job. I've been where she is now, and I know what it's like to be on the receiving end of attention from the wrong kind of man." She taps her temple on the right side of her face and that's when I notice a scar stretching from the middle of her brow almost to her ear.

I swallow thickly at her words and jerk a nod in her direction. "Thank you, Officer Roberts. I appreciate your dedication in helping find my wife." With that she leaves. I shut the front door and turn to Sara. "Now what?"

"Now I think I'm in the mood for some fancy cocktails. Let's go see if we can find any dirt on this guy at the bar where he works."

TWENTY-FOUR

CALEB

WE HAVE TO WAIT UNTIL THAT EVENING BEFORE WE CAN GO TO Stellina. The little speakeasy only opens during dinner hours and closes at midnight. Sara comes up with a plan to try to get some information about Drew so we can do more digging on our own while waiting for the police to do their job. When we walk into the bar there is a young female bartender working behind the bar and one more carrying drinks to one of the tables on the floor. It's early in the evening and the place is mostly empty so Sara and I sit at the bar to make it easier to have a casual conversation with the bartender.

"Hello! I'm Sam, I'll be taking care of you tonight. What can I get you, folks? Tonight's drink special is the Barrel Aged Black Manhattan, a new take on an old classic featuring small batch bourbon, Averna, orange bitters and black walnut bitters. We also have a lovely take on an Old Fashioned made with orange infused honey and a doubleoaked bourbon." Sam flashes us a genuine wide smile that speaks to someone who enjoys their work. We order the Old Fashioned just to keep things simple and attempt to engage her in conversation.

"This is our first time here, Sam. We've heard good things though, have you worked here long?" I ask, casually. I want to get her comfortable enough to chat before diving in and asking direct questions about Drew.

"I've been here since it opened about two years ago. I get to help design all the drinks and specials alongside the boss. We take a lot of pride in crafting bespoke cocktails that are new twists on a lot of old favorites." I nod along with Sara, acting interested in Stellina's origin story.

"My friend was in here the other week, and she said she saw the hottest guy working here. Said he looked like that actor that plays Aquaman." Sara chimes in, leaning in, whispering conspiratorially with the bartender like they are sharing a secret.

"Oh, that's the boss. He works behind the bar when one of us needs a night off." Sam replies as she slides our drinks across the smooth copper bar top. Sara makes a big show like she's looking around for him.

"Is he here tonight? I just got dumped by my ex and could definitely use a DC Superhero to help mend my broken heart." The bartender looks between me and Sara, her face scrunched in confusion, clearly she assumes we were on a date. "Oh, this guy? I'm not his type." Sara jerks a thumb at me and winks at Sam. "Cal here is my work husband but alas that is all we'll ever be. I'm just keeping him company while his beau is out of town." Sam the bartender laughs and shakes her head.

"Sorry to let you down but he's not working tonight. He mentioned something about going to his cabin for a few days. I bet he will be around next weekend though if you want to come back and try your luck then. He's a tough one to nail down though. Trust me, I've seen many women shoot their shot with him when he's working."

Sara's mouth forms an exaggerated pout. "Well damn." She mutters at the same time I let out a derisive snort.

"It's probably for the best Sara, guys that hot are usually assholes anyway." I take a sip of my Old Fashioned and wait to see if the bartender speaks up in his defense or confirms my theory.

"Drew? You're probably not wrong. He's a great boss but he's one of those guys who knows what he wants and has no problems going after it. He spent a year charming the pants off the old widow who used to own this building before she finally sold it to him. She didn't want to let it go since it was her husband's first bar, but Drew eventually won her over. He's persistent as hell when he wants something. A guy like him doesn't get told 'no' often." With that Sam moves down the bar to take care of some new patrons that just sat down. A chill slithers down my spine as her words replay in my mind. *"A guy like him doesn't get told 'no' often."*

TWENTY-FIVE

ELOISE

I ROLL OVER AND NAUSEA SWEEPS THROUGH ME. I LET OUT A LOW groan as my consciousness slowly comes back online. My mouth is dry, my head feels like it's being split in two and I'm two seconds away from losing the contents of my stomach. I try to open my eyes but even the dim light from the setting sun is more than I can handle. I throw my hand over my face to block out the light.

I feel the bed shift next to me and a warm hand grasps my own and pulls it away from my face. "Hey darlin', you need some water. Drink this." He lifts me up into a sitting position and presses a glass to my lips. I take a tiny sip before pushing his arm away.

"I'm gonna be sick..." I clamp my hand over my mouth and desperately try to hold it in. He holds up a small trash can for me to throw up in, and I let it go, heaving the remnants of my breakfast, from hours before, into the wastebasket. Drew holds my hair back with one hand while keeping the trash can in place. He murmurs soothing words until I'm done retching and then offers me the glass of water again. I take a large swig, swish it around and then spit it out into the bin, before chugging the rest of it down. He sets the wastebasket to the side and that's when I fully start to take in my situation.

First, I notice his naked back as he's turned away from me. It's well-muscled, covered in tattoos, all the way down to his bare ass. His bare ass...shock jolts through me when his nakedness finally registers in my brain. It's then that I realize I'm also naked, with only a sheet covering my body. I jump out of the bed and stumble backward, dragging the sheet with me. I land on the ground in an ungraceful heap but keep crawling backward, away from him until my back hits the wall.

The movement sends shockwaves of pain ricocheting through my brain and almost causes me to vomit again. "What did you do? WHAT DID YOU DO? OH GOD, OH GOD...NO..." I bury my face in the sheet and curl up in a ball. I feel his hand on my shoulder, and I instinctively jerk away from his touch. "DON'T FUCKING TOUCH ME!" As I try to move further away from him, I slowly start to realize my body hurts all over. I feel bruised and battered on my hips, between my thighs and on my neck. Tremors wrack through my body and I let out a sob.

"Baby, calm down. I didn't do anything you didn't ask for. I made you feel so good. You're so beautiful when you come. Don't you remember falling apart for me?" Drew is crouched in front of me holding his hands out like he wants to touch me but is thinking better of it, like I'm a wild animal that might bite him. He's not wrong. If he does touch me, I will bite him. I'll bite his fucking dick off.

"Stay away from me you fucking rapist. You drugged me!" I try to get to my feet to get away from him, but my legs give out on me before I make it halfway up. Drew catches me before I hit the ground again, but I jerk out of his hold and spit in his face. "Don't you dare put your hands on me." My breath comes out in harsh gasps as I try not to succumb to the panic rising in my chest.

"Eloise! Calm down. I'm not going to hurt you." Drew grabs my shoulders in a bruising grip and gives me a rough shake, causing my head to snap back and another wave of debilitating pain to sweep through my skull. I clench my eyes closed and wait for the pain induced wave of nausea to pass.

"Please, don't touch me...leave me alone." The tenuous hold I have on my tears finally slips and they start to flow freely. I feel the warmth of them stream down my cheeks as I rest my head against the wall. I bring my legs to my chest and wrap myself into a tight ball. I can't bear to feel his touch or see him looking at me. I can't bear to be in my own skin right now. The only thought going through my head right now is that this is all my fault. I never should've tried to deal with this on my own. I should've spoken up sooner. I should've gone to the police. I should've told Caleb the truth. All the should haves in the world can't change my fate now. He's never going to let me go, not now that he's marked me as his.

TWENTY-SIX

I stay curled up in a ball on the floor for what seems like hours. My muscles become stiff from lack of movement and my eyes start to dry out from hours of blankly staring at the wall. Distantly in my mind I recognize this as shock, but I can't bring myself to snap out of it. The sun sets outside and the only light in the bedroom comes from the moonlight spilling through the floor to ceiling windows. Drew stays downstairs and I have no intention of going down to join him but soon my bladder starts aching, and much to my dismay it seems like the only bathroom is downstairs with him.

Slowly I unfurl my limbs and force myself to stand up. My muscles scream in protest as I stand up and stretch out. I gather my clothes up and put them on, donning them like a suit of armor. The nausea has mostly passed now but my body aches in so many places. I feel like I've been brutalized and dimly I realize that I have been. I was drugged and raped and there's no telling how rough he was with me while I was out of it.

Warm tears track down my cheeks and my vision goes blurry. The shock is wearing off and the full weight of what has happened causes my knees to buckle forcing me to collapse down on the bed. I bury my face in my hands and take in a few desperate deep breaths trying to get my emotions back under control. After a few minutes of practicing some box breathing, a calming technique, I read about in one of my smutty books, I finally feel calm enough to make my way downstairs.

I descend the stairs slowly, scanning the room for Drew. My eyes land on him behind the counter, chopping fruit with the precise strokes of a professional chef. He looks up at me and watches my slow descent down the stairs without pausing his knife. Dread pools in my gut as I realize how much danger I'm in; not only am I alone with him in the middle of nowhere, but he has access to weapons. His eyes track my movements like a lion tracking a gazelle. I'm afraid if I make any sudden movements he will spring into action and take me down.

Once I reach the bottom of the stairs I freeze and wait for him to make a move. We stare at one another for what seems like an eternity. His expression is an inscrutable mask. I decide my only course of action for now is to play a good captive until I can get him to let his guard down.

"Um...where is the bathroom?" My question comes out in a hoarse whisper. My throat is raw from crying and screaming at him earlier.

He points to the door behind me with the knife. "There are towels and soap out if you want to shower. Dinner is almost ready." His voice is even, no sign of irritation, anger or remorse for what he did. He sounds like this is just any normal date he's been on, and it is his eerie calmness that unsettles me the most. I nod at him and quickly retreat into the bathroom.

I am finally able to let out the breath I didn't realize I was holding once there is a locked door between us. I hold no notion that the flimsy door will be enough to keep him away, but the illusion of safety allows me to release some of the tension in my shoulders.

The first thing that I do is look for a way out. There is one window in the bathroom but it's up high, narrow and I'm not entirely convinced my thick thighs could fit though it. Plan B, it is. After I take care of my most pressing needs, I scour every drawer and cabinet in the bathroom looking for anything that I can use as a weapon. Scissors, razors, tweezers...I'll settle for anything sharp or pointy. Unfortunately, my search is fruitless. Unless I plan on pelting him to death with toilet paper I'm out of luck.

I turn to the mirror and take in my reflection. I don't even recognize the woman with the harrowed look on her face. There are dark circles under my bloodshot eyes, my cheeks and nose are red from all the crying I've done, there is a bruise in the shape of a bite mark at the juncture of where my neck meets my shoulder, and my bottom lip is slightly red and swollen from where he bit it.

Suddenly, I can't handle the lingering feel of his touch

on my skin, so I strip down and step into the shower to scour him off. I turn the water as hot as it will go and let it scald me. I take the bar of soap and start scrubbing everywhere he touched me but no matter how hard I scrub the bruises don't go away, leaving a painful (literal and figurative) reminder of what happened. In the back of my mind I know I'm probably washing away vital evidence but at this stage I'm not sure I'll be getting away from him any time soon and I'd rather be clean. Washing between my legs I feel the sticky evidence of his cum and my stomach pitches with revulsion. I have an IUD, so pregnancy isn't a concern but the fact that he came inside of me without knowing that makes my blood run cold. The idea that he may be trying to trap me with a pregnancy makes me weak in the knees all over again and panic begins to rise in my chest.

A knock at the door brings me out of the rising tide of panic threatening to take over my faculties. I shut the water off and clutch a towel to my chest like it's some sort of useful shield against the maniac holding me captive here. Drew's voice comes through the door, "Dinner's ready darlin'. Come out and eat." Again, his voice is warm and smooth like honey. I can't reconcile this doting, gentle, man with the one that drugged and raped me just a few hours ago. It's discordant enough to make me feel like I'm losing my mind. I take my time getting dressed before I rejoin Drew in the main living space.

He's leaning against the back of the couch, watching me with an intensity that feels like he's stripping me bare with nothing more than a look. I glance at the table beside him, unable to withstand the heat behind his gaze. There's a charcuterie board laid out with a selection of meats, cheeses, fruits and pickles. No knives or forks or anything I could use as a makeshift weapon. Just simple food we can pick up and eat with our fingers.

"Come sit and eat, Sweetness. You've got to be starving." His voice is soft and placating as he reaches out and grabs my hand to lead me to the table. My back stiffens at his use of Caleb's pet name for me.

"You do not get to call me that." I bite out the words before I even think them through. A flash of darkness crosses over Drew's face but passes in the blink of an eye. He gives my hand a tight squeeze before tugging me over to the table and forcing me to take a seat. When I'm seated, he places both hands on my shoulders and leans in to whisper in my ear.

"Let's get one thing straight, darlin'. I'll call you whatever I want. You are mine now. I marked you. I fucked you. I claimed you. There is no going back now. The sooner you accept that, the sooner we can begin to build our life together,"

"You are out of your goddamn mind if you think I'm just going to pretend to be happy and play house with you. You fucking raped me!" I try to jerk out of his hold but his grip on my shoulders is unrelenting. Drew wraps my hair in one of his fists and jerks my head back, so I'm forced to look up at him. His other hand leaves my shoulder and wraps around my neck, applying the barest amount of pressure; a threat of what's to come if I don't watch my tone.

"Eloise, I just gave you what you wanted. Give it time and it'll come back to you. The way you ground that sweet pussy against my face and the way it clutched my cock when you came on it told me everything I needed to know. I'm going to give you a chance to eat dinner like a good girl without my intervention but if you don't start playing nice then we can do this the hard way. I just want to take care of you and make you feel good darlin'. Let me do that. Be my good girl."

During his speech Drew's grip on my neck gets firmer, and firmer until he cuts off my air completely. Blood starts pounding in my head so loudly I almost can't hear him when he asks me, "Are you going to be my good girl?".

I jerk a nod and he instantly releases his chokehold on me. I take in a deep gasping breath as he moves to start making a plate for me. I clench my eyes shut and sit on my trembling hands, trying to hide just how terrified I am right now. I don't know how I'm going to get out of this, but I know I can't let him get me unconscious or in an altered mental state again. I need my wits about me if I'm going to make it out of this alive.

We sit and eat in silence. Drew keeps one possessive hand clamped on my thigh while I manage to choke down a few crackers and pieces of fruit. Everything tastes like ashes on my tongue and my stomach protests every bite. I don't know if it's the remnants of whatever he gave me, the stress, or lack of real food for almost the whole day but the combination makes eating almost unbearable. I force myself to eat a few more of the bites he offers me because I know I need food to keep up my strength, knowing I can't let myself get weak and give up.

However, I draw the line at the glass of wine he brings to my mouth, I turn my face away and refuse to drink. After being roofied in his presence twice, I don't trust any beverages offered by him. In my heart I know now that he set up Business Douche Brayden so he could take advantage of me and play the hero. Drew is sick, unhinged, and dangerous and I have to play my cards right to get out of this situation.

"You need to drink something, darlin'." The pressure of his grip on my thigh tightens with his request.

"Can I get myself some water please? I can't handle anything stronger right now." I force myself to look at him imploringly, hoping he will have enough decency to let me do this for myself. He looks at me for a long moment before jerking a nod and releasing his hold on my thigh. I let out a breath and quickly stand up to go over to the sink. I take my time filling a glass of water and drinking it at the sink, all the while scanning the counter tops for any knives or objects I could use as a weapon. My heart sinks when I see the counters are pristine and free from clutter, the knife Drew had been using earlier is nowhere to be found.

Disappointment floods through me when I realize how meticulous he's been about this whole situation. He's not leaving any potential weapons out for me to use against him, he's already drugged me once and there is no doubt he'll do it again if I give him a reason to, and I haven't even seen my shoes since coming back downstairs so making a run for it will be even harder.

I must get lost in my own thoughts for too long because Drew comes up behind me and cages me with his arms around my body, pulling me against him. Startling, I drop the glass in the sink, and it shatters. Before I can reach in and grab the largest shard of glass, Drew pulls me away from the sink and walks me back to the couch where he sits and pulls me onto his lap. He nuzzles into my neck, planting gentle kisses as his hands run up and down my arms, caressing me.

"Baby, I need you to stop fighting this. You know how good we can be together, and I am going to take such good care of you." His hands cup my breasts, and he flicks his thumbs over my nipples. My whole body is stiff and unyielding to his touch, bile rises in my throat again.

"Drew, please stop. I don't know why you think this will work. Relationships aren't built like this. You can't force me to love you. Please, just let me go. I'm begging you." Tears blur my vision and my voice cracks. I don't know if he has enough humanity left to be affected by them but it's the only play I have at the moment; to try and appeal to whatever human decency he has left.

"Give me a chance, darlin'. I'll make it all better. We can start over again. Me and you, out here just getting to know each other. I know I failed you before, but I'll get it right this time. Let me make it up to you." One of his hands snakes under my t-shirt and caresses my breast while his teeth graze gentle nips along my neck.

A lump forms in my throat and goosebumps pebble all over my body. *Failed you before, I'll get it right this time.* What is he talking about? Is he referring to Cassidy? Is what happened with her the root of his obsession with me? My mind is whirring with questions and possibilities. Do I keep him talking and hope that I can make him realize I'm not Cassidy? Will talking about her set him off and make him angry? I decide at this point I don't have anything else to lose, so I jump off the cliff and hope I'm not wrong.

"Drew, I'm not her. I'm not Cassidy. You haven't failed me. You failed her." His body stiffens, his hands ceasing their movements. I hold my breath, my racing pulse thundering in my head while I wait for his reaction. Before he has a chance to respond a knock sounds at the front door and relief floods through me. Thank God. Someone else is here. I open my mouth to call out for help, but he clamps his hand over it quieting me.

"I'm sorry darlin', I don't want to do this, but I've got to keep you quiet." He wraps his other hand around my neck and squeezes, cutting off my oxygen supply. It doesn't take long for my vision to start darkening and sounds to get muffled. The last thing I hear before I pass out is "Police, we need to ask you some questions."

TWENTY-SEVEN

THE NEXT MORNING I'M AT MY LAPTOP SCOURING THE PUBLIC GIS website trying to determine if Drew owns any of the properties on the mountain. There are over 100 cabins in the area, and I've only gone through half of them so far. After I dropped Sara off at home, I spent the night doing some detective work on my own and figured out his last name, and that he's the owner of Stellina. Knowing his full name will go a long way helping in my search.

I keep my phone next to me with the ringer volume turned up in case Officer Roberts calls with any information. My eyes are heavy, and my hands are jittery from my 4th cup of coffee. I've gotten barely two hours of sleep since yesterday. Every time I close my eyes, I picture Eloise being scared, alone and trapped with this asshole. I should have fucking laid him out when he came by the house. I clench my hand into a fist as I wait for the urge to punch something to subside. The ringing of my phone brings me out of the fog of anger settling over me. I glance at the screen and see that it is Officer Roberts' number.

"Hey, this is Caleb. Do you have any updates? Did you find my wife?" I answer in a rush and immediately start peppering her with questions.

"Hello, Mr. Fitzpatrick. We took a squad car up to Mr. Jameson's cabin last night to see if your wife was with him. He was alone in the home and let us come in to verify. I was present with another Officer, and we saw no evidence of your wife being on the premises. We did a sweep of the property and there was no sign of her. We're going to keep looking and Mr. Jameson is still a person of interest in the ongoing investigation. I just wanted to give you an update on where we were." Officer Roberts' tone is professional but empathetic. She knows she's giving me disappointing news.

"What about her phone location? Were you able to track that any further?" I ask, feeling panic claw its way up my throat. I know he has her. There's no way she would go M.I.A. like this without talking to me first.

"Unfortunately, with her phone being off we could only track it to the last cell tower it pinged from, which is where you showed me on your phone. We are not giving up, Mr. Fitzpatrick. We will find her. You did the right thing getting us involved. Are there any other friends or family members she might be staying with? Any reason at all to suspect she's just taking some time for herself?" Irritation courses through me at her line of questioning. I know she's probably just covering her bases but the implication that Eloise is choosing to be away from me rankles.

"I've already checked in with her sister. She hasn't spoken to Eloise since last weekend. He's got her Officer Roberts. I know he does. Eloise and I don't cut each other off like this. We talk through things, and we've never gone this long without speaking to one another. Are you sure he didn't have her hidden somewhere?"

"Unfortunately, without a search warrant we couldn't do a more thorough search of the property. We are working on getting one, but we've got to provide enough probable cause for it to be issued by a judge. If you have anything else to tell us that would help with proving his infatuation with your wife that would help." I blow out a frustrated breath knowing I've already given Officer Roberts everything I know.

"No, I've told you everything I know…" With that she offers me a few more platitudes and reassurances before hanging up. I go back to my computer and resume my search for Drew's mountain property. Now that I know he has a cabin out there I know my search isn't fruitless. Officer Roberts wouldn't give me the address, but I have no issues with finding it and paying him a visit myself.

An hour later I finally hit pay dirt. There is a 300 acre property at the top of Mt. Regis with a Mr. Richard Jameson listed as the owner; I can only assume that it is someone related to Drew. Before I head out the door I grab my keys, the stun gun and pepper spray Eloise had purchased. I have a gun, but I know without a shadow of a doubt there is a high likelihood that I will shoot the motherfucker on sight, and I have no interest in going to jail so I leave it behind.

Forty minutes later I turn off the main road and start following the gravel winding road up the mountain. At first, I'm passing driveways leading to cabins and campsites with regular frequency but eventually the driveways taper off and I pass a No Trespassing sign posted on a fence post. I assume I've reached the edge of the Jameson property. According to the GIS map, it covers the top third of the mountain with a national forest surrounding it with no other nearby cabins for close to a mile. I drive up carefully, taking every detail of the property in.

When I'm about 100 yards from the cabin I park in a copse of trees and hope that Drew hasn't heard my car approaching. I don't want to give him a heads up that I'm coming and let him have the opportunity to hide Eloise again. I approach the cabin on foot cautiously and quietly. There are lights on the lower level and his black SUV is parked off to the side. The back half of the cabin backs up to the cliff edge, so it looks like the only way in or out is through the front door.

I step up onto the porch and peek in through one of the front windows. I see Drew pacing back and forth in the kitchen area, running his hands through his hair, looking agitated. Clearly the visit by the police was not in his plan and he's worked up now. There is no sign of Eloise in the living room or kitchen area. I pull the stun gun out of my back pocket and turn it on, readying to use it. I take a deep calming breath before banging on the front door loudly to get his attention. I stand off to the side and wait for him to open it to take him by surprise.

It feels like an eternity passes before I hear the lock turn and the door open. Without hesitation I whip the stun gun around and jam it into his chest and send 16 million volts into him. "What the fuc—" Drew collapses with a heap, halfway hanging out the doorway. I don't waste any time in throwing my fist into his face two-three-four times, further incapacitating him before the effects of the stun gun wears off. While he's unconscious I take my belt and use it to restrain his hands behind his back. With Drew neutralized I turn my attention to the cabin, it's a large open floor plan layout with a loft bedroom with limited hiding places.

"Eloise! Answer me! Where are you? Eloise!" I yell as I run up the stairs looking for my wife. The bed is unmade but empty, and no doors lead off of the bedroom. "Eloise! Can you hear me?" I'm nearly screaming as I run back downstairs and start opening any doors I see. The bathroom is empty, there's a small pantry by the kitchen that is also empty. As I turn to leave the pantry, I hear a muffled thump from below. Stopping, I turn and look down and almost don't see the hidden cellar door that blends into the floor. There is a rug partially obscuring it, but it looks like it's been moved, as if someone has accessed the cellar recently.

"Eloise! It's Caleb! Are you down there?" Another muffled thump sounds from below. I tear the rug away and throw the cellar door open, revealing a small root cellar barely big enough for a person to stand in. Eloise sits at the bottom of the stairs, duct tape on her mouth with her hands and feet bound together. Tears stream down her dirt smudged cheeks and my stomach rolls at the sight of her bound and gagged in the dark alone.

"Oh god...baby. No no no..." I stumble down the stairs and wrap my arms around her as she sobs into my chest. "Ssh, ssh, I'm here. I'm here, Sweetness. I've got you." Her body trembles against mine as sobs rack through her. I kiss the top of her head and stroke her face gently. "Hey baby, let me get this tape off your mouth, ok? It's going to hurt but I'm just going to rip it off. Nod if that's ok." Eloise frantically nods her head and grabs onto my shirt, bracing for the pain. The tape comes off with a loud rip and a scream tears from Eloise's throat. "I'm so sorry, I'm sorry baby...Ssh, I've got you." I kiss her face all over and clutch her to my chest. My heart is racing frantically but relief is crashing through me at finding my wife alive.

"Caleb, please untie my hands. I can't feel my fingers." Eloise's words come out in choked sobs. Shaking my head, I mentally berate myself for not doing that right away.

"God, of course. Sorry, Sweetness." I begin working on the knots tying her hands and feet together and soon I have her free. "Can you stand? Do you need me to carry you?" I massage her hands, helping the feeling return to them. Her fingers are swollen and purple, angry red welts lacing across her wrists from how tightly he had her bound.

"I think I can stand...just hold on to me. Please get me out of here. He left me down here all night..." More sobs tear out of my shattered wife as I help her to her feet. Slowly we make our way back up the stairs and back into the main part of the house. She holds on to me like I am her life raft. Her body trembles from fear as we both take in the room in front of us. I look to the front door expecting to see Drew still unconscious on the floor. My blood chills when the only thing I see is the small puddle of blood left from where I broke his nose.

TWENTY-EIGHT

WHEN I COME TO, I'M BOUND AND GAGGED IN A SMALL, DAMP and dark space. I try to move but my hands and feet are tied together. My hands are already tingling from the tell-tale sign of circulation loss. I hear muffled voices and footsteps. It sounds like multiple people are talking. I can barely make out anything they say but I hear Drew's booming voice usher the newcomers further away from me. I try to cry out but the duct tape across my mouth prevents me from doing much more than letting out a muffled grunt. The voices keep moving further away and soon I hear the thud of a door closing. My heart crumples as I realize my potential rescuers are leaving.

Sometime later a bright light shines down from an opening above me. Drew is standing at the top of a short staircase looking down at me. His face is dark with anger, rage emanates from him in waves. "Someone reported you missing, darlin'. Any idea why that might be?" Drew comes down the stairs until he is right in front of me. He crouches down and lifts my chin, so I am forced to look him in the eye. "Apparently your husband hasn't quite gotten the message that you've left him. Now, why is that? You told me that it was done." Drew's jaw pulses with irritation, his grip on my chin turning bruising. I can't respond thanks to the tape; all I can do is try to pull away from him.

"Unfortunately, darlin', now I have to leave you down here until I'm sure they're not coming back. That could be awhile. Why don't you sit down here and think about how devastated your husband is going to feel once he watches that tape of me fucking that tight little hole of yours? I told you, if you weren't going to leave him, I was going to do it for you."

A sob fails to escape from my throat. Bile rises up and I desperately try to swallow it back so that I don't throw up. Drew leans in and presses a kiss to my forehead. "Ssh, it's ok. When you come out, we'll start fresh again." With that he leaves me in the dark. Tears silently track down my cheeks as I lay my head back against the cool dirt wall, the crash from the adrenaline high pulling me to unconsciousness like a tide returning to sea.

Muffled shouts and thuds bring me back to consciousness hours later. My whole body aches with cramps from not being able to move. My heart races at a gallop when I hear a muffled *"Eloise! Answer me!"* I start screaming as loud as I can through my gag and kick my feet against the floor, desperately trying to make as much noise as possible. I kick harder and scream louder when I hear *"Eloise! It's Caleb! Are you down there?"*

Seconds later the hatch is thrown open and bright light from above streams down. Caleb is staring down at me, his chest heaving, right hand covered in blood. The relief and shock that passes over his face matches my own emotions. I lose the battle to keep hold of my emotions and the dam breaks loose just as Caleb stumbles down the stairs. My whole body trembles with relief as he buries me against this chest. His soothing words barely register over the sobs trying to break free. *"Ssh, ssh, I'm here. I'm here, Sweetness. I've got you."*

Caleb rips the tape from my mouth, and it feels like the sweetest relief and sharpest pain all at once. The first thing I do is beg him to untie my hands. I'm terrified I've lost circulation from them for too long and there will be permanent damage. When he releases the rope, the pins and needles begin shooting back through my hands and I cry out in agony. He asks me if I can stand while he massages the feeling back into my fingers. I nod, desperate to get out of this pit of hell as quickly as possible. Together we gingerly make our way back up the stairs, my legs barely able to hold me up, leaving Caleb to do most of the work.

When we make it back up to the kitchen, I feel Caleb's

entire body stiffen next to me. He is staring at the front door, where a sizable puddle of blood is congealing. "We gotta get out of here, Sweetness. How fast can you walk?" Caleb turns to me, and I can finally see the panic in his eyes. He's terrified, Drew isn't where he left him and now he's on the loose. I nod in understanding and let him half carry me to the front door. When we get to the porch Caleb pauses and reaches into his back pocket. He hands me the can of pepper spray.

"Babe, I'm parked a mile down the hill. I'm going to throw you on my back, and we are going to run for it. If you see him spray him in the fucking face, ok? I'm going to get you out of here." Caleb crashes his mouth against mine for a brief, searing kiss. I let him help me onto his back and we take off running down the hill. I whip my head side to side scanning the trees for any sign of Drew and it feels like I can't catch my breath the entire time we race to the car.

When the car is in sight, I tap Caleb on the shoulder and tell him to let me down. I can feel how hard his heart is pounding and how labored his breathing is. Reluctantly Caleb lets me down and we hobble together the last 50 yards to the car. When we reach the vehicle Caleb leans me against the car while he fishes his keys out of his pocket. My eyes don't stop scanning the tree line behind him, watching for Drew.

When I hear the sound of the doors unlocking my heart bottoms out. We are so close to getting out of here. Before I know it, Caleb is shuffling me into the car and slamming the door behind me. I hold my breath until he rounds the front of the car and gets into the driver's seat. We sit in silence with only our frantic heartbeats and heavy breathing for a soundtrack as he turns the car around and guns it down the drive. As I stare out the window numb from shock, Caleb simply clutches my trembling hand in his as he drives us away from a literal nightmare.

CHAPTER
TWENTY-NINE
ELOISE

"I've got to take you to the hospital, baby. Do you want to go to your hospital or somewhere else?" Caleb's question brings me out of the daze I was lost in. I blink slowly, taking in the surroundings and realize we are almost to the town limits again. The entire drive off the mountain and back I've been completely zoned out, unable to process any of the events of the last 24 hours. The idea of my co-workers knowing what I just endured sends a wave of shame coursing through my body.

"Take me to B.F. General." My voice is barely louder than a whisper. Between the screaming, sobbing and being choked out, a whisper is all I can manage. Caleb gives my hand a reassuring squeeze before turning the car away from Birch Falls Memorial. His thumb rubs gentle, soothing circles on the back of my hand, and he doesn't let go for the entire drive to the hospital.

When we pull up to the Emergency Room entrance,

Caleb parks the car and hops out to help me get out before I even have a chance to unbuckle my seatbelt. When we walk through the door I freeze, suddenly realizing everything I'm going to have to recount in front of him. I don't know if I'm ready for Caleb to know everything that happened in the cabin, or how Drew raped me. My body starts to shake uncontrollably as the numbness finally starts to wear off.

"Can we get some help over here?" Caleb calls out to a passing nurse as he guides me to a wheelchair to sit in. She takes in one look at my dirty, disheveled appearance and immediately snaps to attention.

"Hey, hon. I'm Arianna, can you tell me what happened?" She squats down in front of me, getting eye level with me. She clasps my wrist in her hand and begins taking my pulse as she takes in my haggard condition.

"I-I...I was attacked..." The words don't want to come out past the lump in my throat. Her eyes go round, and she glances up at Caleb with a wary gaze. "Not him...he's my husband. He saved me." Arianna nods in understanding and gets behind the wheelchair to push me into the triage room. "Sir, I'm going to start her intake. Can you talk to patient registration and give them her information?" Caleb looks distressed at the thought of leaving my side but I'm quietly relieved by the idea of talking to the nurse without him present.

"Can't that wait-?" He begins to protest but I cut him off.

"It's ok, Cal. It won't take you long...please. Do what

the nurse asks." Caleb looks like he wants to fight about this but thinks better of it and nods in resignation.

"Ok, I'll be right there. I won't be long, Sweetness." He leans down and kisses the top of my head before heading over to the registration desk. Arianna wheels me into the triage room and starts the process of documenting my vitals.

"Tell me what happened, hon. Were you raped?" I can see Arianna taking in all of my injuries. I know my throat is bruised and my wrists are chapped and raw from the rope. My whole body aches like I've been hit by a truck and the soreness between my thighs from Drew's assault is still present.

Taking in a deep breath, I nod my head. I can't look at her directly and see the pity in her eyes so instead I stare down at my hands.

"Ok, do you want your husband present for the forensic nurse exam?" Her tone is soft and understanding. I shake my head, my vision blurs from tears. I can't bear the thought of Caleb seeing me like this, broken and battered. "It's ok hon. Tell me your name. I'm going to talk to him and let him know it'll be a few minutes before he can come back."

"My name is Eloise Fitzpatrick." I manage to rasp out. She gives my hand a squeeze.

"Ok Eloise, I'm going to talk to your husband and get a doctor and we are going to do an exam. I'll be right back." I nod mutely and stare down at my feet, unable to look her in the eye. I hear her softly close the door behind her and the muffled conversation she has with Caleb. I hear his hissed cry of dismay at not being allowed in, but Arianna holds firm and insists he has to wait outside. She suggests calling the police while she and the doctor proceed with my exam. I know he's not happy about being shut out but emotionally I cannot take on the load of dealing with his anger and heartbreak on top of my own. A few minutes later she returns.

"We have you admitted now, and we are going to move you to a proper exam room to do the forensic nurse exam. I'll be there with Doctor Lambert the entire time but if there is anything at all you're uncomfortable with, just let me know, ok?" Arianna gives my hand a reassuring squeeze before she wheels me into a larger, private room. She has me change into one of those awful, scratchy blue hospital gowns that don't actually fit anybody properly, before Doctor Lambert comes in. Doctor Lambert is on the younger side, probably only in his early 40s, with mostly black hair with a bit of graying at his temples. He wears black frame glasses and has a kind smile that probably puts patients at ease under normal circumstances.

"Hello, Mrs. Fitzpatrick. I'm Doctor Lambert. I'm here to do your exam with Arianna. If at any point you feel uncomfortable or feel like you need to stop, you just let me know. Arianna can do it, if you'd prefer." His hands are warm as he takes mine into his and he looks me in the eye with the sincerest expression of empathy I've ever seen.

"Let's just get this over with." My voice is still a hoarse whisper, now tinged with resignation. I lay back on the table as they set up the tray with the equipment they'll need and wait for the second most invasive experience of my life to begin.

"Alright, Eloise. We're all done. Do you want your husband to come in now?" Arianna puts her hand behind my back and helps me sit back up. They asked me questions as they documented each of my injuries and I did my best to recount my experience without breaking down. I know this is only the first of many times I'm going to have to tell my story, so I start to build a mental barrier to help shield myself from the trauma of having to relive the worst night of my life.

I give Arianna a quick nod of my head and she pokes her head out of the room to call for Caleb. "Mr. Fitzpatrick you can come in now." Caleb rushes into the room and immediately wraps me up his arms and buries his face in my hair. I cling to him like he's the only piece of driftwood in my ocean keeping me afloat as we both succumb to the overwhelming devastation we are feeling.

Caleb holds me for what seems like an eternity, gently stroking my hair, refusing to give me even a millimeter of space, as if I might evaporate like a mist and disappear on him again. He murmurs sweet reassurances in my ear as his arms cradle me gently, yet securely at the same time. I just soak up his strength and warmth and bury my face in his shoulder as I try to hide from the world a little longer. I know on the other side of that door a police officer is waiting to ask me questions that will force me to relive my worst nightmare and I just need a little more time to prepare for the ordeal of facing it.

Once we have a handle on our emotions, Caleb invites two officers into my room. One is a young, pretty woman with a mass of curly hair on top of her head and the brightest gold-colored eyes I've ever seen. She almost looks feline with her ebony skin, graceful cheekbones and cute button nose, but the scar over her right eye tells me she's lived a harder life than the average pampered house cat.

She's accompanied by an older man, with short cropped gray hair and deep lines carved into his face from time and stress. One officer at the beginning of her career, and one nearing the end of his. In my head I mentally picture them starring in some zany buddy cop movie and I have to force myself to hold back a snicker. I think the stress of everything is finally getting to me and I'm starting to crack up. The two uniformed officers exchange a look at what I'm sure is the weird face I'm pulling in an attempt to not burst out laughing. In my head the older officer's tagline is definitely the same as Danny Glover's from the Lethal Weapon movies.

"Mrs. Fitzpatrick, I'm Officer Roberts and this is Officer Randall." The young pretty cop introduces herself and her partner. "We'd like to ask you some questions about what happened at Mr. Jameson's cabin. Do you mind telling us what happened?"

I'm not quite sure where to begin, so I start from the beginning. Caleb stands by my side, holding my hand as I tell the story of how Drew and I met at the bar and how he kept popping up and pursuing me even when I kept turning him down. I told them about the pictures and the text messages and the threats.

I told them about the night I was roofied the first time and how he held the video of him going down on me as leverage to get me to leave my husband. When I look up at Caleb his face is ashen and tears silently stream down his cheeks, at this part of the story he wraps his arms around me and squeezes me until it feels like my ribs might break.

Once I get to the part at the cabin, I falter. This is where things get hazy for me again. I know Drew and I had sex, and I know he drugged me again but the shame from feeling like I initiated it and enjoyed it makes bile rise up in the back of my throat.

"It's ok baby, take your time. We can stop and you can tell the rest later if you need to." Caleb kisses my temple as he runs a hand along my back in soothing strokes. I glance up at Officer Roberts looking to her for guidance. Her lips are pressed in a tight line and worry creases her brows. Officer Randall next to her has been taking notes the entire time.

"If she's ok with it, we'd like to get her whole statement now." The older man chimes in, without looking up from his notepad. I see Officer Roberts give him a side eye before issuing a curt nod in agreement.

"It's ok, babe. I can finish it." I take a deep breath and plunge into the final part of my story, finishing with Drew choking me out and me waking up in the root cellar. As I tell this part I see Officer Robert's face go ashen, and that's when I know she was one of the officers who stopped by. I can see the flash of guilt cross over her face for not finding me when she was there.

"So, you're saying none of the encounters you had with Mr. Jameson were consensual?" Officer Randall speaks up, skepticism lacing his voice.

"Absolutely not. I kept telling him I wasn't interested and that I was married."

"Then why did you tell your husband you needed time apart?" Randall asks, his tone completely lacking in empathy.

"Did you fucking miss the part where he was black-mailing her?" Caleb snaps out, anger simmering under the surface of his tone.

Randall looks unimpressed by Caleb's ire. "I'm just asking questions."

I chime in before Caleb can get into a fight with the officer. "I was afraid if Drew showed Caleb the video of him going down on me, Caleb wouldn't believe me when I said I didn't remember it. I was afraid of him hating me for cheating on him. I thought if I could get some time to reason with Drew, I could get him to leave me alone or that he would get bored once he realized the chase was over...and that I'd still have a chance with Caleb once he was gone. I just didn't want my husband to hate me..." This is the point where I break down in sobs again.

"Alright we're done here. I'm taking my wife home and if you need to talk to us you can wait until tomorrow." Caleb wraps me up in his arms and dismisses the officers from the room.

"Alright, we will be in touch. We have officers checking out the cabin and the surrounding property now. I'll make sure we have a car posted outside of your residence too until we find Mr. Jameson. Mrs. Fitzpatrick, I'm so sorry you had to endure this." I peer over Caleb's shoulder and see Officer Roberts' warm honey-colored eyes shimmering with unshed tears. She cuts a scathing look to her partner before jerking her head indicating for him to follow her out.

Once they leave the room, Caleb turns to me and cups my face in his hands. "Sweetness...I'll always believe you." My heart crumples at his words and a different kind of devastation sweeps over me. The devastation that I brought this on myself by not trusting in my husband's love for me.

CHAPTER

THIRTY

CALEB

WHEN WE GET HOME IT'S AFTER MIDNIGHT. I GUIDE ELOISE up the stairs to the bedroom and set her down on the edge of the bed before crouching down in front of her. "Hey, I'm going to run you a bath, ok? I know you're tired but maybe this will help you relax some before bed."

Eloise nods her head but doesn't say anything. She doesn't look up to meet my eyes either. She hasn't said much of anything once she was done recounting her story to the police, other than to answer the doctor's questions with one-word answers and to beg to be discharged. Doctor Lambert wanted to keep her overnight for observation, but Eloise insisted that she just wanted to come home. Secretly I agree with Doctor Lambert and wish she would've spent the night but after what she went through, I'll support Eloise in any way she needs to get through this.

I go into the bathroom and start filling the tub. I dump

in some bath salts, some smelly bubbles and a few other bottles of oils and perfumes. I don't know what any of it does, I just want Eloise to feel safe and relaxed back in her home. When we renovated this house the one hill Eloise was willing to die on, no matter what it did to the budget, was to have a bathtub large enough to soak in properly. After years of renting apartments with small bathrooms and tiny tubs all she wanted was a proper bathtub she could relax in. So now we have a bathroom that provides a spa-like experience with a large, deep soaking tub, and a separate shower with a rainfall shower head and jets that shoot out from the sides, and for the first time I'm grateful we spent the extra money.

After checking the water temperature for the third time, I go back into the bedroom, Eloise is still in the same position I left her. She's sitting on the edge of the bed, staring down at her hands, her hair hanging limply around her face like a curtain.

"Hey, Sweetness. The bath is ready. Do you want me to help you?" I take her hand and she allows me to pull her into the steamy bathroom. She still won't look up at me, so I put a finger under her chin and gently lift her face up so I can look at her properly.

"Lo...whatever you need, I'm here. I don't want you to hide from me anymore. I love you. I'll leave you alone if you really want me to, but I hope you'll let me stay and take care of you. I need to be close to you, I need to know you're here with me. We are going to get through this together, ok?"

Tears shimmer in Eloise's eyes, making the blue of them appear so bright it almost doesn't seem real. Her chin quivers as she loses her fight to hold back the sob that wants to escape. She catches me off guard when she wraps her arms around my waist and buries her face in my chest as she breaks down.

"Ssh, ssh, baby. I've got you. I'm never going to let you go." I kiss the top of her head as I stroke her hair and let her tears soak into my shirt.

"Will you get in with me? I just need you to hold me." Relief crashes through me at her request. I didn't realize how terrified I was of her shutting me out until she asked me to stay.

"Absolutely, Sweetness. Come on, let me help you get undressed." I take my time, peeling her clothes off. She turns away from me when she's fully naked, I don't think she's fully ready to let me see her injuries but as long as she lets me hold her, I'm ok with that. I quickly strip down, and we climb in the tub together. She settles in between my legs with her back pressed against my chest. Her nose wrinkles a bit as all of the various scents in the water assault us.

"It smells like you dumped a whole ass Bath and Body Works in here, Cal." I look sheepishly to the products lining the shelf and notice all the clashing smells. Lavender, coconut, cucumber mint, vanilla, sandalwood, rose hips...

"Um, I might have. I wasn't sure what to use so I used everything." Eloise's body shakes against mine and my heart swells when I realize it's with laughter and not tears.

I wash her hair and body, this time with the correct products. She sighs under my touch as I massage the shampoo into her scalp. Selfishly I am thankful Drew didn't ruin her to the point of not wanting to be touched by another person. I need to touch her to reassure myself she's here with me now and nothing is going to take her away from me. I rinse out the suds and run her cucumber mint conditioner through the ends of her hair. I inhale deeply, letting every one of my senses fill up with Eloise. Her scent, her touch, the sound of her soft sighs. I press my lips to her neck in a gentle kiss, needing to taste her too.

We stay in the tub until the water cools and her breathing falls into the soft rhythm of sleep. I nudge my lips against her temple and kiss her. "Hey, Lo. Time to get out. Let's go to bed." She lets out a sleepy mumble but allows me to help her out of the tub and dry her off. I dress her in her favorite soft cotton pajamas and tuck her into bed before drying myself off and climbing in behind her. I pull her tight against my chest, spooning her from behind and resume stroking her hair until her breathing evens out again as she drifts off to sleep.

As tired and desperate for sleep as I am, sleep eludes me. I lay there for hours, listening to Eloise breathing softly as the events of the last 24 hours refuse to stop running through my mind. Anger, relief, terror, frustration, shame, all cycle through me in an unrelenting torrent. I want to kill Drew. I'm ashamed and frustrated that Eloise felt like I wouldn't believe her if she came to me with her story. I failed her as a husband if she truly thought there was any way I could ever hate her, infidelity or not. Terror at the knowledge that he's still out there. The relief of having her back in my arms.

A soft whimper draws me out of my dark spiral and I feel Eloise shudder against me. "No...no...stop." She mumbles in her sleep as she suddenly flings my arm away from her body. I move back as she jerks away from me and kicks out her feet trying to push me away.

"Eloise! Baby, it's me, Caleb. It's a bad dream. You're safe." I grab her hands that are attempting to scratch my chest. "Eloise, wake up!" I yell a little louder and this time her eyes pop open. Her chest is heaving, and she looks up at me in confusion for a few moments before her brain catches up to reality.

"Oh, Caleb. I'm sorry. I...I thought I was back in that cabin...I thought Drew had me again..." She crumples against my chest, and I cradle her in my arms, sshing her and stroking her back.

"It's ok, Sweetness. It's just me. You don't have to apologize to me." Eloise rests her head against my shoulder and threads her legs through mine, and wraps her arms around my body, hugging me like she's an octopus. I squeeze her tightly and start humming her favorite song, "Everlong" by the Foo Fighters. Eventually her breathing evens out again as she drifts off to sleep. This time my eyes close and I follow her into oblivion.

THIRTY-ONE

ELOISE

WHEN I WAKE UP AGAIN, BRIGHT MORNING LIGHT IS POURING through the windows. I roll over and reach for Caleb but find nothing but an empty bed beside me. Sitting up I look over to the clock and see that it's nearly noon. Before I get the chance to climb out of bed, Caleb returns holding a large mug of coffee and a plate of eggs and toast.

"Hey, Sweetness. I was just coming to wake you up." He flashes me the boyish grin that made me fall in love with him 12 years ago before leaning down and kissing me on the lips. It's a soft, gentle kiss that doesn't insist on being more than it is and I appreciate the hell out of him for it. He knows it's going to take time for me to move past what happened with Drew and he won't push me. Caleb has always been respectful of boundaries, and I couldn't be more grateful than I am to have him as my partner right now.

"Thanks, babe." I take the mug of coffee from him and

take a big drink. Caleb sets the plate of food down on the nightstand and climbs into bed next to me again, wrapping his arm around my shoulders.

"I took the liberty of calling your work and telling them you won't be in this week. I told them you were sick. I also called Harold and told him I wouldn't be coming in this week either. I'm not leaving your side until the police find this Drew fucker. I'm going to be clinging to you like your own personal barnacle."

I choke on the coffee I was in the middle of swallowing. "Jesus, Cal. That's a bit much." I laugh as I elbow him in the ribs.

"No, it's not. It'll never be enough. Not while he's still out there. Lo, he took you from me. I am not going to allow that to happen again. I'm never going to let you feel like you are alone or have to face this world on your own. I'm your husband and I am here to protect, cherish and love you until we die. If that requires me to quit my day job and become your own personal bodyguard then just go ahead and call me Kevin Costner. I already put work ahead of you once and look what happened...I'm so sorry, Lo." His voice breaks on those last words and I set my coffee to the side so I can look into Caleb's eyes.

"Hey...it's not your fault. Cal, it was a fucked-up situation that no one could've seen coming." I cup his cheek and press our foreheads together as we both fight back tears and work to regain our composure.

Once we have our emotions back under wraps, Caleb hands me my breakfast and I nibble on it, even though I'm not hungry. I can tell he feels like he needs to be doing something, so I let him feed me and comfort me. I need his reassurances as much as he needs to provide them. When I'm almost finished with my breakfast, Caleb's phone rings. He grabs it off the nightstand and checks to see who the caller is.

"I think this is Officer Roberts. Let me see what she needs." Caleb answers the phone and puts it on speaker so I can listen in.

"Hello, this is Caleb."

"Hello, Mr. Fitzpatrick. It's Officer Roberts. I was calling you with an update. We found your wife's purse and phone in Mr. Jameson's vehicle on the property during our search. Do you want us to drop it by your house?" Caleb looks to me and I give him a quick nod.

"Yeah, that would be appreciated. Have you found Drew?" Caleb asks, venom dripping from his voice when he says Drew's name.

"No, not yet. We've had officers and a team of dogs out looking for him on the mountain but so far nothing has turned up. We are going to keep a car stationed at your house until we find him."

"Good. Is there anything else, Officer Roberts?"

"Yeah, we'd like Eloise to come by the station and make a formal statement and she may want to consider filing a restraining order against Mr. Jameson too."

"Do you really think a piece of paper is going to keep that crazy fucker away from my wife?"

"No, but everything helps. There are steps we can take

to make sure he faces the maximum penalty under law when we catch him, and if he violates a restraining order it will make her case stronger." Officer Roberts' tone remains neutral and even. She doesn't react to Caleb's frustration.

Before he can speak up, I put a hand on his arm and chime in. "I'll come and make a statement. I want to do whatever I can to make sure he gets locked up forever so no one else has to go through what I went through." My voice sounds much stronger today. I can speak at a normal volume again and it doesn't sound so raspy.

"Eloise, I didn't realize you were there. How are you doing?" Officer Roberts' voice softens up as she addresses me.

"I'm holding up." Caleb gives my shoulders a tight squeeze as he drops a kiss to my head. I look up at him and give him a soft smile.

"Ok, we should be able to drop your things off in the next hour or so. Could you come by the station tomorrow morning? You can take today to recover. I don't want to push you, but the quicker we build this case against Mr. Jameson, the better."

"Yeah, I can come tomorrow. Thank you for everything you're doing, Officer. Whatever you need from me to make sure he gets locked away, I'll do it, just let me know."

With that we say our goodbyes and Caleb tosses the phone to the side. "I'm so proud of you, Lo. I hope you know that." Caleb takes my face in his hands and looks me in the eye. I see nothing but the pride he speaks of, shining in his eyes. "I mean it. You are so strong for wanting to do everything you can to help. Shutting down would be a completely valid response to what you just went through."

"It would be, but it won't help anything or stop it from happening again. Caleb, you don't know how much of a monster he is. It's not just the physical assault; he's a manipulator and a master at gaslighting. He made me believe I was asking for it and that you were going to leave me...I was so scared you would find out and believe him. He made me doubt my own mind and had me almost believing I was seeking him out. He is dangerous. I don't think he was going to let me go until he had broken me completely."

Caleb engulfs me in his arms and drops another kiss to the top of my head. "I will always believe you, Lo. Always. I know I wasn't here when I should have been, but that changes now. I'm not leaving you. Not for work, not for anything." We sit there, just holding each other, basking in the comfort of being together again.

Later, after another shower, because I'm not entirely sure there will ever be enough showers to wash away the grimy feeling of Drew's touch, I make my way downstairs to wait for the officer to drop off my belongings. Caleb is sitting at the dining room table at his laptop, glasses on, his shoulders bunched up with tension.

"Hey, what's up?" I come up behind him and rest my

chin on the top of his head and look at the computer screen. There is a news article up from the local paper, the headline reading - "Missing Local Woman Found" with a picture of me.

"Why is there a news article about me?" My knees go weak, and I take a seat next to Caleb. I want to help the police, but I am absolutely not prepared to deal with the press in any way.

"I'm not sure. Sara and I did report you as a missing person to the police but I'm not sure how this made it to the news so fast. It doesn't have a lot of detail in it, just that you were reported missing by your husband and found. It doesn't mention Drew or the cabin. I don't know if some journalist was just trolling the police radio and just caught some of the info. Do you want me to call Officer Roberts and see if she knows?"

I shake my head. "It's fine. It's not like she can do anything about it now." Just then a knock sounds at the door.

"I'll get it." Caleb stands and makes his way to the front door. When he opens it, a young cop we haven't met yet stands there holding my purse and phone.

"Mr. Fitzpatrick, Mrs. Fitzpatrick, I'm just dropping off your belongings." Caleb takes the purse and phone and thanks the officer before sending him on his way.

When Caleb hands me my phone I nearly toss it to the side before remembering the email I had sent to Cassidy Grainger's sister. After my experience with Drew there is no doubt in my mind, he had something to do with her disappearance. I attempt to power on my phone but it's completely dead.

"Shit." Caleb's brows furrow in confusion at my exclamation.

"What's wrong?"

"I need to charge my phone. I sent an email the other day and I need to see if I got a response."

"An email? What's so important about an email?" It's then I realize Caleb doesn't know about Cassidy. I pull him over to the couch and make him sit down so I can fill him in on what I found out about Drew and his missing girl-friend. As I talk, Caleb's normally bronze complexion goes ashen.

"Fuck...Lo. Are you saying you aren't the only woman he's done this to?"

I shrug my shoulders, "I don't know for sure but based on my experience with him, I'm thinking it's very likely he had something to do with Cassidy's disappearance. I think he fixated on me because I reminded him of her. I look like her, just with purple hair. And he kept saying things about how he wasn't going to fail me again...Caleb, I think he was trying to relive whatever happened between them with me."

With that I go off to find a charger for my phone so I can see if Cassidy's sister got back to me. I also need to check in with my family. I don't know how much Caleb told them while I was gone but if they see that news article they're going to be blowing up my phone.

Sure enough, as soon as my phone comes back on

notifications for missed calls and texts start flooding in. I see missed calls from Caleb and Sara at first but then from this morning I see several from my sister, several unknown numbers, and work. "Shit, I need to call Liv." I hit dial on her contact and wait for the call to connect. She answers on the first ring.

"Lo! What the fuck is going on? Are you ok? I've been freaking out all morning. Caleb called me asking if I had seen you over the weekend but didn't elaborate and then I saw in the newspaper that you were missing? Where the hell did you go? Are you guys having problems? Did you leave him?" Olivia's voice is frantic as she pelts me with questions.

"Liv, it's a long story and I'm not ready to get into it just yet. But I'm home now with Caleb. We are fine. I'm not leaving him. But if anyone from the press comes sniffing around, please don't talk to them."

"The press? Lo, you need to give me a little bit more to go on. What the hell happened?"

"Liv, I was taken by someone against my will. Caleb found me. He got me back safe, but the guy is still on the loose and the police are looking for him. I have to go by tomorrow to give a formal statement. I'm not really up for recounting the whole thing right now, but I just needed to let you know I'm safe now." I hear the shocked gasp right before Liv bursts into tears on the other end of the line.

"Y-you...were taken? Like kidnapped?"

"Yeah."

"Did he hurt you?" I look up at Caleb, who can clearly

tell where this conversation is going. He comes over to me and wraps his arms around me in a comforting hug.

"Yeah…he did. Look, Liv, I need to go. I'll check in soon, ok? I love you, give the kids a big hug from Auntie Lo, please."

Olivia takes a moment to get her emotions back under control before responding. "Sure thing, Sissy. I love you too. Can we come by and see you soon?"

"Of course. Let me just get things sorted out first with the police. I don't want you bringing the kids by until this guy is caught. I don't want him seeing them if he's still stalking me. I have to go now, please hug the kids for me." With that we disconnect, and I pull up the email app to see if Cassidy's sister responded. Right at the top of the list is an email from S. Grainger.

"I got your email regarding my sister's case. You said you might have some information that might be of use. I'm still in town and can meet. When and where is good for you?" -Stacy

I read the short email two more times; Caleb stands next to me reading over my shoulder.

"Are you going to meet up with her?" He asks me.

"I have to. After everything that happened with Drew, I have to find out what she knows about her sister's relationship with him and what he was like back then. Maybe we can connect the dots enough that the police can nail him for Cassidy's disappearance too." Caleb nods in understanding.

"See if she can meet tonight. Maybe you should both go to the police tomorrow once you talk." I nod my head in agreement.

"That's a good idea." I shoot off another email to her asking if she can meet us at the Starlight Diner at 5pm. It's still early enough in the day that I hope she will see my email and respond.

I don't have to wait long. Five minutes later my phone chimes with an email notification. It's Stacy again, agreeing to meet with Caleb and me tonight. Once that is done, I realize my hands are shaking again, this time with nerves. I can't believe my experience might help lead to the resolution in a near decade old cold case. If anything good can come from being kidnapped and raped by Drew, it will be providing closure to Stacy about what may have happened to her sister.

THIRTY-TWO

ELOISE

At a quarter 'til five, Caleb and I are waiting in a booth at the Starlight Diner. A waitress approaches to take our order but we wave her off until Stacy arrives. Neither of us have much of an appetite at the moment with the heaviness of the conversation we are about to have weighing us down. Just before 5, a woman close to our age walks into the diner. She has long brown hair, and a face so similar to her sister's there is no mistaking who she is. She stops at the door and takes a moment to scan the diner looking for us. I wave her over to our booth and she approaches with equal parts trepidation and hope crossing her features. Stacy slides into the seat across from us and Caleb and I offer our hands in introduction.

"Thank you for meeting with us, Stacy. I'm Eloise and this is my husband, Caleb." Stacy shakes our hands and gives us a quick once over, curiosity written all over her face as she takes us in.

"You said you might have some information about my sister's case?" Stacy gets straight to the point. I can't say that I blame her. I'm sure she's had a lot of false leads that have led nowhere over the years, so she probably isn't in the mood for pleasantries.

"I might...what do you know about your sister's relationship with Andrew Jameson?" Stacy sucks in a sharp breath at the mention of Drew's name.

"I know he was obsessed with her. They met at B.F.U. and dated for two years, but things were rocky during the last few months before she disappeared. They kept breaking up and getting back together. It was volatile and I told her to stop taking him back, but she was convinced she loved him, so every time he came back and apologized, she would take him back." Stacy rolls her eyes and snorts out a bitter huff.

"Why did they keep breaking up?" I ask, my spine stiffening at hearing how toxic Drew and Cassidy's relationship was.

"Drew was jealous. Cassidy was in a sorority and in a lot of clubs. She was super popular and was a party girl. Drew didn't want her going to frat parties and kept her on a tight leash, so sometimes she'd get smart and get tired of his bullshit and she'd break up with him. Then he'd come around and sweet talk her and they would get back together." Stacy narrows her eyes at me. "Why are you asking about her relationship with Drew?"

I glance at Caleb, and he grabs my hand under the table to give it a reassuring squeeze. "Let's just say I've had a run in with him. I saw there was a police report filed on him for a domestic disturbance when he was with Cassidy. What was that about?"

Just then the waitress returns to take our orders. We each order a coffee and skip the food for now. Stacy studies me for a moment before she answers my question.

"Cassie was out at a party one night, drunk off her ass. One of Drew's friends shared a live video of her grinding up on some frat bro online and Drew saw it. He showed up at the party and got in a fight with that guy and drug Cassie out of the party with her screaming like a banshee about him never letting her live her life. Someone called the cops, and they showed up and took Drew in. Somehow, he convinced Cassie to come out to the station to tell the cops it was a big misunderstanding and they let him go. Two weeks later on her way home from another party Cassie went missing." Silent tears stream down Stacy's cheeks as she focuses on her coffee mug.

"He was never a suspect in her disappearance?" I ask, my hands wrapped around my own coffee mug to keep them from shaking. Stacy shakes her head.

"No, supposedly he had an alibi for that night, and he wasn't at the party." Stacy looks up again and meets my gaze. "Why are you asking about Drew?"

I take in a deep breath, preparing myself to share my story. "Drew recently became obsessed with me. He stalked me, drugged me, blackmailed me, and ultimately kidnapped and raped me. If he is capable of doing those things to me, I have to believe he had something to do with your sister's disappearance." Surprisingly I don't start crying again at my admission of what I just went through. Caleb's warm hand on my thigh gives me a gentle squeeze reminding me that he's right here with me. Stacy's mouth drops open in shock as she takes in my words.

"Where is he now? Is he in jail? How did you get away?" Her questions come out in an excited rush. Clearly, she thinks I got away and Drew is in jail now. I hate that I'm going to burst her bubble.

"Caleb found me. He found Drew's cabin up on the mountain and rescued me. Unfortunately, while he was busy helping me out of the basement where I was being held, Drew got away. We don't know where he is right now. He's out there, still on the loose. The cops searched his property but he's not there."

"Oh my god..." Stacy's skin takes on a slightly greenish tinge like she's going to be sick. She closes her eyes and buries her face in her hands, her shoulders shaking with silent tears. "I fucking knew it...I knew he was bad. I never could prove it. He never left bruises on Cassie, but he manipulated her so much she almost couldn't make a decision on her own. It was so bad there at the end she barely even talked to me because he had her convinced I was trying to break them up." Stacy looks back up at me and I reach across and take her hand in mine.

"That's his M.O. He's a master at gaslighting, manipulation, and isolation. He threatened to tell Caleb I was cheating on him, even though Drew was the one forcing himself on me. He was so persuasive he had me convinced that there was no way Caleb would believe that none of it was consensual. He even called my work and tried to get me fired. He was trying to isolate me away from my friends and family. Sounds like he did that with Cassidy too."

"I'm so sorry you had to experience that." Stacy and I just sit for a moment, letting our mutual trauma wash over us. Caleb speaks up finally for the first time.

"Lo is going to the police tomorrow to make a formal statement. We thought maybe if your sister's experience with Drew was similar that maybe this new information coming to light might be enough to get Cassidy's case reopened." Stacy nods her head excitedly.

"It's got to be, right? There's no way they wouldn't reopen her case. This has to be enough to take another look at him."

"That's what we are hoping for. We want to nail his ass to the wall, not only for what he did to Eloise but for what he did to your sister as well." Caleb responds, his tone firm and determined, like he's not planning on settling for anything less than Drew spending the rest of his natural life in prison.

We spend the next half hour filling in gaps for each other on what we know about Drew's pattern. We exchange numbers and agree to let Stacy know once I'm done making my statement to the police. I plan on telling them what I know about Cassidy and that Drew made references to her when I was with him, hoping it will spur them into action on her case.

"But what if they don't find him?" Stacy bites her bottom lip, worry etched across her face.

"I don't think he's going to be able to stay away. He doesn't seem like the kind of guy that leaves unfinished business," I say solemnly, knowing in my soul that he isn't done with me yet. That kind of obsession doesn't just disappear overnight and there is no way Drew is just going to walk away from what he thinks we have. "If I have to play bait to get him to show himself, I will. I will not allow what happened to me or Cassidy to happen to another woman." I surprise myself with the amount of steel in my voice and by how much I mean what I say. I will dangle myself like a worm on a hook if that's what it takes to lure Drew out of hiding.

Caleb jerks in surprise next to me. "The fuck you will, Lo. We are going to let the police handle this."

"Caleb is right, you can't put yourself in danger again. He will mess up and the police will get him." Stacy grabs my hand and gives it another squeeze. I'm not sure I believe her considering how long her sister's case has gone unsolved and how thorough Drew was in his manipulation with me. I don't argue though. I just nod my head and let them think they win this argument, knowing deep in my soul I will do anything to make sure he doesn't hurt another person the way he hurt me.

It's the next day, Caleb and I are leaving the police station after giving our statement about what happened with Drew at the cabin. There still hasn't been any sign of him since he disappeared while Caleb was rescuing me. The longer he goes without being found, the more on edge I get. I don't know if I'm more afraid of him turning back up or going somewhere else and starting all over with some other woman.

When I mentioned what I knew about his relationship with his previous girlfriend, how he acted strangely about her with me, and her disappearance, the detective I was speaking to said he would encourage the cold case unit to investigate it. He hedged my expectations about anything coming of it, saying everything is circumstantial so far, so he couldn't promise what happened to me could lead to Drew being linked to her case. I can't say I'm not disappointed, but I half expect a response along those lines.

"Do you want to go get some lunch?" Caleb asks me as he links his fingers with mine as we walk to our car. He's been doing his best to encourage me to eat since coming back home. I think he feels frustrated and helpless that he hasn't been able to help in a tangible way so feeding me is the next best option. My appetite hasn't fully returned since waking up drugged and nauseous after my rape, but I nod my head and give Caleb a smile that doesn't reach my eyes.

"Sure babe. Where were you thinking?"

"How about that Vietnamese place with the really good Pho? It's on this end of town and I know you love their spring rolls." He's not wrong, I do love that place. Pho seems like it would be easy enough to stomach so I nod and let him lead me down the block and around the corner. The restaurant is a short walk from the police station, and it gives us a chance to take in the gorgeous summer weather and pretend we are a normal couple out on a normal lunch date during the week.

When we are almost to the restaurant, a noise in the alley we are walking by catches my attention. I stop suddenly and look down the alleyway and see a tall man leaning over a much more petite woman, his arms caging her body against the brick wall. My body tenses as the memory of Drew having me in the same position slams into me. My breathing grows shallow as goosebumps break out all over my body. Caleb stops walking and turns to see what has me so anxious. He peers down the alley, following my line of sight, his hand tightening around my own. He can see the panic attack threatening to take over, so he turns me away from the couple and forces me to look him in the eye.

"Lo, it's ok. She's fine. It's just a couple having a private moment. She's laughing. Can you hear her laughter?" He cups my face in both of his hands and his steady gaze holding my own helps calm the overwhelming sound of my heartbeat enough that I can hear the woman's laughter. I close my eyes and take in a few deep breaths, trying to will my racing heart to calm down. "Stay with me, Lo. You're here with me. He's not here and he can't get you." Caleb presses his forehead against mine and we stand like that, blocking the sidewalk for God knows how long, parting the workday lunch crowd milling around us like the Red Sea.

"I'm fine...I'm ok." I give my head a quick shake and pull away. Caleb gives me a wan smile before pressing a kiss to my forehead and tucking me under his arm. Once we are seated at a table waiting for our lunch, Caleb grabs my hand and clears his throat.

"Um...have you thought about maybe seeing someone about what happened? Like, a therapist? Or talking to someone at one of those crisis centers? Or maybe calling the sexual assault hotline?" I can tell Caleb is nervous about bringing up this topic. We haven't spoken about my assault other than what he heard me recount to the police. I think he's afraid that bringing it up will send me into a spiral, and I'm not entirely sure that it won't. I've been doing my best to wall off the memory of Drew's touch and how my body responded to him even when it felt all wrong. I take a sip of my ice water, trying to buy some time before responding.

"Lo, I'm just saying, I think you need to talk to someone. You don't have to go through this alone. If you want to talk to me, you can. I'm here. I'll always be here for you. But I think maybe you should see a professional to work through your trauma." Just then the waitress reappears with our food order and it feels like there is a lead weight sitting in my stomach now. I don't think I can stomach anything to eat with the reminder of what Drew did to me now in the forefront of my mind.

"I...I will. I know I need to talk to someone. I'm just not ready to relive what happened just yet." I don't look at Caleb when I speak, instead grabbing my spoon and stirring my pho around in the bowl. I take a small sip of my soup, but the normally flavorful broth tastes like nothing. Disappointed, I set my spoon to the side and bury my face in my hands as I fight back the urge to cry.

"Hey, hey...Don't cry. It's ok. You can go when you're ready. I just want you to be ok, Sweetness."

A soul crushing weight falls over me as I think about how I don't deserve him or his patience or goodness. I put myself in that situation because I didn't have enough faith in my husband or his love for me. A wave of nausea rolls over me and I leave the table abruptly to find the bathroom. I barely make it to the toilet in time before getting sick.

Hovering over the toilet with tears streaming down my face and bile in my throat, I feel like I haven't even left the cabin at all. I can still feel Drew's touch on my body and the rough burn of his stubble on my neck. It's then I know Caleb is right; I am going to have to talk to someone if I have any hope of getting through this.

THIRTY-THREE

CALEB

A WEEK PASSES WITHOUT ANY SIGN OF DREW OR BREAKS IN THE case. We've kept in touch with Stacy but unfortunately the updates have been sparse. Eloise has been withdrawing more as time passes. The strength she possessed when she first came home has waned and the trauma from her experience has settled in. She spends a lot of time in bed and has closed herself off from me. I've looked into rape counselors and therapists in the area but unfortunately with this being a college town with a fairly large frat population the sexual assault specialists stay booked out.

I know she's blaming herself for what happened and no amount of reassuring from my end will make her see she isn't at fault. I blame myself for not manning up a long time ago and finding a way to be home with her instead of letting Harold run me all over the country. I'm getting ready to go upstairs to see if Eloise is hungry when my phone rings. I pause my ascent and take a look at the caller ID. I see that it's Officer Roberts' number.

"Hey, this is Caleb. Do you have any news?" I turn around and go back down the stairs and towards the back of the house, so Eloise doesn't overhear. I don't want her to be disappointed if there isn't any news.

Officer Roberts hesitates before she responds. "Well, yes. We're going to need you to come into the station for some questioning."

"Questioning? We gave our statements days ago." I run my free hand through my hair as I pace through the kitchen.

"Well, yes, but Mr. Jameson has turned up and he's pressing charges against you for battery, breaking and entering so we are going to need you to come to the station willingly so we can talk, or we will have to come pick you up."

"ARE YOU FUCKING KIDDING ME?" I shout into the phone, before realizing Eloise might hear me. I lower my voice again. "He kidnapped my wife! He had her tied up in a fucking basement!"

"He also claims it was a consensual sexual fantasy they were acting out. He has...some compelling video evidence." Roberts' voice sounds strained, like she's not entirely buying this bullshit either.

"There's no fucking way any of that was consensual!" I grip the phone so tightly I'm sure I'm close to cracking the screen. My heart is racing and I'm fighting the urge to throw a punch at the closest hard surface.

"He went to the hospital in the next town over after you attacked him. He's been there most of the week recovering from the injuries he claims you gave him. He said you tried to kill him and he's very adamant about pressing charges. We need you to come in so we can talk. Mr. Fitzpatrick, please don't make me have to come pick you up in a squad car."

"If I go to the station, am I going to be allowed to come back home? There is no way I'm leaving Eloise alone with that animal on the loose." I can feel my chest tightening in panic at the thought of being separated from Eloise. That's got to be his angle. Get me away from her and possibly locked up so he can finish what he started.

"I can't make any promises, but I will do my best to make sure you get to go home. I don't like this anymore than you do, but I'm being overruled on this." A small sliver of relief threads its way into my chest knowing I've got Officer Roberts on my side.

"Let me call a lawyer, I'll be there as soon as I can." I say, resigned to doing this. I don't want them to come pick me up and make it harder to get back home. We hang up and when I look up, Eloise is standing at the kitchen doorway looking at me like her world is crumbling all around her.

"Why do you need to call a lawyer, Cal? Where are you going?" She grips the door frame like it's the only thing keeping her upright. I hesitate for a long moment debating on how much to tell her. Do I worry her with this nonsense and cause her to freak out more? Do I tell her so she can be prepared for the possibility I might not be coming home? "Caleb, talk to me. What is going on?" She snaps out, her voice wavering as she fights to keep calm.

"I need to go to the police station to answer some more questions. Drew has turned up and is telling a different version of the story and they just need me to come in and answer some questions." I try to keep my voice light, like this is no big deal. I don't want her to panic about anything, she's already been through so much already. "I should only be gone an hour or two. Do you want me to call Sara to come over and stay with you while I'm gone?"

"He turned up? He went to the police and he's not the one in jail right now? What the fuck is happening Caleb?" Eloise's voice is shrill as she shrieks in indignation.

"That's what I intend on finding out. Believe me, I'm going to do what I can to make sure his ass gets thrown behind bars. Lo, I've got this. I'm going to get it sorted."

I stride over to Eloise and wrap her up in my arms and kiss the top of her head. She freezes in my embrace momentarily like she always does now, before thawing and letting her body melt against mine. I hate that what Drew has done to her has fucked up our intimacy, but I'll be as patient as I need to be with her. "I've got this, Sweetness. I'll be back soon. Do you want Sara to come over?"

Eloise shakes her head. "I'm pretty sure she and Derrick went out of town for their anniversary this weekend. Just go, I'll be fine. There is still an officer stationed outside."

"I dunno, Lo...I don't like it. You shouldn't be alone." I don't say it, but I also don't want to take her in case he is at the station. I don't want him seeing her or vice versa. I'm not sure what seeing him will do to her at this stage of things and I don't want to risk pushing her further into her depression.

"Cal, you can't babysit me forever. You'll have to leave the house eventually. I'll be fine. I've got pepper spray and a stun gun. I'll lock myself in the bedroom until you get back. Have Harold call his brother, I'm pretty sure he's a good criminal attorney. He should be able to help you. It's not like Harold doesn't owe you."

I nod. "Good idea, babe. I'll call him. Look, I'll be back as soon as I can. Please don't leave this house." I kiss her softly on the lips, for the first time since the night we came home. I hesitate for a moment before deepening the kiss and her mouth parts, letting my tongue enter. I can't walk away from her without knowing when I'll get to come home without tasting her one last time. My tongue sweeps into her mouth and she lets me taste and lick inside her mouth like she's ready to be devoured.

I run my hands through her hair until my hands are grasping the back of her head and I angle our mouths so I can delve deeper into this kiss. Her hands that were pressed flat against my chest are now gripping my t-shirt like she's afraid I'll float away if she lets go. I turn us so her back is against the door frame, and I push against her body so she can feel how desperate I am to touch her again. She arches her back and presses her body more firmly against mine and my heart soars at the thought that she may be ready to be touched by me again.

"Fuck, Lo. Hold that thought baby. I've gotta get going." I pull away panting, desperately wishing I could just stay here and bury myself in my wife.

"Just think of it as an incentive to hurry back. Come back to me Caleb." I nod and press one more kiss against her swollen, puffy lips.

"You know I will. Stay inside, I'll be back soon, Sweetness."

When I get to the station, Jerry, Harold's brother, is there waiting to meet me. I called him on my way over, having already had him on retainer in case we needed a lawyer for this whole Drew mess. I just hadn't expected to use him for my own defense. "Hey Jer, thanks for meeting me here on short notice." I shake his hand and follow him into the station.

"No problem, Cal. If everything happened the way you said it did, we shouldn't have to be here long. It's a pretty clear-cut case of self-defense. I'm not sure what this asshole thinks he's trying to pull." Jerry is a lot more brash and foul-mouthed than his older brother Harold. He's a pit bull in a courtroom while Harold is a complete golden retriever in a boardroom. I'm glad he's got my back going into this.

"Listen, don't answer any questions without my go ahead. I don't want you accidentally stepping into some sort of trap that will make it easier for the cops to drop your case against this fuckhead. You're not in the wrong and we are not going to let this injustice stand. Let me do the talking." Jerry claps his huge hand on my back and pushes through the entrance to the police station like he owns the place. I imagine he spends a lot of time here so he's infinitely more comfortable here than I am. Jerry handles talking to the officer working the front desk and she pages someone to come get us. Instead of seeing Officer Roberts like I expected, Officer Randall and another man come around the corner to collect us.

"Mr. Fitzpatrick, Mr. Jones, this way please." Randall directs us to a small interrogation room. I don't like this, and I feel the hairs on the back of my neck stand up at how different the vibes are this time around.

"Randall, is this really necessary? You know full well my client was acting in defense of his wife who was assaulted by that monster." Jerry immediately jumps into pit bull mode.

"According to the story told to us by Mr. Jameson, your client showed up at his private residence in a jealous rage and attacked Mr. Jameson because Mrs. Fitzpatrick had left him. Mr. Jameson states everything that happened between him, and Mrs. Fitzpatrick was 100% consensual and he had video evidence to back it up."

I can't hold my tongue any longer. "What video evidence? What the fuck are you talking about?" I slap the table with my hands. Jerry grabs my shoulder and gives it a warning squeeze.

"What my client is trying to say is, what video evidence could you possibly have?"

"Video evidence of his wife willingly climbing into Mr. Jameson's lap and making out with him and letting him carry her up to his bed? Video evidence of a consensual sexual encounter between two adults, one of whom might be having some buyer's remorse?"

"She was drugged!" I leap out of my chair and Jerry immediately shoves me back down.

"Allegedly. The labs from her exam at the hospital didn't show any drugs in her system."

"Bullshit! What about the bruises? The fact that she was tied up in the basement?" Rage is coursing through me right now. I'm not entirely sure I will be able to make it back home tonight. The urge to punch Officer Randall in the face is almost overwhelming.

"Like I said, he alleges it was a consensual sexual fantasy they were playing out that got disrupted when you showed up." Randall's voice is tired and annoyed like he's explaining why the sky is blue to a child.

"If that's the case, why did he have her hidden away when Officer Roberts and Officer Clinton showed up to search the premises? Why wouldn't he explain what was going on when they were there?" Jerry leans forward, resting his elbows on the cold metal table, leveling a no bullshit glare at the police officer. Officer Randall shifts uncomfortably, knowing Jerry has a point with his questions.

"Like I said, he's got video of them, and everything looks like it's consensual. She even initiates the encounter. There's also footage of Caleb showing up and tasing Mr. Jameson before brutally beating him without even talking to him first." Sensing my impending outburst, Jerry cuts a glare my way and places a hand on my forearm, warning me to keep my mouth shut. I bite my tongue so hard the taste of copper fills my mouth. Fuck.

"Is there audio to go along with this video?" Jerry asks.

"No, only video. Just a few basic home security cameras set up, but they aren't wired for sound."

"Well, that's awfully fucking convenient." I mutter under my breath.

"Do you know what you did to Mr. Jameson? You gave him a concussion, fractured his orbital socket, knocked out two teeth and fractured several ribs that resulted in a punctured lung. He spent five days in the hospital after crawling away from your assault and getting help.

Before I can say I wish I had killed him, Jerry interjects. "He was acting in defense of his wife who he had reported missing."

"Did his wife call him, asking for help? Did she or did she not leave under her own power saying she needed some time apart? According to Mr. Jameson, they had been carrying on an affair for a couple of weeks and Caleb found out about it and acted out in a jealous rage. They even saw one of Mrs. Fitzpatrick's friends that afternoon before going to the cabin and she never said anything about needing any help. The waitress that served them at the coffee shop even gave a statement about seeing them together and how cozy they looked."

Red clouds my vision as rage takes over. This fucker is still manipulating and gas lighting to get his way. "She doesn't want to be with him! If she did, why was she terrified and crying when I found her?" It's taking every ounce of self-control that I possess to not completely lose my shit on the officer sitting across from me.

"Maybe she was scared of your reaction? You do seem to have quite the temper on you. Have you ever hurt your wife before?" Officer Randall stares at me placidly like he didn't just utter the most ridiculous question I've ever heard. My mouth drops open in shock, and I am unable to form a coherent thought that isn't just full on screaming at a police officer.

"Look, are you charging my client with anything or not? We are done here if not. This is ridiculous and we will not humor this line of thinking."

Officer Randall lets out a humorless laugh. "Oh, we are far from done here, Mr. Jones. You better settle in and get comfortable because this fucker isn't leaving until I'm satisfied with his story."

My heart drops when I realize there is a slim chance I'm going to be walking out of his police station tonight and not spending the night behind bars.

THIRTY-FOUR

CALEB HAS BEEN GONE FOR NEARLY TWO HOURS. I'VE SPENT THAT entire time pacing around my bedroom chewing my fingernails down to the quick. The fact that Drew is out there and not behind bars has my stomach in knots. I know how manipulative he is. I know what he is capable of. I'm terrified that he's managed to come up with a way to twist things to make it look like he's the innocent party.

A sudden, overwhelming desire to break shit comes over me and I pick up the closest thing to me and hurl it across the room. The lamp crashes against the wall with a satisfying smash. It doesn't relieve the anxiety building in my chest, so I try again, throwing several hardback books sitting on the nightstand. They land against the wall with a series of unsatisfying, dull thuds before falling to the floor, covers askew and spines dented.

"FUCK!" I scream before flopping onto the bed. I'm so angry. I've spent the entire week in a fog, trying to pull myself out of the hole of self-deprecation and blame I'd been buried in and now I can feel rage taking over as the primary emotion. Caleb getting dragged into this shit-storm and possibly becoming a victim of Drew's manipulations was the trigger I needed to shake off the overwhelming weight of guilt and blame I had placed on myself.

The sound of something falling downstairs has me sitting straight up again, my heart pounding in my chest. I glance at the clock. Caleb has been gone for a while; is he home already? I jump up and run out of the bedroom to go see him and ask how things went. Surely if he's back already then things must've gone ok. "Cal? Is that you? Did you get it all cleared up?" I call down the stairs as I rush down to meet him. There is no answer. "Caleb? You in the kitchen?"

I make my way through the living room to the kitchen in search of him. Just as I pass through the doorway a hard body grabs me from behind and a large tattooed hand clamps over my mouth and nose. In front of me the window overlooking the backyard is shoved open and the vase that had been sitting on the ledge is knocked over, spilling the brightly colored bouquet of flowers across the floor.

"Hey there, darlin'. Miss me?" Drew's gravelly voice rasps in my ear as he jerks me against his body, immobilizing me. I try to kick my legs back to get at him, but he spins us around and smashes my front against the wall while pressing his body more securely against mine. He shoves one of his legs between mine, making it impossible for me to kick him or shove off the wall. The hand he has covering my mouth snakes down and wraps around my throat, effectively cutting off my oxygen supply.

"Eloise, your husband interrupted us before I was done with you. I don't appreciate being interrupted. Now he's really going to pay for not letting you go." Drew is practically growling in my ear right now.

My lungs are screaming for oxygen and the only mantra running through my mind is, *"No, no, no, no, no, not again."* Over and over. I can't let him take me out of this house again. There's no way I'm getting out of his clutches alive a second time. A whimper escapes my lips as I try to squirm out of his hold. My vision is starting to go black around the edges and I know I only have seconds before I pass out from lack of oxygen.

"Are you going to be a good girl for me, darlin'? Or are we going to have to do this the hard way?" I try to nod, hoping he will ease up and let me breathe again if he thinks I'm agreeable. My chances of escape aren't great either way, but if he makes me go unconscious then they go down to zero. The grip he has on my throat lessens just enough for me to take in a desperate gasp of breath.

"Please..." I try to choke out a plea, but his grip tightens again.

"I didn't say you could talk, darlin'." Drew's voice is filled with venom as he jerks me away from the wall and walks me through the house and forces me to go up the stairs. He's not taking me out of the house. That's good, right? Or is it bad because I don't have a chance to signal for help outside? *Shit...shit...shit.* My mind is reeling from panic right now and I'm close to hyperventilating.

He finds our bedroom with ease and pushes me into it, kicking the door shut behind him. He shoves me across the room, and I crash land on the bed. The sound of his belt getting dragged through the belt loops of his jeans pulls me from my panic enough to get me to scramble across the bed and fall to the floor on the other side, keeping the large piece of furniture between us.

My heart catches in my throat when I take in his appearance. His face is a riot of colors from the beating Caleb gave him at the cabin. One eye is still mostly swollen shut and there are cuts along his eyebrow and his nose looks like it was broken. The look on his face is nothing short of rage. He is pissed at Caleb, and he is fully intending on taking it out on me.

"Darlin', I'm sorry, but this is going to hurt." Drew wraps his belt around his fist as he stalks towards me. I scramble backward until my back hits the wall and my hand lands on a pile of broken glass from the lamp I threw earlier. I hiss in pain as a shard stabs into my palm. I glance to the side and see a decently long shard of glass just inches from my hand. If I can get close enough to him I can stab him with it.

"Get the fuck away from me, you goddamn psycho! You're a fucking lunatic!" I spit at him, lunging forward enough to palm the broken glass. Drew reaches down and grabs me by my hair and yanks me off the ground. He loops the belt around my throat but before he has a chance to fully cinch it tight, I swing my arm up and drive the glass shard straight into the muscle where his shoulder meets his neck.

"FUUUUUUCCCCK!" He roars, his grip on my hair loosening, allowing me to fall to the floor again. I waste no time and scramble to my feet and run towards the door. I don't know where my phone is, and the pepper spray is in the bedroom. I'm desperate to get space between us so I run down the stairs in a flash. If I can make it to the hall table by the door, I can get the gun Caleb has taken to storing there for protection. Just as I'm about to reach the bottom of the stairs, my foot slips and I slide down the last 3 steps with my left leg catching underneath me. I feel and hear a pop in my left knee as I hit the floor and a pained scream tears out of my throat. My vision goes black momentarily as agony rips through my knee.

"Shitshitshitshit..." I chant, trying to breathe through the pain. Just then a loud thump at the top of the stairs draws my attention and I see Drew leaning against the wall, blood pouring from the wound I inflicted. The fury written across his face is terrifying and I know I can't let him get his hands on me again. I try to stand but my leg won't bear any weight now.

I frantically use my good leg to drag myself across the floor to the table where the gun is hidden. I should go for the front door, but the lock is higher than I can reach now without being able to stand, and I'm not sure if the rookie they put on duty to watch our house is even out there paying attention since Drew managed to get in, in the first place.

Just as my fingers graze the drawer pull on the table, I feel a hard yank as Drew grabs the end of the belt still looped around my neck. My finger catches the drawer pull and I manage to pull the drawer free from the table and it clatters to the ground inches away from my reach. My hands grasp at the belt loop around my neck, now cinched tight, frantically clawing at it, trying to make space between the belt and my skin. I feel blood vessels burst in my eyes as my air is choked off again. Drew tugs me against his body and I feel the hot, sticky, moistness of his blood soak into my shirt.

"Darlin', you are going to regret that. I was really hoping we could do this the easy way. By the time I'm done with you, your fucking twat of a husband isn't going to be able to recognize you to identify your body." I reach back with my right hand, desperate to inflict any sort of damage on him and rake my nails down his face. I feel them scratch across his bruised and swollen eye and I dig in, trying to blind him or distract him enough to loosen his grip.

"FUCK!" His pained shout in my ear nearly deafens me but he releases his hold on the belt loop, and I collapse back on the floor again. The belt slackens enough that I can breathe again, and I crawl across the floor with my eye on the drawer holding my only hope for survival.

Just as I dive for the gun, Drew grabs my left foot and yanks me back towards him. Excruciating pain shoots through my left leg as the throb in my knee intensifies to a near blackout level of agony. By some miracle I manage to grab the gun, and as he tugs me back to him, I roll onto my back and squeeze the trigger. My aim goes wide with the first shot, and it hits the wall behind him. Drew rocks back on his heels, letting go of my leg. Shock is written all across his face when he realizes I have a gun.

My ears are ringing from the shot fired and my hands are trembling uncontrollably. I know my aim is going to be shit but I have to hope just me holding the gun on him will be enough to keep him at bay. I pray one of the neighbors or the officer outside heard the gunshot. "Back the fuck up or the next one goes into your gut."

Drew tilts his head as he takes in our new dynamic. Aside from the initial shock of the first gunshot, he doesn't seem to be intimidated by me. Why would he be? I'm shaking like a leaf and on the verge of completely losing my shit in a panic attack. A shit eating grin slowly spreads across his face as he raises his hands in a placating manner. He knows I'm terrified of him, and he presses his advantage.

"You really think you have what it takes to kill me, darlin'? I don't think so..." He stalks forward, forcing me to awkwardly scoot back while holding the gun on him.

"I said, back up! I'm not asking again!" My voice cracks and it hurts to talk after nearly being choked to death. I still feel like I'm suffocating with the belt loop around my neck, but I don't dare take either hand off the gun while I have it trained on Drew.

"Darlin', you might as well put that down before you hurt yourself with it." Drew's voice drips with patronizing insincerity as he takes another step forward. If he gets any closer, he will be able to reach out and snatch the gun from my hands.

"FUCK YOU!" I shout as I take a deep breath and squeeze the trigger again. This time the shot hits him in the bicep, and he roars with pain.

"YOU LITTLE BITCH!" He dives on top of me and back-hands me with his uninjured arm. Stars explode across my vision, but I don't let go of the gun. It's trapped between our bodies now as he presses down on me, completely covering me with his muscular bulk. Blood pours from the wound on his arm as he presses his forearm against my neck, once again cutting off my ability to breath. What is it with this fuckface and his choking fetish? I feel his other arm snake between us, trying to fish out the gun.

My only thought at this moment is that I can't let go. I can't lose this gun or it's all over. I keep a death grip on the handle of the gun but relax the muscles in my arm so he can more easily drag my arm free from between us. Just when the hand holding the gun slips free and I feel the weapon angle upwards, I squeeze the trigger again. There is no missing this time. The barrel is pressed directly against Drew's ribs, part of it still wedged between our bodies. I feel the blast of heat from the shot and then a gush of warm stickiness as more blood pours from the wound.

Drew lets out a garbled cry of pain as he slumps

forward, completely covering me with his limp body. His heavy body is crushing me and I'm not sure I'll be able to shove him off me. I can still feel the faint beat of his heart with his chest pressed against mine. I don't know if the wound will be fatal, but I need to get free of him if it's not. Just then a loud pounding at the front door grabs my attention.

"Mrs. Fitzpatrick? Is everything ok in there? It sounds like shots were fired." The rookie officer stationed across the street must have heard the gunshots. Thank fuck. "Help me!" I scream out, hoping he doesn't need more incentive to force his way in.

"Stand away from the door if you're near it! I'm going to kick it open!" Three swift kicks later and the young officer clambers though the busted front door with his weapon drawn. His face goes white with shock when he sees the carnage in the house and our bodies tangled up on the floor.

"Please get him off me! Help me!" Just before the officer reaches us, I feel Drew's arm that was fighting me for control of the gun shift. His hand grasps the handle, tilting the gun down this time and his large finger crushes mine as he pulls the trigger. It feels like I'm being ripped apart when the bullet slams into my gut. The last thing I hear before passing out from the excruciating pain is another shot being fired. Then my world goes black.

THIRTY-FIVE

CALEB

We are going on hour three of this bullshit interrogation when a knock at the door interrupts the stare off between Officer Randall and myself. He keeps trying to goad me into watching the footage of my wife being raped by that monster, and I keep refusing to watch. He's trying to incite some sort of reaction out of me that he can use to keep me here, but I am refusing to play into his game. Jerry's calming presence is damn near the only thing keeping me from leaping across this table and assaulting a police officer. That and the thought of Eloise being alone if I get thrown behind bars.

"We aren't finished here yet." Officer Randall threatens as he stands to go speak to whoever is at the door. Just before he slips out, I hear a feminine voice say, "There's been an incident, sir.".

My head snaps towards Jerry, his eyebrows raised like he heard the same thing I did. "Jer, I need to get out of here. I swear to God, if something happened to Eloise, I won't be held responsible for my actions." Jerry nods and walks over to the door. Just as he's getting ready to knock to get the officer's attention the door opens, and Officer Roberts comes in.

Her mouth is set in a grim line, and her eyes shine with worry. I jump out of my seat, instinctively knowing if she's here to deliver some news, it's going to be bad.

"Mr. Fitzpatrick–"

"What happened?" We speak at the same time.

She stares at me for a beat, and it feels like an eternity before she speaks again.

"There was an incident at your house. There's been a report of gunfire and two individuals have been taken to the local hospital." Her voice is somber and full of sorrow. She knows more than she's letting on right now.

"IS MY WIFE OK?" My knees feel weak, and I lean against the table to keep myself from collapsing to the floor. It feels like I can't get air into my lungs and my vision begins to blacken.

"She's been taken to B.F General. They've rushed her into emergency surgery."

"Can I go? I need to go be with my wife! You can't keep me here!" I'm nearly screaming, my chest constricting with the rising panic.

She nods. "You can go. I can escort you to the hospital to get you there quicker." I nod dumbly, as Jerry slaps his hand on my shoulder.

"You go, I'll stay here and make sure we don't have to

come back and deal with this fuckery. I'll catch up to you at the hospital. Do you want me to call anyone for you?"

"Olivia. Call her sister." I rasp out as I begin to follow Officer Roberts out of the interrogation room.

As we walk down the hallway, I see Officer Randall standing off to the side, talking to his silent partner that had been present during my questioning. I see red and lunge out, shoving him against the wall. Pressing my forearm against his windpipe, I spit into his face. "I swear to fuck, if my wife dies because of your fucking bullshit interrogation, she won't be the only one. I will fucking kill you." Surprisingly Officer Randall doesn't react to my threat, he simply nods in acknowledgement, and I let Officer Roberts pull me away from him.

"Come on, Caleb. We need to get to the hospital." Her use of my first name lets me know right now, she isn't just Officer Roberts. She's just a good person, trying to make sure I make it to my wife before it's too late. She grabs my arm and leads me through the station at a brisk pace and outside to her squad car. She flips on her lights, and we speed out of the parking lot, racing to B.F. General.

"What do you know? Please, tell me what happened."

"The officer stationed outside of your house heard several shots fired. When he went to investigate, he heard your wife call for help. When he kicked open the door he saw a large male intruder, laying on top of your wife. Before he could get to them, the male moved and managed to fire the gun one more time. That bullet struck your wife in her abdomen. Officer Thomas then fired again at the male, subduing him and called for assistance.

"It was Drew." It's not a question, it's a statement. I know it was him. She nods without taking her eyes off the road. "Is he dead?"

"I'm unaware of his current status." We ride in silence for the rest of the trip to the hospital. My mind is racing with all the potential outcomes of Eloise's surgery. When she pulls up in front of the Emergency Room entrance I jump out of the car before she even has it in park. I'm through the doors in a rush, desperate to find someone to give me an update on Eloise's condition. When I make it to the front desk, I hear my name called out. I turn and see Arianna, the nurse who took care of Eloise during her last visit, waving me over.

"How is she? Is she ok? Is she alive?" My words come out in a frantic, jumbled mess as I get close to Arianna. Officer Roberts joins us a moment later as Arianna takes me by the arm and guides me over to an empty exam room.

"She's in surgery right now. She came in with extensive injuries, including a gunshot to her abdomen, a dislocated knee with a torn ACL, multiple contusions, and injuries consistent with choking. She's a fighter though, Caleb. She's in good hands with Dr. Henley. He's one of our best trauma surgeons."

My knees finally give out on me, and I collapse on the ground, burying my face in my hands. The tears I had been fighting back the entire ride over finally break free, my heart cracking open at the agony Eloise must be experiencing. I hear Arianna and Officer Roberts talking in hushed whispers over me, but I can't make out what they are saying over the sound of my pulse pounding in my ears.

"Caleb, hey, I'm going to take you to the waiting room for the surgery wing." Arianna places her hand on my shoulder, pulling me from the dark spiral I was lost in.

"I'm going to see if I can get an update on what happened at your house, Caleb." Officer Roberts pats my shoulder before stepping out of the room and making her way back out front.

I let Arianna guide me to a waiting room deeper in the hospital. It has a few people waiting for updates on their own family members, none of them looking nearly as distraught as I am feeling right now. They cast concerned glances my way as Arianna leads me to a seat in the far corner away from prying eyes.

"Can I get you anything? Do you need me to call anyone?" She sits next to me, holding my hand in hers. Arianna's presence is so calming. She isn't caught in the frenzy of panic that I am lost in. This isn't the first trauma or distraught family member she's had to console, and it shows.

"My lawyer was supposed to call her sister, Olivia. Can you make sure she gets back here?"

Arianna nods, "Of course. Is there anyone else we need to call? Do you need anything? Something to drink?" I shake my head.

"Not yet...I want to know how she is first. How long has she been in surgery?"

"Not long. They brought her in about 40 minutes ago. They did a quick assessment in the E.D. then rushed her back for surgery. It'll be a while before we know anything." Arianna squeezes my hand and gives me a sympathetic smile.

We sit in silence, me staring at the clock on the wall, watching the seconds tick by. My whole body is tense and my jaw hurts from how hard I'm clenching. I feel like a spring wound way too tightly and I know I won't be able to relax until I get word that Eloise is ok. I zone out and lose track of time until a distraught cry brings my focus to the door of the waiting room. Olivia rushes towards me and I stand, wrapping her in a hug. We cling to each other, her tears soaking into my t-shirt.

"How is she, Cal? Is she ok? Is my baby sister still alive?" Olivia pulls back and looks up into my face, her eyes red rimmed and face puffy from crying.

"We haven't heard anything yet. She's still in surgery right now." Behind Olivia, I see Arianna stand up.

"I'll go see if I can get an update for you." She leaves, giving us privacy to grieve together.

"How did this happen? What happened?" Olivia and I sit down again, she takes my hand and looks at me imploringly, seeking answers. I tell her what little I know.

"I was at the police station being interrogated. Apparently Drew popped back up claiming I assaulted him, and he was trying to press charges against me. I guess his plan was just to separate me from Eloise so he could get to her again. Somehow, he got inside our house and attacked her. Eloise got my gun and shot him, but she's been hurt too." Bile rises in my throat, and I pause, trying to swallow back the urge to vomit, before continuing. "The officer stationed at our house heard gunshots and went in to investigate. Before he could get to her, Drew got the gun and shot Eloise."

Olivia lets out a choked gasp and covers her mouth with her hand. "Oh my god..." She bursts into fresh tears, and we huddle together, trying desperately to find comfort while we wait for an update. Eventually, Arianna returns with a grim look on her face. Olivia and I jump up simultaneously, our hands clasped together, waiting for the bad news.

"How is she?" Olivia gets the question out first. Her body tense next to mine, like she's bracing herself for impact.

"She's stable. There was quite a lot of damage they need to repair from the gunshot wound. The bullet missed a lot of the major organs, but it did nick her spleen. They're removing it now, and then will assess for any further damage. They will let her rest after this surgery and keep her in the hospital for a few days before going back in to take care of her knee. Her other injuries aren't life threatening, but he had choked her with a belt. We aren't sure of any damage to her vocal cords yet, she was unconscious when she was brought in. We will get an ENT specialist in to see her in the next day or two, to assess that damage."

"How long until they finish her surgery?" Olivia is taking control now, asking the important questions while I stare mutely at Arianna, feeling like my entire world has been knocked off its axis.

"Probably another two or three hours. Maybe you two should go to the cafeteria to get something to eat and drink. It will be a while before we hear anything else, but I'll stay close by, waiting for updates." I look up and really take in Arianna's appearance. She looks tired and haggard, like she's at the end of a long day.

"Don't you have other patients to take care of?" I ask, silently giving her permission to go back to her actual job.

"Eloise came in at the end of my shift. I was on my way out when I saw her get wheeled in on a stretcher. I remembered everything she told me from her last visit, and I knew I had to stay to wait for you. I'm not going anywhere until I know she's ok."

Olivia lets go of me and wraps the nurse up in her arms in a warm embrace. "You are truly an angel." Arianna smiles as she returns Olivia's hug.

"You two go eat. I'll come find you if I hear anything." Arianna moves to the side and motions for Olivia and me to go. "The cafeteria is on the 2nd floor. It should still be open for dinner for another hour or so." I give her a tight nod and we make our way out of the waiting area and up to the cafeteria.

When we get to the canteen, we both grab some coffee

and a couple of sandwiches but when we sit neither of us make a move to eat them. "Caleb, tell me what the fuck has been going on? Eloise has been radio silent since the last time we spoke, and I've been out of my mind with worry. All I know is you reported her missing and some dickbag kidnapped her and now she's in the hospital after being shot! Tell me the truth, I deserve to know what is going on with my little sister!"

The idea of going through the whole sordid tale makes my stomach pitch and roll, but Olivia is right. Eloise is her only sister, and she deserves the whole story. I take a deep breath and launch into the tale, not giving myself a second to rethink or brush her off. When I finish, Olivia is looking at me with silent tears streaming down her cheeks.

"Oh god.... why wouldn't she ask for help? She should've said something!" Her indignation and outrage at being excluded causes my hackles to rise in defense of the woman currently laying on an operating table.

"It isn't her fault, Liv. This guy is a fucking master manipulator and had her all twisted up. She was terrified he'd convince me that she was cheating with him, and she was afraid of losing me. If anything, it's my fault for letting her ever become that insecure in our marriage and my love for her."

Olivia snakes her hand across the table and takes mine in hers. "No, Cal...you're right. It's not her fault, and it's not your fault either. All the blame lies on that fucked up piece of shit stalker. He better be dead because if he isn't I'm going to kill him myself." The fierce protectiveness in Olivia's tone sends a shot of pride coursing through me.

"Get in line, Liv. I've got dibs." I mutter darkly, as I feel the venom of hate seep into my bones when I think about how I plan on peeling the flesh from Drew's bones if he isn't already dead.

THIRTY-SIX

CALEB

When we make it back to the surgical waiting area, Arianna and Officer Roberts are sitting in the far corner with their heads bowed, speaking in hushed whispers. Arianna notices us first and stands up to greet us. Officer Roberts rises too and tips her head at me like she wants to speak privately. I look to Arianna first and ask, "Any updates?". She shakes her head.

"Not yet. We probably won't get an update until they're closing her up." The phrase 'closing her up' causes my stomach to roil with nausea and I squeeze my eyes shut, breathing deeply, waiting for the feeling to pass. I nod at Arianna then turn to Officer Roberts.

"Do you know what's going on with Drew?" I ask, not entirely sure if I'm hoping he's dead or worrying death would be too easy of an out for him. She takes my arm and guides me out of the waiting room and down an empty corridor away from prying ears.

"I called back to the station. According to Officer Thomas he was taken over to Memorial. My sister is a surgical nurse there, so I called her. This is completely off the record right now, because you're not supposed to know shit, so keep your mouth shut or my sister can get fired. But he was still alive when they brought him in, three gunshot wounds plus a stab wound. He's been rushed to surgery, but it sounds like he lost a lot of blood, and his outcome is uncertain."

"She shot him? And stabbed him?" I lean back against the wall, holding on to the handrail to keep myself steady. I am both shocked and amazed at Eloise's ability to take on a madman who has 6 inches and a good 50 pounds on her.

Roberts nods, her lips turning up at the corner with a proud smirk of her own. "Your wife is a fighter, Caleb. She stabbed him with a broken piece of lamp in his trapezius muscle and then managed to shoot him in the arm and through his torso. Officer Thomas got the last shot off, hitting him in the shoulder. Unfortunately, that was after Drew had gotten his hand on the gun and fired on your wife." The pride in Officer Roberts' eyes dims a little as she remembers my wife is still fighting for her life. "Needless to say, whatever charges he was trying to press against you are being dropped. I already called and spoke to Randall and told him to drop that nonsense like a flaming bag of dog shit. He didn't argue with me."

"You know, your partner is a real piece of work. He kept insisting Eloise was asking for it and tried to make me watch the video of her being raped. He's lucky I didn't break his fucking nose." I say with bitterness lacing my tone.

"Believe me, I'm aware. Men like him are the whole reason I went into the force. I know how much of a boys club it is and how hard it is to get someone to believe you. I've been there and it's why I do what I do now." She gives me a grim smile but the haunted look in her eyes tells me there's a lot to her story that she isn't telling me. "Speaking of, I have an excellent therapist that specializes in PTSD related to sexual trauma. I can give you his information if you think Eloise is going to need it. I'm sure he'd work her into his schedule as a favor to me."

I nod, choked up with thankfulness that we have someone like Officer Roberts on our side. "That would be amazing. I've been calling around trying to get her an appointment, but no one is taking any new patients." Tears prick at the back of my eyes, and I blink them back.

"Yeah, I know that struggle too. I'll send you his contact information. Just tell him I gave it to you, and he will work her in ASAP. "

Just then a weary looking doctor in green scrubs walks by and heads into the waiting area. We turn and follow him in, hoping he's there to provide us an update on Eloise's status. He heads directly for Arianna and Olivia in the corner, and I pick up my pace to be there when he starts talking. I see Arianna motion to me, and he turns to acknowledge me.

"Mr. Fitzpatrick? I'm Dr. Henley. I'm the one that's

been working on your wife." He reaches out to shake my hand. His demeanor isn't somber, like he is here to deliver bad news, he just seems exhausted from being in a grueling case.

"How is she? Is she going to be ok?" Olivia rises to her feet and comes to stand next to me. She clasps my hand as we wait with bated breath.

"She's doing well. She will be in recovery for another hour or so and then we will move her to a room. We will keep her sedated for the night as she's gone through some major trauma and she's going to be in pain. We still need to have an Ortho surgeon come in and take care of her knee but that can wait a few days while her body starts to heal from this. We did have to remove her spleen. She can survive just fine without it, many other organs can take over the functions of the spleen, but she may have a harder time fighting off infections, and she will be at increased risk of getting sick. She will have to stay on top of her vaccinations to help prevent serious illness in the future." Relief washes over me as I take in the doctor's words. I feel Olivia tremble next to me as sobs wrack her body.

"What about her knee?" I ask, still afraid of the other shoe waiting to drop.

"I'll have the orthopedic doctor come by and assess her in a day or two. It was dislocated and we went ahead and put it back into place, but she will need surgery to repair the tear in her ACL. She will likely need a few months of physical therapy to regain her mobility but there's no reason for her not to get back to her normal activities after that."

Olivia wraps her arms around me and begins to sob in earnest into my shirt. I hold her close and let my own tears fall. "Thank you, Dr. Henley. I can't tell you how grateful I am..." My words trail off as I get choked up again. Dr. Henley gives me a warm smile and pats my shoulder.

"The nurse will come get you when she's in her room. Like I said, we are going to keep her sedated tonight, but she will be awake tomorrow morning, and you'll be able to talk to her then." He gives Arianna and Officer Roberts a tight nod and leaves us in the waiting room.

Olivia peels herself away from me and pulls out her phone. "I'm going to call Derrick and our parents. Now that I know Eloise is going to be ok, I think I can handle that call...I didn't want to deal with their worry until I knew she was going to be ok..." She looks abashedly down at her feet.

"Liv, it's ok. It's not like they could've done anything while she was in surgery anyway. I'm sure they'll be on the first flight from Costa Rica, so you just bought Lo some more recovery time before Hurricane Helen hits her." Olivia lets out a little laugh at my nickname for their mother who is known for sweeping into their lives, causing complete chaos in a short amount of time and then sweeping off again on her next great adventure. Currently she and their dad, Charlie, were spending half the year in Costa Rica, enjoying their golden years exploring the rain forest. Olivia wanders off to make her phone call and Officer Roberts bids her farewell next.

"I'm going to get back to the station. I'll call you with any updates I get." She surprises me by giving me a quick hug before departing.

Arianna stays with me until Olivia gets back from her calls. "Alright, they should be coming to get you soon. I've got a shift in eight hours so I'm going to head home. I'll come by and check on you guys tomorrow, ok?" I pull Arianna in for a tight hug and thank her for staying with me. With our friends gone, because that is exactly what Arianna and Officer Roberts are now, Olivia and I resume our vigil, waiting for our first chance to see Eloise with our own eyes.

THIRTY-SEVEN

ELOISE

Everything hurts. My mouth feels like it's full of sand. It's so dry I can't even swallow and it feels like someone set fire to my insides while forcing me to huff gasoline. My head throbs but feels spacey at the same time.

"Ughhhhh..." I let out a pained groan when I attempt to open my eyes, but the harsh fluorescent lights force me to shut them again immediately. I hear some sort of shuffling nearby and a warm hand envelops mine.

"Lo? It's me, Caleb. I'm right here, Sweetness." I hear Caleb but his words sound muffled, like one of us is under water.

"C-c-leb...." I try to speak but my throat hurts like it's been in a vice grip and the dry mouth makes it almost impossible to talk.

"Ssh, ssh. Don't try to talk, Sweetness. You've been through a lot and the doctor said your vocal cords might be damaged."

"H-rts….water." A second later I feel a straw press against my lips, and I take it into my mouth and sip. At first the water is soothing but then feels like glass when it goes down my esophagus. I wince at the pain and Caleb brushes a hand against my temple.

"I'm going to let the nurse know you're awake." He brushes a gentle kiss against my temple and steps away. I immediately feel chilled by his absence. I open my eyes again, blinking against the bright lights. I take in my surroundings and realize I'm in a hospital room. I hear the beep of machines, and the muffled noises of people milling around in the hallway. The blankets are the standard scratchy medical-grade, bleachable fabric and the room smells like antiseptic.

"Hey hon, I'm your nurse, Amanda. I let Dr. Henley know you're awake and he's going to come by and see you shortly. Don't try to talk yet, you have some extensive swelling and bruising around your neck, and we want you to heal up some before you try to talk too much. Can you nod if you understand me?" The nurse is an older heavy-set woman with fire engine red hair that reaches halfway up to God, but she has kind eyes and warm, soft hands. I nod the minuscule amount I can tolerate, and she seems satisfied by my answer.

"Are you in any pain right now? If you can make a number with your hands, that would be helpful."

It takes a minute for me to remember how to make my fingers work but I slowly put out seven fingers.

"Ok hon, I'm gonna push some more pain meds for

you. We had to keep you sedated after surgery so you will probably feel like you're getting over the worst kind of hangover. I'll give you some more fluids and that should help." I nod again and wince when it sets off another lightning bolt of pain through my head.

"Head hurts..." My voice is barely a whisper, and it comes out as a rasp. I watch Nurse Amanda push buttons on the IV pump next to my bed as she adjusts my medications.

"That might take a while to go away. We think you got a concussion during your struggle, along with your other injuries. Just keep trying to rest, sweetheart."

I feel Caleb's weight settle next to me on the other side of my bed. As gently as I can, I turn my head and look up at my husband. He looks about as good as I feel, with dark circles under his red eyes, his hair is a complete disheveled mess and he's wearing the same clothes I last saw him in before he left to go to the police station. Still, he is the most beautiful thing I've ever laid eyes on.

I feel like I want to cry but my entire body is so dried out I'm not sure if it's physically possible for me to shed any tears right now. Just then I see a tall man in navy scrubs and a white lab coat walk into the room. He's lanky, with salt and pepper hair, wire rimmed glasses and the calming air of a surgeon about him. He looks up from the tablet he's carrying and smiles at me when he sees I'm awake.

"Ahh, hello Mrs. Fitzpatrick. I'm Dr. Henley. I'm the one that performed your emergency surgery last night.

How are we feeling today?" Dr. Henley directs the question to the nurse who is still standing by my bed.

"She said her pain is at a seven, and that her head hurts. I swapped out her fluids and pushed the next dose of her pain meds. BP, pulse and O2 are all normal right now."

Dr. Henley nods and makes a note on his tablet, probably charting what Nurse Amanda just told him. "You've been through the ringer, Eloise -", he pauses, "Do you mind if I call you Eloise?" I shake my head and he continues on. "We had to do emergency surgery to repair the wound from the bullet. You got lucky in the sense that no major organs were damaged, but we did have to remove your spleen. We also reset your dislocated knee, but I have an orthopedic surgeon coming by to check you out later. You've got a torn ACL and that will likely need surgery to repair. You also have a concussion and quite a bit of bruising and swelling around your throat from the belt he choked you with. It's hard to tell yet if there will be any lasting damage to your vocal cords from that, so try to avoid talking as much as you can until the swelling goes down."

Considering it hurts to even swallow, I don't anticipate having any trouble following that particular instruction. I give him another tiny nod as I look up to Caleb as he takes in everything the doctor is saying. Worry lines his face and instinctively I know he hasn't slept at all since getting to the hospital. I grasp his hand in mine and squeeze it with as much strength as I can muster. In spite of the pain I'm in, I can't help but feel grateful that I'm still alive.

"We are going to keep you here for a few more days for monitoring, Eloise. I won't lie, you have a rough road ahead of you. Wounds like yours will take a while to heal and you'll have a lot of PT in your future for your knee, but I don't see any reason for you to not make a full recovery."

Caleb's shoulders slump and his head bows in relief, as if those were the words he had been waiting to hear. I see him tremble slightly as tears start to trickle down his cheeks. My heart swells with how much I love this man and I can't believe he's still mine after all of this.

"I'll be back to check on you later, but rest up as much as you can, ok?" I give the doctor a thumbs up and he smiles at me and gives my right foot a gentle pat in a reassuring manner before leaving the room. Caleb turns and stares at me with complete awe on his face, like he's just as surprised as I am that I'm still here. We stare at each other, our eyes saying everything we can't speak out loud yet, until the nurse clears her throat awkwardly.

"I'll leave you kids to it. You heard the doctor, get some rest. Sir don't keep her up. Eloise, if you need anything just hit the call button on your bed and I'll be in, ok?" I nod and smile at Nurse Amanda before she retreats from the room as well.

"Fuck, Lo. You scared the shit out of me. I thought I was going to lose you." I mouth *'sorry'* back to him, trying my best to follow the doctor's orders. "Shit, you don't have anything to be sorry about. I'm sorry I left you alone. I knew that fucking piece of shit was separating us on purpose and he used the cops to do it. I could've killed Officer Randall when I heard that Drew had gotten to you. I still might."

I see the rage flash across Caleb's face, and I know he means every word. I shake my head at him and mouth *'he's not worth jail time'*. Caleb grins down at me with that smile I love so much. "You're right, he's not. But fuck...he should at least lose his goddamn badge for such an epic fuck up. You could have died!"

He leans down and peppers kisses all over my face. When he gets to my mouth, I kiss him back and I can taste the saltiness from his tears. My heart cracks open at the thought of how worried he must have been while I was in surgery. Caleb shifts until he's lying next to me in the bed, careful to avoid touching me too much afraid of causing me more pain, but eventually he settles next to me with his head resting on the pillow next to mine.

"Get some sleep, Sweetness. I'm not going anywhere. I'll be right here when you wake up." With his comforting presence surrounding me, I do exactly that and let my eyes drift closed, falling into a peaceful, dreamless sleep.

The next three days pass in a blur. Doctors and nurses come at all hours of the day and night. Between their visits and the pain that hasn't dulled much, sleep is hard to come by. On the fourth day of my stay Dr. Henley comes by with Dr. Renaldo, the orthopedic surgeon. They have me on the schedule for the next morning to repair my ACL and if all goes well, I will be allowed to go home the following day.

Relief floods through me at the thought of finally getting to go home. I'm so tired of the constant beeping of monitors, endless chatter in the hallway, and that god awful hospital smell. My sister and her family have come by to see me a few times, as well as Sara and Derrick. Mom and Dad are flying in from Costa Rica and should be getting here by the time I get home. Even Officer Roberts and the nurse Arianna have stopped by to check on me. As nice as it's been to see everyone, I am so desperate to get back into my own bed and actually sleep in a completely dark room I'm tempted to offer one of the doctors a blowjob if it will speed up the process.

Slowly the swelling has gone down in my throat, and I've been able to speak and swallow without too much pain. I'm still on a strictly soft, bland food diet while my insides heal but it's nice to not feel like I'm swallowing glass every time I take a sip of water. I can talk now in short sentences before my voice starts to give out. It's a low, smokey rasp now, and it's yet to be determined if that's just how I'm going to sound from now on. I joked with Caleb that if I will always sound like this, I'll at least have a future as a sexy book narrator to look forward to. He did not find my joke as amusing as I did.

Updates on Drew's condition have been sparse. Officer

Roberts, or Serena as she's insisted we start referring to her, has told us what little she's allowed to. He survived his injuries and initial surgeries, but he has been in a medically induced coma the entire time. She assures us he is going to be looking at a mandatory life sentence once he's healed enough to stand trial. The cold case team has reopened Cassidy Grainger's file and have been in touch with Stacy about their progress. They did find some journals from his time with Cassidy, tucked away in a closet at Drew's cabin that read like the ramblings of a crazy, obsessed stalker. Those, along with the confession they hope to drag out of him once he's awake should ensure justice for Cassidy. There's no doubt in anybody's mind that he had something to do with her disappearance. Especially not after what he put me through.

Once the surgery on my knee is done, true to their word, the doctors discharge me and let me go home. As Caleb is wheeling me out of the hospital, I look up at him, and see a lightness on his face that hadn't been present inside the hospital walls. "I'm so happy to finally get out of there. If I had to slurp down one more bland meal of applesauce or mashed potatoes, I was going to scream."

"As if, you can't even scream louder than a chipmunk now." Caleb jokes and I shoot him a death glare.

"Too soon, asshole."

He grins at me before leaning down and planting a kiss on the tip of my nose. "So, I talked to Olivia, and we think it'll be best for us to stay at her house while you recover. Our house is nothing but stairs and you can't use crutches yet until your abdomen heals. I already had her and Micah pick up some of our clothes and toiletries and they're going to let us crash in their first-floor guest room. Your parents are going to stay at our place while they're in town.

I pout at the thought of not being able to go straight home, but Caleb isn't wrong. There are stairs that go up to our front door and our bedroom is on the second floor. Being wheelchair bound makes it impossible for me to get around our house. My sister lives in a sprawling ranch style house with a spacious open floor plan on the first floor and will be much easier to navigate.

"Plus, I want to rip out the floors and redo them. I don't want a single thing of that fuck wit's in our house. Including his fucking blood stain. I'm going to renovate our bedroom, living room and entryway. That'll take several weeks." Never in my life have I been so grateful to be married to this thoughtful, amazing man.

When we get to Olivia's house, I am surprised to see Sara, Derrick, Mom, Dad, Arianna, Serena and Stacy waiting for me. Sara and Olivia are holding up a huge poster board sign that says, "CONGRATULATIONS ON NOT DYING!" on it and I can't hold back the laugh that bubbles out. Leave it to my sister and best friend to make a joke about my near-death experience. I fucking love them for it.

CHAPTER
THIRTY-EIGHT

ELOISE

THE NEXT SEVERAL WEEKS PASS WITH LITTLE TO NO ACTIVITY, other than constant phone calls from the press looking for an interview or quote to use in their news stories. I refuse to talk to any of them until I have more time to process everything first. I want to make sure I'm in the right frame of mind before I do any interviews. I don't want to unintentionally blame myself for what happened and influence any other women in a similar situation.

Caleb does an amazing job at shuttling me to therapy appointments, both physical and mental. Serena had given him the name of her own therapist and Dr. Jensen immediately opened up a spot in his schedule just for me. I've been seeing him twice weekly for the last three weeks, slowly working through my guilt, grief, shame and trauma. When I first saw him, I couldn't shake the feeling that everything that happened had been my fault, and Dr.

Jensen has worked stoically to undo the gaslighting that Drew inflicted on my psyche. He has been a godsend.

I wish I could say the same for the physical therapist that I've been seeing for my knee injury. I'm convinced Olga is a demon sent from hell with the torture she puts me through three times a week, but I am hellbent on getting my mobility back, so I dutifully show up for every appointment.

"Hey, Lo, do you want to go out for dinner tonight?" He knocks on the bedroom door where I'm currently holed up, writing in my journal Dr. Jensen assigned me to write in. I hear a shriek of an excited little girls behind him as Poppy and June chase each other through the house. While it's been nice staying with my sister while I recovered, now that I'm on crutches I am more than ready to go back home. As much as I love my sister and her family, I am ready for some peace and quiet. Once the renovations to our house are finished we are moving back in. It should only be a few more days and I am counting down every second.

"Please. I need to get out of the house for a while." I give Caleb a grateful smile as I reach for my crutches. Aside from therapy and doctors' appointments we've kept a low profile, staying in most of the time, to avoid the general public and press. My case has been big news, not just locally, but nationally as well. Two other women came forward when Drew's pictures were splashed across the TV, saying they had been stalked by him as well. Not quite to the extent I had, but enough to hopefully let the prosecutor for his case establish a pattern of behavior.

Once Drew was recovered enough, he was sent to a local facility to await arraignment for his trial. He was denied bail, so it's been a little easier to breathe knowing he's stuck behind bars. He has still refused to give up any information about what happened with Cassidy, but the journals found in his cabin point to her possibly being buried on the land the cabin sits on. The police have had cadaver dogs combing the area but considering how much ground there is to cover, and how long ago she disappeared, it seems unlikely they will find her. I keep hoping for Stacy's sake that they do, so she can finally get some closure.

Caleb helps me out to the car, and we head into town. "Where do you want to go, babe?" He reaches over and grabs my hand while he steers with the other.

Caleb has been amazingly attentive during my recovery. He took a leave of absence from work and made Harold promise him when he returns, he will be able to work from home most of the time. Harold agreed with no hesitation on his end and even gave Caleb a promotion and raise to incentivize him not to leave. Personally, I think Harold is feeling more than a little responsible for the situation, even if it's not his fault.

"How about that little rooftop bar that just opened downtown?" It's a beautiful late summer evening. One of those days that starts off sweltering but as soon as the sun goes down you can start to feel a hint of fall in the air. I am desperate to just be outside and breathe in the fresh air, and just enjoy living again.

"Sure thing, Sweetness. Hey, what do you think about trying again for that trip to the Poconos? It sort of got forgotten about when...well you know. I was thinking maybe we could go for our anniversary in October. Hopefully by then you'll be free of the crutches." I see him give me a shy, hopeful look out of the corner of my eye.

It's clear Caleb isn't completely over when I walked out of our home and out on him, even if I did it under duress. We haven't been able to be intimate during my recovery and I am more than ready to show my husband how much I love him.

"That sounds perfect, Cal. Let's do it." I lean over and give him a kiss on his cheek. We continue on to the restaurant in comfortable silence.

"So have you thought about if you're going to go back to work?" Caleb asks as we share an order of calamari and a bottle of white wine. I've been on short term disability since leaving the hospital. It will be a while yet before I'm cleared to go back to work, but I've been considering other options.

"I'm thinking about going back to school. I'm considering going back for a degree in either criminal justice or psychology. I want to be able to help more women and men who are going through what we went through...It's not right how hard help is to come by when you're a victim. Especially when the people that are supposed to help, won't. I want to advocate for victim's rights." Caleb looks at me with pride shining in his eyes.

"That's amazing, Lo. I fully support that decision. I can support us both with my raise. You can focus on school. I'll back you up no matter what path you decide on." Caleb leans across the table and gives me a quick peck on the lips. Before he gets a chance to pull away, I grab his shirt collar and pull him in, deepening our kiss. I slide my tongue along the seam of his lips, and he parts them letting me in. I can taste the sweetness from the wine on his tongue and I let out a satisfied hum.

"Babe, we need to get back into our house. As much as I love my nieces and nephew, I need to be in bed with you without worrying about what they might overhear." A blush creeps over Caleb's cheeks as he sits back down.

"Say no more, babe. We will be home by the weekend."

True to his word, Caleb lit a fire under the contractors' asses and our renovations got finished by Friday morning. When we walk into the house, I take in the new light bamboo flooring throughout the entryway and living room. A new colorful area rug brightens up the space and the walls are a calming shade of sea-foam green. "It's gorgeous Cal! You picked all of this out?" Caleb gives a little bashful shrug of his shoulders.

"I wanted to remove every reminder I could of that

awful day. This is our home, Lo, and I won't let that bastard taint it." I turn to my husband and wrap my arms around his neck. I pull him down for a kiss that starts out gentle and soft, but quickly turns hungry and desperate, driven by our need to finally be together again.

"Take me upstairs, Caleb. I need you." My still husky voice comes out in a breathy whisper.

Caleb wastes no time in picking me up in his arms and carrying me up to our bedroom. I don't even see the changes to our bedroom, I am so completely consumed with kissing Caleb. Our lips are fused and our tongues dance together to a rhythm only we know. He sets me down gently on the bed and I immediately tug my shirt off and pull at the hem of his, indicating for him to do the same. Caleb rakes his eyes over me in a hungry gaze and licks his lips, before complying with my silent demand. Once his shirt is gone, he quickly loses his pants, leaving him only on his sinfully tight black boxer briefs.

"Are you sure you're ready for this, Sweetness?" Caleb kneels down in front of me to help me out of my knee brace.

"God, yes. I won't be up for any reverse cowgirl or doggy style, but we can still fuck. I need you inside of me, Caleb. I need to feel every inch of your body covering mine. I can't stand the thought that the last man to be in me is Drew. I need it to be you." I bite my lower lip and give him what I hope is my sexiest come-hither look.

"Fuck, babe. When you put it that way..."

Once my knee brace is off, Caleb takes his time peeling

my leggings off of my body, leaving me only in my pale pink bra and panty set.

"Goddamn, Sweetness. You don't know how much I've missed this." He leans in and places a reverent kiss on the inside of my thigh before doing the same to the other. Then he runs his nose up the seam of my damp panties before nipping at my clitoris right through them. "I need to taste you."

Caleb shocks the hell out of me by ripping my thin lacy panties right off my body with one swift tug. Then he descends on my pussy, completely feral for the arousal already leaking out of me.

Caleb licks along my entire slit from bottom to top. When he's at my hole he plunges his tongue in and fucks me greedily with it while his hands clamp my thighs tightly to his shoulders. When he has his fill of tongue fucking me, he flicks up to my clit and sucks the swollen nub into his mouth, sending fireworks shooting off behind my eyelids.

"Oh god, yes! Keep doing that!" I grind my pussy down on his face and his grip tightens on my legs. I feel him alternate between sucking on my clit and flicking it with his tongue in a mind-numbing rhythm that sends me careening off the edge. "Yes, fuck...yes!" My body seizes and it feels like I might crush him between my thighs.

It's been months since my last Caleb induced orgasm and it feels like heaven. It feels like my soul leaves my body briefly and a light tapping on my thigh brings me back to awareness. I realize I'm still clenching around

Caleb, keeping him buried in my pussy. "Oh shit, sorry babe." I laugh as I finally get my legs to relax.

"No worries, Sweetness. There are definitely worse ways to die." The grin he shoots me sends a jolt of lust straight to my core and I scoot back on the bed, giving him room to crawl on top of me. He kisses me like a man possessed and it is amazingly hot with my wetness completely covering his face. He tastes like him and me combined and it's the sexiest thing I've ever tasted.

"I need to fuck you now, Lo. Let me know if I start to hurt you, but I can't wait any longer." I nod my agreement and cant my hips so my core brushes up against his erection still covered by his briefs. With one hard shove, he pushes them off his hips freeing his impressive length. He's so hard and already slick from the pre-cum dripping from the tip. With a gentleness that seems to be straining every ounce of self-control he has, Caleb lowers himself on top of me, before he slowly begins to rock his length into me, one agonizing inch at a time. He peppers my neck and chest with kisses, before working his way lower and take one of my peaked nipples into his mouth. He nips, licks and sucks on one breast before switching and giving the other the same attention.

"Cal...I need you to fuck me...for the love of god, stop playing just the tip and fuck me properly." With my good leg, I push my heel into his backside and urge him to plunge deeper into my greedy cunt.

Caleb needs no further encouragement. He bites down lightly on the nipple in his mouth sending an electric shock straight to my pussy as he shoves his cock the rest of the way in, bottoming out. He immediately picks up a punishing pace while rolling his hips, allowing his cock to hit me just in the right spot. I quickly feel the pressure of a second orgasm begin to build in my lower belly and I tighten my thighs against his hips to hold on for the ride.

"I'm gonna come, Lo...Come with me." He rasps out as he presses his palm against my lower abdomen, increasing the pressure on my g-spot as he continues to pound it. With a few more thrusts we both detonate with our release. I feel the warmth of Caleb's cum fill my pussy as my muscles continue to clench around his cock, milking it of every drop. After a few minutes of heavy panting and waiting for our heartbeats to return to normal, Caleb rolls us to our sides, so we are laying face to face, with him still anchored inside of me. We fall asleep like that, finally whole and at peace again for the first time in months.

EPILOGUE
ONE YEAR LATER

ELOISE

"I don't think I can do this...I feel like I'm going to be sick." I pace nervously in the green room of the television studio, swiping my sweaty palms down the front of my black sheath dress. Caleb comes up to me and envelopes me in a reassuring hug, grounding me and pulling me out of my panic spiral.

"Sweetness, you've got this. You've done dozens of interviews. This one is no different." He cups my face and forces me to look up at him. I give him an exaggerated eye roll.

"No different? I'm going to be interviewed by Keith Morrison! He's like...the Grand Poohbah of true crime news stories! Oh god, I have the flop sweats." I start flapping my arms around, trying to keep pit stains from showing up on my dress.

"Babe, calm down." Caleb halts me before I start panicking again and crushes his mouth against mine. He kisses me hungrily, like he's a starving man in the middle of an all you can eat buffet. All thoughts fly from my head as he plunges his tongue into my mouth and pulls my body against his until I can feel the evidence of his arousal through his trousers. He palms the back of my head with one hand while the other snakes its way down my body until it is cupping my ass. He kisses me like that until my knees are weak and I forget what I was even stressed out about. He pulls away and gives my bottom lip a playful nip. "Better?"

I nod, breathless and a little dizzy. "Better…" I look up at him and see my red lipstick smeared all over his mouth. "But…you got a little something…here." I rub my thumb across his bottom lip and smirk at him. We both let out a relieved, hysterical laugh before fixing our appearances.

This is my biggest television interview to date. I've done a few interviews for some local and regional TV stations, but Dateline is my first nationally broadcasted interview. Drew's trial was wrapped up just two days ago after being dragged out for the last three months. He didn't even go to trial until six months after everything that happened, but the prosecutor was waiting for the police to find Cassidy's body so they could charge him for her murder, to ensure he would never get out of jail. Unfortunately, in this day and age, rape still does not carry a long enough sentence to ensure he would never get parole, so going for the murder charge was essential in keeping him locked away.

After weeks of searching the entire mountain top property, Cassidy's body was finally discovered by cadaver dogs. Stacy was understandably distraught when she was found, and we spent the entire day together comforting each other, but the closure of finally knowing what happened to her sister was absolutely necessary to help her move on. It was worth it though, to hear the jury read out the guilty verdict and see him sentenced to life in prison without the possibility for parole, for the murder of Cassidy Grainger; along with the 20 years he was sentenced to for kidnapping, rape, attempted murder, and other various charges brought against him in my case.

Just then a knock at the door brings us out of our little bubble and the director's assistant, Natalie, pops her head in, "Five-minute warning, Eloise! Are you ready?" I nod at Natalie.

"Yup, just fixing my lipstick." I shoot Caleb a sly smirk and he covers his mouth, trying and failing, to hide the smeared lipstick still staining his lips. She shoots us a thumbs up and backs out of the room again, leaving us alone.

The last year has been a whirlwind of police interviews, television interviews, doctor's appointments, therapy appointments, trial dates, going back to college and taking classes, and focusing on my relationship with Caleb. This is the last interview I plan on giving about my ordeal before hopefully going back to my normal, quiet life. The dark cloud that had been hovering over me while waiting for Drew's trial to finish has finally lifted and I feel like I can finally take in a full, clean breath for the first time since everything started.

Caleb has been my rock through it all; never wavering during the darkest, lowest points of my recovery, never leaving my side when I would attempt to push him away in a fit of guilt and self-doubt, and most importantly, holding me together anytime I needed to fall apart. We are closer than ever, and our relationship has survived and even flourished in the aftermath.

"Let's go, Sweetness. You don't want to keep the Great Keith Morrison waiting." Caleb winks and gives my ass a light smack, ushering me out the door.

CALEB

I stand off to the side of the stage watching Eloise handle the interviewer's questions with a sense of poise and grace that is awe inspiring. She never wavers in her story. She holds her truth close to her chest and places all of the blame firmly on Drew and his fucked-up obsession. It took Dr. Jensen months to undo the gaslighting and manipulation that Drew had used on Eloise, but she is healthy and whole now. She is the strongest person I know, and I can't believe the strides she's made in her recovery in such a short amount of time.

In spite of everything our relationship is stronger than ever. As fucked up as it is, a small part of me will always be a little grateful that this ordeal brought us a closeness that no other experience ever could. We survived, bonded, healed and are thriving now and nothing will ever split us apart again. I watch the interview wrap up, with pride swelling in my heart.

After we are done here, I have a surprise planned for Eloise. I'm surprising her with a trip to New Zealand. She's on break from classes until the next semester begins, and I got everything planned with the help of her sister and Sara. We will be gone for two weeks, and it seems like the perfect reset button after this interview and the trial finally being over. This trip has been her number one bucket list trip to take since we were in college, and I can't think of a more ideal way to celebrate surviving the most difficult year of our lives.

Eloise stands up, accepting a handshake from Keith. While she waits for someone to come unclip the mic attached to her dress so she can finally be free; she looks my way and gives me a thumbs up, indicating she's happy with how the interview went. When she makes her way over to me, I wrap her up in a tight hug and kiss the top of her head.

"I told you, you were going to do great. I'm proud of you, Sweetness." She squeezes me back as she lets out a contented sigh.

"I'm just glad it's over. I don't want to talk about that cuntmelon, or the shit he put me through, ever again." I chuckle at her insult for Drew. She's taken to referring to him in a variety of colorful insults and swears to avoid saying his name. I can't say that I blame her. The less space he takes up in our lives, the better.

"Hey, speaking of, I've got a surprise for you." Eloise pulls back and looks up at me with a hopeful look.

"Is it shooting target practice with his ugly fucking mug again?" She gives me a wicked grin and I can't hide my amusement at her viciousness.

"Better. We are going to New Zealand for two weeks." Lo's mouth drops open in shock and she looks around, as if she's expecting this to be some sort of joke.

"What?! When? How? Why?" She splutters, completely taken off guard.

"Now, by plane and because you deserve it. Let's go. Sara and Liv have already packed for you, the bags are in the trunk and our flight leaves in three hours."

Lo is completely dumbfounded, and her mouth keeps opening and closing like she wants to say something but can't because of the shock. I push her chin up with my finger, closing her mouth.

"Come on, Sweetness, we've got a plane to catch." I kiss her lips lightly before grabbing her hand and tugging her along behind me so we can leave.

When we get to our car, Eloise surprises me by grabbing me by the arm, turning me around so my back hits the door and she pushes up against me. She reaches up on her tiptoes and presses her mouth against mine, demanding entry into my mouth with her tongue. I oblige because I'm not an idiot, and she kisses me until we are both panting and breathless.

"I fucking love you, Mr. Fitzpatrick." She whispers against my lips. I smile and move my mouth to her ear.

In a low, husky whisper I reply, "I fucking love you too Mrs. Fitzpatrick. You are mine now and forever, don't you ever forget it."

The End

ACKNOWLEDGMENTS

First of all, I need to thank the Nerdy Girls Collective for all of their support on my journey to write my first book. They have been with me, every step of the way, cheering me on, giving me feedback, helping me learn the publishing process and connecting me with all the resources I needed to get this book out into the world. I cannot thank you enough, Amy, Amanda, Trish, Kymberlie, Courtney, Lyndsey, Vallene, and MJ. Without Nerdy Girls and the Kismet team, this book never would have been made.

Thank you to my Beta readers, Adára, Candice, and Erin. You were the last line of defense between the general public, all of my typos and general complete lack of understanding of how commas work.

To all of my ARC readers, thank you for your feedback, gif reactions, error posts and support. I couldn't have asked for a better team as a first time novelist and you guys are a big part of making this book what it is now.

I also must give a shoutout to Drew, for not being too terribly upset at me for borrowing his name for one of the worst book bad guys ever. Sorry about besmirching the good name of Andrew. I'll make it up to you somehow!

Thank you to Amanda from Eternal Geekery for the amazing cover design. I still can't believe you created something so stunning based off of my half-assed Pinterest board. You are a magician, woman.

Nat, thank you for all of your help along the way. Even if it did take you the longest to read my book. I still love you.

Thank you to all of the readers who chose to read Astray as well. I appreciate so much that you gave me your time to read the words that I wrote, and I will be eternally grateful for that. I know there are so many amazing books out there to read and the fact that you chose to read mine means the world to me. Putting this book out into the world is a dream come true and I will always be thankful for anyone who chooses to spend their time reading the nonsense that came out of my brain.

And finally, to all of the women who have suffered a fate similar to Eloise's: I wanted to write a story of hope and a story of a woman recapturing her power after being a victim of sexual assault. I hope I did her, and your, story justice.

ABOUT THE AUTHOR

Poppy Fitzgerald is an emerging author of romance novels. Poppy calls the beautiful Blue Ridge Mountains home, with her husband, two sons, mostly absentee cat, and overly affectionate Golden Doodle.

Poppy enjoys any and all romance genres and tropes, but loves to play around with popular tropes and turn them on their heads to come up with something not commonly seen.

When she's not writing she usually has her head buried in her kindle, reading smut. She also communicates fluently in GIFs and sarcasm and loves making her readers cry.

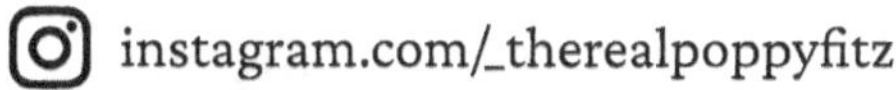 instagram.com/_therealpoppyfitz